FIEND

KETLEY ALLISON

BRIARCLIFF UNIVERSITY STUDENT PLAYLIST

Call You Mine - The Chainsmokers

i miss you (with Au/Ra) - Jax Jones, Au/Ra

Feel it Coming On - Contessa

Trampoline (with ZAYN) - SHAED, ZAYN

Past Life (with Selena Gomez) - Trevor Daniel, Selena Gomez

Bridges - Aisha Badru

WOW - Zara Larsson

Wildfire - SYML

Where We Come Alive - Ruelle

Lonely Hearts Club - Winona Oak

Hurricane - Tommee Profitt, Fleurie

Find the rest of the playlist on Spotify:

http://bit.ly/briarcliffsociety

1

———

y death is silent.

On the outside, the quiet is suffocating. My ears are clogged. My limbs hit nothing. My voice is strangled and without breath.

I'm sinking into the black, but my eyes are wide open.

Bubbles of the remaining life I cling to escape my lips, though I can't see them, not even when I tilt my head skyward, my hands curled into claws, desperate to grab *something*.

Water runs through my fingers, thick and viscous, but not tangible enough to lift me to the surface and gasp for air.

I can't swim.

My mind understands this, but my body refuses to concede. It jerks, seizes, *flails*, and yet I'm sinking, down, down...

Inside, I scream. Inside, my heart refuses to die. It

pounds against my ribcage, my rebellious pulse transmitting the frantic message to my neck, banging against my eardrums and shrieking into my mind: *Swim! Swim, damn it!*

I try. Oh God, I'm trying, but nothing ripples above. There's no break in the black, the sea claiming me as easily as a stone plinking into its depths.

Chase.

My last thought is of him, the tightening in my chest swelling to unbearable levels. I'm choking because I'm refusing to allow my body to do what it does best: breathe.

There's no oxygen down here. No life.

But I...

My chest seizes. My eyes pop wide. I stop flailing and wrap panicked fingers around my neck, my instincts taking control.

Don't try to suck in air. Don't breathe.

My mouth opens.

Lake water fills the one spot it hasn't claimed, rushing into my lungs.

I gag.

Squeeze my throat.

Burn from the inside out.

A strand of hair tickles the side of my cheek as I stare into the horror of dying...

Hands clamp under my arms.

I've curled inward, my eyes rolling back into my head, but a small spot at the base of my brain communicates a crucial fact: *Someone has you.*

Water splices against my body as I'm pulled, up and up,

a sliver of moonlight piercing the surface of the lake the closer I'm led to the top.

Those same hands switch to my waist, propping me against their side until my head breaks through the water.

A horrible, grotesque noise I've never heard before escapes through my airways, my nose and throat spluttering. Lake water warmed from my lungs is vomited out.

I scramble for a handhold as I cough with painful heaves, hollowed-out barks escaping my throat as my eyes stay scrunched shut.

They won't open after being stretched to their limits, the underwater prison creating an ironic dry grit that scrapes against my lids every time I try.

"Easy," a voice says behind me. "I got you."

They guide my hand to a piece of wood, curling my hands around its edge. "Hold on tight."

"Wh—wh—..." I'm seized by another coughing spasm.

"Slow breaths," the same person says, rubbing my back as I move to grip the dock with both hands. Water laps at my elbows. I'm exposed to the air from my shoulders up, but too much of me remains buried in the deep.

"Let me—" I gulp. "Get me—get me out. Lift me up."

"I ... I can't, Callie."

That voice, the musical, familiar lilt of it, starts to make sense. I blink, scrunching down hard, then force my eyes open.

At first, all I see is a panel of wood, moist and slippery from mildew and reeking of the same scent. But I twist my neck—*oh*, until the person holding onto the dock beside me, the one who saved me, centers in my view.

"...Ivy?"

Her ice blonde hair is slicked back and flat against her head, wisps of it floating around her shoulders where the lake still claims it. Thick, dampened eyelashes border her wide, worried gaze, droplets of water clinging to her brows, her nose, the crease of her upper lip.

She doesn't say anything, just continues to regard me with that anxious, frightened stare.

"How..." I clear my throat. "What's going on? Who pushed me?"

She licks her lips, a bead of water dissolving on the tip of her tongue. She glances up, over the dock, then back at me.

"You got what you wanted," she whispers.

"I—what?"

"Calla Lily Ryan," another voice says. "My, oh my..."

The careless tone stiffens my shoulders, despite my feet treading uselessly underwater.

Shoes clomp closer, stopping at my fingertips. A heavy, golden cloak flutters around the ankles, and I know, before I continue my upward survey, who owns this unconcerned gait.

"Falyn," I grit out. My hands clamp harder around the dock's edge, readying for her heel to come down on my fingers and send me screaming back into the murky depths.

A full-body shudder overtakes that thought, and I swallow the impending bile.

Ivy's here, I reason. *She won't let that happen to me again.*

But why *is* she here? And why did she allow it to happen the first time? I could blame the grogginess of almost drowning, but in truth, my subconscious has collected more suspicions about Ivy than my present mind ever did.

"Did you find the answers you were looking for down there?" Falyn asks with a smile.

Every molecule in my body wants to *get out*, get dry, get *away*, but Falyn blocks my scuttle to the ladder by laying the tip of her shoe on my fingertips.

She says to Ivy, "Has your time with this water-logged possum softened your heart so much that you couldn't leave her without a swim buddy for two seconds?"

Ivy tips her chin to Falyn, adding a glare. "You shouldn't have pushed her. It's too dangerous. Callie doesn't know the docks like we do. She could've swum up and hit her head. Or been caught in the anchoring ropes. It was a stupid move, Fal."

Ivy and I lock eyes over the rippling water against our jawlines, her expression stiff with a silent, desperate message she tries to send my way. I read the warning through her squinted gaze.

Falyn has no idea I can't swim.

I give Ivy a minuscule nod.

"Everything we do is dangerous," Falyn says. A breeze ruffles her cloak, pushing the hood wider, and I catch the twisted glee written across her features. She looks down at me. "And the beginning of a serious awakening."

My fingers ache with their hard clench. The adrenaline drifts away with the same speed, and I kick my jellied legs in an attempt to raise myself higher. "Not to be a buzzkill, but can we finish your life lessons on land?"

Instead of being insulted, Falyn answers with a low,

languid laugh. She glances behind her. I follow her gaze to a line of Cloaks, waiting silently ten feet away. Seven of them stand as straight and stiff as chess pieces, save for the ominous movement of their gold-threaded robes, fluttering in the night breeze.

Falyn turns back to me. "I assume you managed to read the two words in your invitation before you were butt-kicked into the lake."

My mouth turns grim. "Yes. I'm in. Now let me up."

She doesn't step back or lay off my fingers. Instead, Falyn's grin grows wider. "I'm guessing you didn't have time to turn the card over."

"*Stop*, Falyn," Ivy says next to me. "We're freezing. Let's finish this when you give us some towels, at least."

Falyn ignores her. "Let me be the bearer, then."

Falyn picks up the thick card that fluttered from my fingers to the edge of the dock when I was pushed.

"It says." Falyn stops to clear her throat. "'If you choose to accept your first initiation rite, you will land on the path to become one of us.' You're not a Virtue yet, Callie."

Controlling the shivers in my voice, I respond, "I'm still trying to pinpoint when I accepted being pushed into a lake."

"Oops." Falyn's lips curve.

My face doesn't betray my thoughts as I scan behind Falyn toward these girl soldiers who must be awaiting Falyn's orders.

Is Falyn really their leader? I find it difficult, even while flailing around half-submerged from her doing, to see her at the top of a secret society pyramid.

"Do you want the key to our temple?" Falyn asks me, her voice candy-coated and thin.

"*Falyn*," Ivy hisses.

"You didn't go through all this trouble for nothing, did you?" Falyn arches her brows as she regards me below her. "Here's something you can accept: Go fetch."

"What?" I look from Falyn to Ivy in hopes Ivy can explain, but Ivy's face is either too numb from cold, or she's too stunned and horrified to move her muscles.

"This isn't good for me, is it?" I mutter to Ivy.

She blinks. Swallows. Her eyes soften, shimmering with warm tears against the cold drops of water in her lashes. "I'm so sorry, Callie."

"You're one of them, aren't you?" I whisper in return, but my words are so much hotter than hers. She doesn't respond, which is answer enough. "How could you not tell me?"

Ivy answers with a moan. "I thought I was keeping you from the worst."

"Are you done with your pep-talk, Ivy?" Falyn asks from above. "Your bleeding heart can only go so far in this scenario. You know the rules. Callie's on her own. Come up and leave her to it."

Ivy braces her hands on the dock.

"You lied to me?" I whisper hoarsely.

Ivy pauses before she lifts out of the lake, her elbows spearing to the sky. She turns her head and whispers through stiff lips, "Kick off your shoes. Underneath the dock are vertical slats of wood. It's what keeps the platform secure and floating. In between those slats are pockets of air."

I find enough space in my lungs to say, "What?"

"Grip those slats. Hold your breath and pop up for air whenever you can. You can do this."

"What the fuck, Ivy—"

Water sloshes when she lifts herself up in a streamlined move. Once her knees are on the dock, she rises to a stand. Her clothes are stuck to her body and soak my trembling hands when she moves to stand beside Falyn.

"Welcome to your first test of allegiance," Falyn says. "You're a late-term pledge, but that doesn't exempt you from what the rest of us had to endure."

Ivy lays a hand on Falyn's robed arm, and my face spasms with the agony of betrayal, but I do as she says. I toe off my shoes and picture them sinking, down, down, and landing silently on the brackish lake floor.

"Your key to our temple is tied under this dock," Ivy says. "Find it, and you'll succeed in becoming a Baroness."

I go cold on the inside, its spreading icicles leaving frost on my numbed skin. "I..."

"Get it over with, Callie," Ivy cuts in. "I'm not going anywhere."

"Or don't," Falyn is all too happy to add. "Frankly, the queen gave you an easy in. If you can't do this much, then you *definitely* don't belong with us."

Queen?

"Who's your queen?" I ask, my throat shrinking in size. Falyn may not know I can't swim and thinks this task is letting me off the hook, but ... and my stomach sinks as I look to Ivy ... what about the person in charge? Did she require this specific hazing because she's aware of my handicap?

A clawing ominousness clamps around my heart as I quietly answer my own question. Falyn's been put in charge of my initiation—that's evidence enough.

Despite every part of me *pleading* with Ivy, she gives a slight shake of her head. Ivy can't—or won't—do anything besides offer silent support.

"You'll meet our queen when she deems you worthy," Falyn says. "Now hurry up and dunk. We've got parties to get to."

My hands turn into Arctic-level claws. I risk dipping my chin into the water, then choke on a terrified squeal and shrink closer to the dock when it laps over my mouth.

I can't do this. I may be as close as I've ever been to uncovering what Piper might've died for, but I can't face my fear. I refuse to willingly drown for—

"Oh, fuck this," Falyn says, then kicks at my fingers until they rip from the dock.

2

don't give into the hysteria of freaking out. It didn't do me any good the first time, and I refuse to be rescued a second time ... if any savior would come.

As soon as lake water covers my face, I scramble for the dock, gripping its underside to keep from sinking.

There isn't enough breath in my lungs. Even if I prepared for Falyn's move, there wasn't time for a big gulp of air.

Meaning, I need oxygen. Now.

My heart pounds against my ears, and a blaring panic alarm lances through my system, but I force myself to give into the quiet and think. *THINK.*

In my desperate scrabble, I'm gripping the bottom of the dock. I have no idea where to turn to find the edge, and I can't swim to find it.

I can't swim.

Ivy's words prod the back of my skull. I'd waste precious

time questioning them, so I release one hand and let it explore for a neighboring slat, my legs assisting as much as they can with hard, uncoordinated kicks.

The backs of my fingers hit a vertical plank, and I grip it with all my might and do an underwater pull-up until my nose is pressed against the slime and decay of submerged wood.

With my lips pursed and jaw working like a fish's, I search for the kiss of air, however small, to meet my lips.

Water peels back from my face, its waves climbing up my cheeks at each small ripple of movement, but it's enough to suck in the stink of limited oxygen and blink my eyes.

Black. It's so black under here, and my ears are submerged and blocked from sound. But I feel footsteps up above, one pair crashing down harder than the others, and I swear I hear a voice hollering *"Where is she?"* through the clogged clamshells of my ears.

My heart crashes and ricochets along the walls of my entire body, emitting the obvious threat to my life in urgent, pulsing bursts, but my emotions won't get me out of this.

I keep Ivy's advice in mind as I gulp in breaths and tentatively move my grip up and back, testing each hand's strength. Flooded, manmade wood is so different than it is on land. Slimy. Soft. Almost pliable. Certainly not easy to use to keep my head above water.

If I slip ... I'm done for.

As if calling on fate, my arms and hands tremble and ache under the strain.

I can't stay still much longer. If I keep my body this stiff, I'll have no hope of clinging to the surface.

Don't freak out.

Falyn said the key is tied somewhere under this dock. What would it be attached to?

Someone must've swum this path before me to leave the key. Would they be adventurous, or would they want to get the fuck out of here like I do?

Ropes. Ivy mentioned ropes.

With that illustrious amount of information zinging through my mind, I move carefully forward, my fingers slipping with each forced maneuver.

When my left hand catches a sharp piece of wood, I cry out and release it on instinct, water cascading back into my lungs.

Nononono.

I struggle for another hold, kicking and thrashing, and manage to find another thin beam and hold on, angling my head to meet another small pocket of air.

Using my legs this time, I swing out, searching to hit something—hopefully a rope tied from the dock to the lake floor. I keep swinging, keep pressing forward, praying either my leg or my hands hit gold.

At last, I feel a tight, thick rope against my thigh. It's angled, probably from one end of the dock and anchored to the floor, so I use it like a monkey and wrap my socked toes around its width to push my body up and give my hands the tiniest break. I balance on it, my knees bent under me, searching with every sense I can for the feel of a key.

I come up with nothing.

Whimpering, I pry my numbed toes off the rope and find another one.

I beg my hands to keep their strength and help me move a little bit forward, but when my foot slips and all of me falls under, I'm close to failing, instead.

Can I die for this?

My body sings its denial. My brain voices its extreme concern. I'm made up of nothing but bickering parts, my conscience and motivations ceding ground as instinct takes over.

I find another hold on the rope and push up for air, and when I do, my toe catches on a ring of something, hard and unlike the scratchy slime of the rope.

The key?

It's near my foot. Somehow, I have to willingly release my grip on one slat, bury my face in water, and get it.

"Callie? Callie!"

The voice is above me, my one exposed ear picking up the hollow clomps of boots.

"Can you hear me?" comes a water-clogged follow-up.

"Yes!" I cry, then cough against the sloshing of water around my mouth.

"Follow my voice. I'll get you out of there."

I sense the sound of the voice drifting left, and I instinctively move toward it, my toes curling over the rope as I use it for a guide.

The key.

Gritting my teeth, I try one time. Just once. My legs have bent enough that I have the right balance, and if I keep my left hand on the wooden beam, gulp an inhale, and dunk low enough to...

My free hand closes on nothing but water. But I persevere, my heart hammering its extreme displeasure.

I scrabble forward as much as I can, swiping blindly for what doesn't belong down here, scraping along the rope and searching for the object.

When I hit what feels like a ribbon tied in a bow, I don't question it. I feel for an end, pull to unravel the knot, then grab the ribbon before it floats down, joining my shoes in their watery grave.

Sharp metal hits my palm.

I burst up with my feet, jerking off balance but maintaining it on the rope, and force my lips not to open too wide as I gasp for more briny oxygen.

"Callie!"

"I'm here! I'm coming!"

After shoving the key under my shirt and in my bra, I follow the voice all the way, ducking into the water only when I hit the next beam and have to pass under it.

Soon, there are no more beams to grip. My hand smacks against the side of the dock, searching, *hoping* this is the end, and when I feel a warm, calloused palm cover mine, I nearly weep with gratitude.

He pulls, and after a loud gulp of air, I let myself go under with my hand enfolded in his.

My body follows the current of his strength. I give one last push, and this time, when I curve around the dock and my head breaks the surface, I'm surrounded by the wide, empty space of air.

Sputtering, I allow hands to come under my arms and pull me up. I hear Ivy on one side, her voice so panicked that I can't decipher what she's saying.

A towel comes around my shoulders, and when a familiar scent envelops me, I finally open my eyes.

Chase's face eclipses the moon as he stares down at me. He's bare-chested with black feathers painted between his pecs. Some kind of costume for the Turkey trot tonight, a party I was hoping we'd attend together, after I met him here. Before...

I've been propped into a seated position, my legs splayed out, and I'm covered in emergency blankets from the boathouse. He swipes his hands down my cheeks, cupping my jaw, his expression urgent. But his eyes are dark with fury.

I'm certain he doesn't say anything because he's too overcome with rage to speak. His lower lip trembles with the same emotion, his jawline rigid and sharp as a knife. He slides one arm under the backs of my knees and the other around my shoulders—

"No," I choke out, despite the shivering, visceral need to fall into his arms and lay my head on his chest. "I can stand."

"You sure?"

His words are soft but laced with a gathering storm.

I shuffle forward. "I can—"

A mocking, disgusted voice sounds out, "Oh, come *on*, Callie, don't use your epic failure to become a damsel and let Chase carry you off into happily ever after. Have some self-respect."

I glance to the side, unsurprised that Falyn is the first to speak, but Willow stands next to her, and so does Violet, their hoods pulled back and their hair glinting under the dock's singular lamplight.

Yet, they appear frazzled, their expressions twitchy and their eyes darting between Chase and Tempest, who stands nearby, glowering with his arms crossed. The other robed Virtues have scattered closer to the boathouse, risking glances, but otherwise whispering to each other and straying from the scene.

"It's not like that was hard," Willow pipes up, but shrinks under Tempest's answering growl.

"You okay?" Chase murmurs near my ear.

I nod, even though I am far, *far* from okay.

"Too bad," Falyn sneers. "I was *really* looking forward to you becoming a member of our society."

"I'm..." I clear my throat from the lingering panic that spreads across my vocal cords like the jagged pieces of coral. "I'm flattered. Because I have your fucking key."

Falyn's expression goes blank. Chase braces beside me.

She says, "Excuse me?"

Ivy, staying near, smiles at the same time her body sags in relief.

Falyn asks quietly, "You what?"

"Hey, you said this was one of the easier tests, right?" With a trembling hand, I loosen the blanket around my shoulders and pull the key out from my cleavage, its silver curves catching the beam of light as it dangles from my fingers.

I'm awed by its old-fashioned beauty, heavy with solid

metal and smooth with its three half-circles at the top. I slide it off the sodden ribbon and into my palm, my fingers curling over the stem.

"I believe this is mine now?" I ask on a rasp.

Falyn's expression goes rigid. She glances at Willow, Ivy, Tempest, Chase—anyone who might have an answer for this unfortunate twist of fate.

When no one offers their opinion, Falyn gathers herself, standing taller. "Fine. Bravo. You've passed the first round."

"Give her more credit than that," Chase says, standing. He crooks out an arm as he rises, so I can take hold and push to my feet with him. My legs ache with the effort. "Since I doubt this was orchestrated by your queen." Chase's jawline cascades with shadow when he pinpoints Willow. "Am I right on that, Will?"

Willow folds her arms into her chest, refusing to meet his eye. Tempest arches a brow at her. "Lies got your tongue, Chancellor junior?"

"Like it matters," Falyn snaps out, then points a shaking finger at me. "She would've had to undergo a similar ritual in the temple. I was just the expeditor. Our queen will be—"

"Pissed," Chase supplies. "But sadly, her ire won't come close to the retribution I'm about to seek."

Falyn's lip trembles. She steps back. "You don't have that kind of power over me."

Chase idly checks his cuticles with his free hand. "Don't I?"

"Being the prince of the Nobles doesn't give you the authority to direct me," Falyn says, but her voice isn't as firm.

"You Virtues." Chase clucks his tongue, and while everything about him appears languid and at ease, the arm I grip is taut with barely constrained anger. "Does our mutual rulebook not say that if a Virtuous member attacks a Noble prince's soulmate, the prince may exact any punishment he wishes?"

Willow gasps.

Ivy steps to my other side but stares over my head at Chase. "Are you serious?"

Tempest slides his fingers along his chin, chuckling mirthlessly. "Should've seen that one coming, ladies."

Falyn's mouth works before she says to Chase, "You don't have a soulmate anymore. And our princess can override—"

"You don't have a princess, either," Chase counters. "She's dead."

I add quietly, "I'm—I'm having trouble following this argument."

"Callie Ryan is *not* your soulmate," Falyn says, drawing closer. "Piper was."

Chase withdraws his arm from mine, wrapping it around my shoulders and pulling me closer. "I've chosen a new one. The rules stand."

"*No,*" Falyn whispers, and casts her glare on me.

Her face contorts with fury, hatred, targeted disgust. Her upper lip peels back. "You don't belong with us. You only have access to the societies because it'd be too obvious if we seriously injured you and left you for dead. Admit it. You have no place as a Virtue."

She's right. All I want to do is take them down. For Piper,

Emma, Eden ... me. And every other girl who's crossed their paths and been veered into their orchestrated trauma.

I'm about to agree—

"Aren't you curious to hear my punishment for forcing Callie to find a key she has every right to?" Chase asks, a soft cadence to his voice. Too lenient.

"You don't choose our members," Falyn hisses at him.

"You're right. The queen does. And she chose Callie." Chase cocks his head. "Get in the water, Falyn."

"*Fuck* you," she retorts.

"Get under the docks."

"I will *not*."

"And hold your breath for as long as I tell you to."

"*I will not!*" Falyn screams, saliva frothing in the corners of her mouth.

Falyn is so outraged that her entire form shudders, and her eyes, stretched so wide, the gray of her irises leak into the white.

Ivy rests a hand on my shoulder, drawing close.

"Back off, Falyn," Ivy says. "Callie's under our protection."

Falyn slow-blinks, her face twisted in grotesque anger. Then, she guffaws, her stare pin-wheeling between Chase, me in the middle, and Ivy. "Protection?" she asks, then starts cackling. "*Protection?*"

"Either you jump into the goddamned lake," Chase says, "or I'll force your Virtues to do it for you."

"Right, the princely Stone would never touch a girl in such a ruthless manner," Falyn says through her laughter. I'm both horrified and fascinated by the sight. "That's not how you assholes operate. You go behind the scenes, don't you? Orchestrate your enemies' downfall with quiet, sightless maneuvers, but they're just as strong, just as *lethal*, as if you laid your hands on Callie in the first place." Falyn locks me in place with her gaze. "No. They're worse. And you're their latest puppet."

Chase releases his hold on me and storms forward. "If you value your place in the Virtues, you will shut the hell up."

Falyn doesn't back down. "Haven't you told your latest *soulmate* how she's inherited that title in the first place? I'd think that would be some crucial information to impart before you strip her and toss her in your bed."

Dread sloshes against my rib cage. I take one step, laying a hand on Chase's bicep. Trying to turn him, he refuses to cede any ground. "Chase, tell me what she's talking about."

Up until this point, I'd been silent during most of their exchange, drinking in their polarizing arguments for later use, but with the way Falyn's face transforms from distressed rage to snide, *winning* confidence, I'm terrified of this new outcome.

"Oh, honey." Falyn turns to me, widening her eyes with feigned, comical sympathy. "You've already fucked him, haven't you?"

Ivy steps between us, her back to me. "Do as Chase says, Falyn, or go tell the queen what you've done to Callie. Neither choice keeps you on this pontoon."

"I'll get to you." Falyn points dryly at Ivy. "Callie, I'm about to make your trip under the docks feel like *paradise*."

Chase rasps, "If you so much as whisper more lies..."

Ivy's shoulders go rigid. "Falyn, don't. Remember the sisterhood."

"The same sisterhood that's failing to defend me?" Falyn counters. She gestures to the cluster of Virtues hovering at the perimeter, their hoods obscuring their faces. Then at Willow and Violet behind her. "You all want to fall in line behind the prince? Fine. I'll face my punishment, but not before I tell Callie that Ivy was *ordered* to befriend her, and Chase was *told* to fuck her as a distraction."

My knees buckle. I falter in automatic recoil, my heels coming too close to the end of the dock but jerk back just in time.

I may have saved my body from another drowning, but my heart teeters over the edge and splashes back into the black depths. "That's not true."

But it can be. It is.

Haven't I learned by now that the students in Briarcliff are not what they seem? Friends are true enemies, teachers are predators, Chancellors are members of secret societies…

Paranoia spreads its spider-legs across my mind, assisting in Falyn's revelation.

Ivy spins to face me. "Don't let her get to you. I can explain."

Chase cups my face. "Falyn's batshit. You hear me? Don't *listen*. I care about you. I do."

The two of them crowd in, and it's with a shredded scream that I push them off. "How could you? *How could you both*?"

"Callie, she's made it out to be—"

"To be what?" Falyn cuts Chase off. "Something other

than the truth? If you care about her so much, Stone, then tell her why you singled her out on her first day. How you beckoned her with your looks and your smile and your sex appeal." Falyn slides her gaze to me. "Unfortunately, you're not the first, honey."

I shake my head. "Shut up. All of you, just shut up."

But Falyn's relentless. "Happy with your key now, Callie? Ivy's only friends with you because she has to be. We were curious about you the minute you came on campus, and you certainly didn't disappoint, with everything you've told Ivy you discovered about us."

I blink at Ivy with wide eyes. "You told them everything?"

Ivy's stare gleams with tears. "You have to understand…"

My chest grows tight. There's no water surrounding me this time, but I feel like I've been deprived of all oxygen.

What did I just fight through all this filth for?

"Your life isn't your own anymore," Falyn continues. "It's ours. We tell you who to be friends with. What subjects to excel in. Who you can *fuck*. We're the Virtuous future, and we've just screwed you *senseless*." Falyn beams after her statement. "So, tell me, Callie, as the soulmate who was, and I quote, 'attacked,' you have the option of nullifying Chase's punishment. Still want me to jump in your water? 'Cause I firmly believe I've baptized the shit out of you in this lake—"

I can't listen anymore. Chase tries to catch me, but I push him off, crying with harsh, damaged vocal cords, "*Liar!*"

He backs off, but Ivy comes up beside him, her face pleading with me to stay.

But I don't. I can't.

My world has shifted, and not simply because Falyn has decided to control its axis.

"Let your trials begin!" Falyn calls after me, her laughter echoing across the lake.

3

 'm not sure I can function enough to make it to my dorm room, but I ask for one more favor from my quivering, battered legs to get us to our final destination, where a hot shower and a warm bed await.

Clutching the scratchy boathouse blanket around my shoulders, I wobble as fast as I can up the trail and scurry through Briarcliff's winding pathway until I arrive at Thorne House.

The night security guard raises a brow as I stumble through the sliding doors.

"Rough trot, already?" he asks through his burly mustache.

I shake my head, my teeth chattering too hard to form a proper response, and like he cares whether or not I've taken part in Briarcliff's students Turkey Trot. All *I* care about is warmth.

"I won't ask for your ID, considering I recognize that

face of yours," he says when I reach the elevator. "You were in the crowd around that Harrington kid who got arrested for her sister's murder."

I manage a nod, but not much else.

"Looks like you've had a rough enough time of it," he mutters when the elevator door dings open. "Stay safe, kid."

I'm forced to face him when I push the button for the third floor, and whatever he sees in my expression makes his chin jerk back. "And warm," he adds. "Your lips are blue."

The door slides shut on the perturbed crunch of his brows, but I think I've had enough of concerned adults who end up providing zero assistance in this shit-hell of a school.

My keycard is somewhere in my back pocket, and I dig for it with numbed fingers while I wait for the elevator to spit me out on my floor. It takes four tries before I'm successful, my grip on the blanket wrapping around my neck like a vise each time I move.

With my jaw in full-on seizure mode, I stumble down the hall, slap the keycard against my electronic lock, and fall inside, the heavy wood slamming shut behind me.

"Jesus, what—oh my God, Callie."

Emma steps out from her room, annoyance warping into wariness as she strides over.

"S-sh-shower," I say through chattering teeth.

"No shit." Emma takes hold of my elbow, guiding me into the bathroom.

I'm shaking too much to properly peel off my wet clothes, but I try, anyway. Emma turns on the bathtub faucet then helps me undress, her deft fingers taking over where I fail.

"Arms up," she murmurs without meeting my eye.

I nod, but even that much movement causes a searing pain into my brain, and I wince.

"Almost there," Emma says, then unbuttons my jeans and peels them off.

I lose my balance when I try to lift my foot, jarring my hip against the sink and my palms slamming down, but Emma does most of the heavy lifting, pulling my feet through the leg-holes as I wobble above her.

A heavy, metal *clunk* sounds out against the floor's tiles when Emma tosses my pants aside. She picks up the ornate key, turning it around a few times in her hands.

"They had a new opening, huh?" she asks, her voice hollow.

"N-n-not anym-more," is all I can manage to say.

Emma's fingers clench over the Virtues' key before setting it on the counter. She ducks under my arm and helps me into the bathtub.

When my toe hits the water, I wail.

Emma nudges me forward. "It feels like fire because you're getting hypothermic. But the water is barely room temp. I promise. Try to slide in."

I grip her shoulders, whimpering, but do as she asks. This isn't the first time Emma's saved me from my own stupid injuries, and it probably won't be the last.

After a few minutes of coaxing and gentle, *gentle* easing into the bathwater, I'm immersed almost to the shoulders, my shivering limbs and joints turning into soft tremors. I breathe deep, closing my eyes, while Emma lays a warm cloth on my forehead.

"When you start to get cold again," she says, "tell me. I'll add warmer water."

I swallow. "They—they—"

"Don't try to talk. Relax. Deep breaths."

I crack my eyes open instead, my jaw too clenched and my teeth ramming together too hard for my voice to be much use. So, I attempt to communicate my wishes with my stare.

Emma avoids my eye, dipping a washcloth in the water and squeezing out the excess with both hands before draping it on the exposed skin of my chest. I wait it out, because she has to look at me sometime.

When she does, I flare my eyes, pleading with her to give me answers. "A-Addiysn."

After reading my expression, Emma sits back on her haunches and sighs. "I'm sorry for cornering you in her room and making you think we betrayed you. We needed Addisyn to believe we were on her side."

I jut out my chin for her to elaborate, the bathwater rippling with my shudders.

"We had to be believable," Emma says. "Otherwise, the Virtues weren't going to buy it."

"The—the—diary," I rattle out.

"Yeah, you found Piper's missing pages in Addisyn's room. But proving she killed her sister wasn't enough."

"But Addisyn was arrested."

Emma cocks her head. "Were you planning on stopping your snooping into the societies once she was arrested? If so, then great, good job. But I thought you wanted more. I thought you wanted the Virtues."

"I do."

Emma nods. When she moves forward to rearrange the cloth on my chest, the planes of her face are cast in the bathroom's light, the burn down one side of her neck mottled and red. "If the Virtues found out that you knew where Piper's lost pages were and that you were planning on breaking into Addisyn's room and retrieving them, they would've protected Addy first chance they got. Eden and I had to serve as a distraction and make them think we would intervene and bring them the pages instead."

My fingers curl under the cooling water. Emma takes that as a sign to drain the tub a little and add a warmer temperature. When she turns the tap and the stream hits my tingling toes, I sigh in relief.

I say, with my head leaning back, "You've been meeting with the Virtues? Are those what your late nights were all about?"

Emma studies me carefully. "Sort of. They're so up their own asses, it wasn't difficult for them to believe Eden still wanted a chance with them."

My chin comes down. "Eden's been meeting with them?"

Emma nods. "She told them your plans—with my okay. I've been giving her advice behind the scenes and helping her infiltrate the society. She said she would intervene and get the pages from you. Addisyn was in the room when Eden told the queen our plans, and Addisyn demanded to be present when you were steam-rolled."

I frown. "You let me trust you, then you went behind my back."

Same as Chase. Same as Ivy.

The utter recognition that no one I've surrounded myself with has worn their true face has me pushing against the sides of the tub and rising from the water.

Emma catches the movement and stands with me, holding my arm, but I shake her off.

"Callie," she pleads.

"No. Thank you for—for this, but I need to be alone."

"Don't you see it was worth it? We took the pages from you," Emma admits, "but Eden and I, we gave them to the police, not the Virtues."

"No, you blew up your spot with the Virtues by going to the police. Now they'll be pissed. You could've just let *me* do it the way I was supposed to, and your covert operation—or whatever it is you and Eden have going—could've gone on." My voice gets stronger as I reach for a towel, though my thighs are gelatinous and weak.

"Callie," Emma says quietly. She motions up and down my body. "Our plans are still in full effect."

I pause wrapping the towel around my torso.

Emma continues, "You're the newest initiate of the Virtues. Do you believe that was an accident?"

Holding the towel with crooked, thawing fingers, I whisper, "I'm so fucking tired."

"I know you are. But stealth is so important when it comes to them. We've been moving the pieces quietly. We had to get Addisyn out of the way and you into the society, but on our terms, without tipping off the Virtues. If we told you outright what we were trying to do—"

"What *are* you trying to do?"

"They are aware of every step you take. They *knew* you weren't about to stop looking for Piper's killer, or the origins of the Virtues."

"Thanks to Chase," I spit. "And Ivy."

Emma's nose wrinkles in confusion. "Ivy?"

"*Yes*," I hiss. "All of you, working together without letting me in, watching me stumble around and—"

"Risk your life," Emma counters, her voice more controlled than mine. "*That's* what you were doing. The closer you got to exposing the Virtues, the harder they would retaliate."

"And so, you, what, think you can bribe my silence by making me a member, the way they tried with Addisyn?"

"You have no idea. *None* ... of what they're capable of." Emma points to her face. Not to the burn, but to the scar on her lip. The one eyelid that's lower than the other. "I was beaten because of what they forced me to do. What the queen forces *all* her favorite girls to do in order to graduate as a Virtue."

The exposed skin of my back presses against the cold tiled walls. Wincing, I move away. "Are you threatening me?"

"No." Emma's breath billows out in an exhale.

"You said it. I'm an initiate because you wanted me to be. Am I the next girl to suffer at their hands?"

"Not if we play this right." Emma steps forward. "Listen to me. They won't hurt you so long as you abide by their rules. They think they can control you now. It's why, once Addisyn was arrested, they had to let you in. Eden was never going to be their next member. But you? You've given them so many reasons to get you on their side."

"They could just kill me."

Emma gives a single blink. "Contrary to what you believe, the Virtues don't go around murdering on the reg. They work too hard on their girls to put them in their graves so early."

I ask through stiffened lips, "What will I really be doing, then?"

"Getting what we need."

I rub one eye with the palm of my hand. "I can't be your—"

"It's not just Eden and me working together to expose the Virtues."

My hand drops to my side. My subconscious predicts the name about to leave her lips, but hearing his name out in the open, having *Chase* echo against the bathroom walls, makes it so much more powerful.

And foreboding.

Until she says the name I'm not expecting.

Emma takes a breath. "It was Piper, too."

4

———

*P*iper.

The girl I lived with for a week, who bullied me relentlessly until the minute she died, still possesses enough of a foothold in this reality to haunt me.

My legs have turned into brittle matchsticks—I barely possess enough energy to balance on my feet, and my eyes are heavy and begging for sleep. But I pop them open to say, "Piper was helping you?"

"Yes."

"Shit." My knees buckle. I plop down on the side of the tub, clutching my towel.

Emma takes pity on me and throws another towel over my shoulders to keep me warm. "She was the only one with access to the temple and the Virtues' documents. When she died, we thought we'd never get back in. None of us had any idea she'd left clues in her diary."

"The library reference code," I murmur.

Emma takes a moment to assess my hunched over form, then scoots to my side. "This is a lot for you to take in. We can reconvene in the morning. You need to sleep."

I don't argue when she lifts under my arm and helps me to a stand. Yet, it's not only lethargy that hangs off my bones. "What happened to you?"

Emma angles her head to glance at me, but instead of answering, speeds us up.

I refuse to be sidelined, so I attempt to ask it in a less personal way. "What do they make all their girls do before graduating?"

"You've had a brutal couple of hours. Can't we leave it for a while?"

"Have you? Left it? After all they've done?"

"Fair enough, but I'm tired, too. I promise. Tomorrow morning, I'll explain more. Until then..." Emma ushers me into my room.

My hand flies to the doorframe. "Wait. My clothes. The key."

"I'll get them."

I let her go, and on my way to my bed, I drag an old t-shirt hanging off my chair back. The towels puddle to the floor as I slip it on, my footsteps heavy, then crawl under my covers, forcing myself to stay awake until Emma returns.

Her shadow flits against my blurred vision. "Here," she says, and something cold presses into my palm. The key to the Virtues' temple. "You earned it."

"Mm." I palm it close to my chest, then bury half my face in my pillow and close my eyes. "What did you have to do? To get yours?"

A few beats pass, then she says, "An abandoned lake house under construction. I had to sleep there overnight and find the key."

"That doesn't sound too bad." I manage to ask, before surrendering to slumber, "Were you afraid of the dark? Is that why they put you there?"

"No." I hear Emma's footsteps pad over to my door. She flicks the light off. "I was afraid of monsters."

Muffled sounds of an argument drift through the black, and I roll over, rubbing my eyes.

"She needs to sleep—Chase. *Chase!*"

I jolt in bed as my door bursts open and scramble up to my forearms, wincing when my sore muscles protest the movement.

"Callie?" he asks as he strides forward.

"I'm—" I clear my throat. "I'd like to be left alone."

He doesn't listen. He sits on the bed, close to my side, light from the doorway illuminating the sharp angles of his cheekbones, the stiff line of his shoulders. Worst of all, it puts a halo around his blond, tousled head.

"I may not be at my best," I say, "but don't think I won't push you off this mattress."

"I came to explain."

"I don't want to hear what you have to say."

"Hate me. Go ahead." His tone turns sharp. "But don't let it be because you listened to Falyn over me."

"I can think for myself." I sit up, wrapping my arms around my legs.

He sets his jaw. "After meeting you..." he sighs. "It's become so *fucking* complicated."

While my heart and my mind war with each other, my hands clench into fists. I'm hurt, hollowed out, and confused, but Chase is here. And he wants to talk.

Falyn's words scythe inside my head, their sharpened blades cutting into my skull with such terrible precision.

Tell your latest soulmate how she's inherited that title...

Chase was ordered to fuck you as a distraction...

Oh, honey. You've already fucked him, haven't you?

I meet his eyes in the gloom with a colorless stare. "So tell me."

"I was told to keep an eye on you. That much is true."

My heart picks up its beats. "By the Nobles?"

His chin jerks down in a single nod. "Piper died, and hell broke loose in our ranks. You were so adamant the society was responsible for her death that my father took me aside and asked me how much you knew."

I frown. "But at that point, I knew nothing."

Chase knuckles his jawline. "You told me you and Piper were working on Rose Briar as your history paper."

"Yeah ... and? The founders are a common topic in BU history subjects."

"You made a connection with the date of Rose's death and Piper's. After that, you started throwing around our society name, then the Virtues'." Chase angles his head to look at me. "Were you expecting them to let you keep tripping over their secrets until you managed to reveal one?"

"I didn't have an inkling of who *they* were until I read Rose's letter that Piper hid in the public library. Then I saw your ritual room and what you do to naked women—"

"If I could explain to you the hundreds of years the society's been given to hone their sexist, masochist ways, I would. But that's not what you want me for. Is it?"

He's right, damn him. I'm not allowing Chase to sit here so I can yell at him about Noble traditions. I'm letting him stay, because... "You were ordered to seduce me."

Chase doesn't bother to deny it. "Yes."

I hug myself tighter. "Then Falyn was right."

"Falyn dilutes the truth to meet her needs, every time."

"Does she? I want to believe that." I'm desperate to cling to his words, to *him*, and forget there was ever a confrontation at the boathouse.

But that would require altering my memories to suit a reality more palatable, more meaningful, for my soul to handle. And I just can't do that to myself.

I force my next sentence to be stronger than the soft edges of my heart. "Then tell me about the first time we slept together."

Chase's back goes rigid.

"Did you sleep with me because you had to? Was that all I was? A task to complete?"

Chase presses his hand against my entwined ones. "It's not that simple."

"Yes or no." My lower lip quivers, but I'm praying for its concealment in the dark.

Chase exhales. "Yes."

I turn my face away so he won't catch the midnight glimmer of my tears. "You can go now."

He doesn't move. He stares at me.

"The *first* time, yes," Chase says. "But the second? Third? Fourth? Fuck, how many times have we slept together? Add them up, because those weren't instructed or ordered. They were mine. I kept coming back to you, because, hell, Callie. Because you shook me loose. You're the first girl who's made me feel like there isn't a collar around my throat, attached to chains against my father's wall."

I hear what he's saying, but he's cloaked in lies. Raised on vehemence and stubborn pride. Chase could form his lips around those sweet nouns for as long as they suit his needs.

"Don't let Falyn come between us. Or allow the Virtues to win." Chase grabs my hands with both of his, holding on tight. "We're *us*, Callie. We don't have to be what they—"

"But do we have trust?"

Chase raises his head. "What?"

"Say I believe you. That we've fallen for each other. That we're attracted and can't resist the need to give in to mutual pleasure. But can you trust me?"

Chase leans back. "I..."

I give a slow, aching nod. "I'm not angry with you for not being able to answer that. I can't answer it, either." I meet his eyes. "And I think that's the problem."

"We can fix it."

"Not right now, we can't. Not with the Virtues and the Nobles trying to direct our every move. We've seen what they can do. *You've* seen more than I ever will. Can you honestly say that whatever information we feed each other, accidental or on purpose, won't reach their ears?"

"That's not fair. It's different now. I'm not their puppet."

"No. You're their prince."

Chase breathes out. "Callie."

"You plan to go against them, remake their values, and that's wonderful. I don't want to be the reason you can't. And they'll use me against you, just like they used you against me."

The shadows caressing Chase's face turn into sharp points on the planes of his cheeks. "I won't let that happen. I'm not under my father's control anymore. I've sided with my sister. I've sided with *you*."

I lift my hand, caressing the dark hollows near his mouth. "You and I, we can't let each other in. Not yet."

And, my heart cries out, maybe we'll never be able to.

Chase takes hold of my wrist, pausing my strokes. "If you can't trust me completely, have faith that I've been doing everything in my power to protect you. Tonight, at the docks..." His billowing breath comes close to a death rattle. "I wrote that letter asking you to come to the boathouse. I wanted to meet you, alone, just you and I, so I could finally be honest with you. If I'd known they were going to use my meeting with you to catch you by surprise ... fuck." He casts his gaze to the ceiling. "Maybe you're right. We're putting each other at risk."

I have no doubts, but I ask anyway, just to hear it in his cadence, a tone he reserves solely for me. "Do you swear you had no idea they were going to push me off the dock?"

"Jesus, Callie—*no*. I wrote that stupid note in my room,

then dropped it off on your bed, thinking I'd embrace my fucking dork and you'd find it cute. Thought you might enjoy a handwritten 'hit me up' instead of a text. Then I was sidelined on my way back to the dorms. By James. He had some shit he needed to sort through at the academy and ..." Chase buries his fingers in his hair. "He played me. Kept me occupied."

The urge to reach up and massage the back of his neck, bend his rigid body into mine, is so strong, but I curl my fingers on my lap instead. If Chase can't even trust his friends, how could he ever think we could ask that of each other?

Maybe, because now is the time he needs you most.

I staunch the thought. Too much has been triggered. "I can't swim."

Chase freezes in scraping his hair back. He grimaces. "The fuck?"

"I can't swim," I repeat. "I don't think being pushed into the lake was a coincidence."

"You can't *swim*?" Chase rears off the bed, then whirls to face me. "And you swished around under the docks trying to find a fucking key? It's a vintage prop the Virtues don't even use anymore! Why didn't you refuse? And who the fuck did you tell your weakness to?"

I wince. "I could ask the same of you."

Chase huffs out a breath.

"You could've refused your dad's demands and ignored me. Maybe then, I would've stayed the harmless possum everybody liked to kick around. Instead, after meeting you, I risked everything to find Piper's true killer. I sacrificed a future where I excel in all my classes in a top-tier private campus because I couldn't ignore that pained look on your face every time your ex-girlfriend was mentioned. And just when I think this whole thing is finished, that Addisyn is in custody, and you and I can finally get to know each other without Piper's ghost behind us, I've been conned into a secret society by your sister and Eden through some twisted belief that my presence in this group can make up for Piper's absence. I can't do this, Chase. I'm not Piper."

Chase presses his hands to my face, tipping it up. He asks harshly, "Is that what you think? That you're some lame glimmer to Piper's falling star?"

I try to nod, but he holds my head firm.

"Listen to me. I have *never*, nor will I ever, want you to take Piper's place. What you and I have—it's ours. Not theirs. Not hers. And I can't speak for Emma, but when it comes to my sister and her plans to take down the Virtues, she'd only involve someone if she knew they wanted it, too."

I choke on a sob, and my words are lost.

Chase murmurs my name. His thumbs stroke my cheeks, painting curved paths through my tears.

"You're a girl who came into my life at the exact wrong time," he says, bending closer. "And made me question everything I wanted. My future. My choices. I thought I had my tomorrows on lock, but the minute I had you, the second I sank into you, I had no fucking idea what the next day would bring." His fingers knot in my hair. "And I ended up craving that uncertainty. And obsessing over my next fix of you."

His gaze darts to my parted lips. Even doused in darkness, Chase's handsomeness calls to the emptiness inside me, hooks it painfully, and draws it forward for him to satiate. His beauty is incomparable to anyone I've ever met—it makes me greedy and gluttonous. I want to stare at it, touch it, lick it until it's mine.

Chase's eyes lift. They sparkle like tiny stars.

My tongue hits my lip.

His lips break into a smile, and I forget to breathe, yet I don't care. I've lost my breath so many times tonight, but this time, I'll gladly give it away. Our chests rise and fall in tandem. He breathes for me.

Kiss me, he mouths.

My nipples *zing* as I read the silent words. He must sense it, because his grip tightens in my hair, tipping my head back and leaning forward until nothing but a sliver of air exists between us.

Chase tugs me closer, and I shiver as his hand slides from my hair down to the small of my back.

When he finds my bare ass, my body jerks with a small gasp, but I use that momentum to press my lips to his.

His silken tongue glides through my mouth, bringing with it his addictive taste—salted mint mixing with a tang uniquely his. I moan, going pliable in his grip, and he braces his arm at my back to lower us onto the bed, then settles between my legs as he devours me, owns me whole.

"Are you still cold?" he asks against my lips.

It's an effort to open my eyes and come out of paradise. "Freezing."

His pillowy mouth curves into mine, his hands start roaming, and my body curves into his every sway.

Chase traces my folds, slick and ready for him. I raise my hips, and on a groan, he sinks his fingers in.

"I want you to feel me inside you," he says between kisses, "as much as I feel you in me."

Whimpering, I clutch his shoulders, matching his pumps, circling my hips with his. When he pinches my clit between his fingers and twists, he catches my cry in his mouth.

Feeling outmatched, I let my hand wander between us, then under his jeans until I meet his dick, curling the pads of my fingers until I trace the thick vein on the underside of his incredibly long shaft. He groans when I squeeze, when I pace my hand pumps to his finger thrusts.

His knuckle brushes across my clit, once, twice, and I'm so swollen, even my throat can feel the pleasurable, aching pulse begging to release.

Chase's smoky voice curls into my ear. "I'm going to make you come, and right when I have you, when you're screaming my name, I'm going to fuck you."

I tip my neck back, allowing him full access. "Yes."

My legs tremble, but not from cold or fear. Pure ecstasy flits through my veins with the lightness of fairy dust, and as Chase brings me to my peak, when that enjoyable blackness coats my vision, I arch my back and give in.

I'm so lost in the ether I don't notice Chase stand and strip off his pants. I barely register the crinkle of an opening condom. I can't see the way his body covers mine, the sheer width of him blocking out the entirety of my room.

But I spectacularly feel when he thrusts into me mid-orgasm.

The sheer intensity of another building orgasm on the tail of my first one is almost too much, and I bite down on my lower lip to stop the scream.

Chase doesn't let up. He pounds into me, his rhythmic thrusts ignorant to my pathetic attempts to be quiet.

"I've loved fucking you from the first second," Chase rasps, nipping and licking my earlobe. "Love the tightness of your pussy, the feel of you clamping around me when you come. I want you to think about this whenever you're questioning our validity. Remember what it's like to have my cock inside you, to go to class still dripping with my cum and your juices, to have panties soaked with your want for me every time I can't give it to you. Because I would. In public view, in the Wolf's Den, on classroom desks, in Marron's fucking office—I'd have you soaking wet in every damned room at Briarcliff Academy."

My voice hitches. I can't garble out syllables, words, meanings. I'm so close to tipping over another brink, I can't even poise his name on my tongue.

"You like that? Me talking dirty? I fucking love it, too. Come on me, Callie. Come all over me and show me what I do to you."

I can't bear it. I cry out as my body dances under another spotlight of ecstasy.

My nails rake down his back as I instinctively bring him closer, absorbing his heartbeats into my own. Chase keeps drilling into me, cursing once before he thrusts as deep as he can and holds himself there. I wrap my legs around his lean hips to bring him as deep as possible, my body capturing his every orgasmic tremor and twitch.

We hold each other as we come down, Chase burying his face in my neck. Through my hazy, sleepy fog, I hear, "I think I got paint all over your shirt."

Laughing, I let my fingers delicately trace the deep route of his spine, the muscles on either side showcasing it like a ravine on his skin. "It's worth the dry cleaning bill."

Chase chuckles near my ear. "That ratty thing?"

"It was my mom's shirt."

Our movements still. Chase lifts his head. "I'm sorry."

"Oh, that's not—I'm not mad." I push pieces of loose hair from his flushed, angular face. "But I guess I just doused cold water on us, huh?"

The mention of my mom coupled with bringing up the topic of water, are two sore subjects I should've let lie. Instead, I've allowed them to flood their unresolved angst into this room. Into us.

Though it pains me to say it, I murmur, "I'd really like to get some sleep."

"Yeah." Chase's hands come down on either side of me, and he swings himself up and out of bed. "Sure."

He stands, the tendons of his arms and ridges of his biceps flexing. Even in this meager light, the full-frontal force of him is startling.

Chase glances down at me. "I gotta say one last thing."

I nod while slipping under the covers, my body still twanging and vibrating from his sudden, addictive devotion. I don't think it'll ever fade. Chase gives me goosebumps just by looking at me, and hell, I'm in trouble now.

"You got their key, but it doesn't get easier from here." Chase leans forward, his pecs coming awfully close to my mouth, and his evergreen, freshwater scent all-consuming. He grabs the key from where it lays on the cold side of my bed and lifts it for inspection. "All this talk of trust between us ... non-legacy members have to prove they're trustworthy. That you're committed to the society. And that whatever happens, you'll keep the society's agenda, their traditions, a secret you carry to your grave."

"Yes," I whisper into the enlarged space between us.

"They will test you the hardest of all, considering what happened today with Addisyn's arrest. You'll have to do things you will never be proud of. Are you ready for that?"

After a moment, I give another nod and sort through my thoughts enough to say, "I need to become one of them to take them down."

Chase studies me in grim silence. When I don't elaborate, he says, "I'll do everything in my power to help you. So will Emma."

He turns for the door, and I watch him leave under the heavy night shadows.

At the last minute, Chase turns. "Callie. I want to stop you from doing this, but I won't force you to back off. Just know that whatever comes next, I warned you."

Then, he leaves.

The white, predatory glitter in his eyes as he turns is the last image that resurfaces before I fall asleep.

5

onday rolls in with an oceanic storm, and I scramble up the exposed pathway to the academy under my lopsided umbrella, balancing the overflow of textbooks in my arms, as well as my bag, straining at the seams as it bounces against my back.

When the corner of a textbook hits one of my kidneys, I curse, buckling under what both tickles and hurts at the same time.

Other students hurry up the same hill, but they have their shit together as they fly by with extra-large umbrellas and roller bags for backpacks.

And ... is that a golf cart I see buzzing up ahead?

Why couldn't I catch one of those?

Hunched over, huffing, and dripping, I make it to the school's entrance in time to see said golf cart smooth to a stop under the covered section of the pavilion. Chase slides from the driver's seat, brushing his hands down his impeccably dry Briarcliff blazer.

Even in a cold winter storm, his golden brilliance stays intact. His blond hair is sculpted away from his forehead with perfect, tousled texture. He fills out his uniform like a god, straining the fabric in all the right places, without a single raindrop marring his Midas aura.

Chase cuts his eyes to the right, catching me in plain sight as I inadvertently ogle him.

Can't a life and death situation stifle, just a little bit, my foolish attraction toward him? Why does a stupid crush have to feel so unshakeable?

I pick up my pace, horrified to be caught in such a weakened position, especially after this weekend.

"Look, man, she's wet for you," I hear James, golf cart passenger, say. "How many times does it take for you to squeal, possum? Huh?"

I expect James's remarks to be followed up by Chase's fist hitting some part of his friend, but only silence follows.

Daring a peek over my shoulder, I notice that Chase merely sidles up to James with a smirk, Tempest coming up behind them. The fourth musketeer, Riordan, barks out with laughter as James says something else I don't catch.

Chase's attention flicks over to me once more, but then chooses to scan the rest of our surroundings in boredom rather than return to my face.

I whip back around, my cheeks hot with embarrassment and hurt, but I remind myself: Maybe this is how it should be, Chase going back to his rule-the-school roots and me returning to my rodent state. It's safer this way. The Nobles and Virtues are less likely to mess with our heads if they think Chase has grown bored with me and stayed friends with James.

I tell myself that on the way to my locker. That Chase's answering smile to James's insult is an act, and not the real him.

This is what you wanted.

I kicked him out of my room for this very reason. Didn't I?

My locker is—for once—a welcome sight when I come up to it, the dark wood varnish a much better image to focus on rather than Chase's cool dismissal. I spin my combination code and swing the door open, dumping my textbooks with a breathy, happy sigh.

I peel off my blazer, too, considering it's more of a damp overcoat than a fashion choice.

My phone dings in its pocket as I fold the collar over the hook, and I fish inside to pull it out before classes start.

When I see the preview on my lock screen, I frown. It's a text with just a small image, too pixelated to get a good look.

Unlocking the screen, I pull up the message.

And cut off mid-gasp.

I glance around, hoping the nearby students who are also dropping off their things and having lingering morning chats before the first bell haven't clued into my sudden freak-out mode.

But *I* have, and I glance at the picture one more time, to make sure it's real.

It's of Eden, changing in the co-ed bathrooms of Richardson House where she shares a dorm room with Ivy.

She's bending down, grabbing a towel off the hook, completely naked. The photo only shows her side, but a picture at any angle, while naked, is still meant to be humiliating if you haven't consented to it.

And Eden is clearly unaware of a lens trained on her body as her damp hair trails down her back, and her tan lines on her shoulders and thighs from a bathing suit are on full display.

It took mere seconds to catalogue the terrible intent of this picture, and my brain screams *delete delete delete* well before my finger hovers over the screen.

But then another message pops up.

Private Number: Create a finsta and share this pic with the entire student body. Caption: FORMER SWIM CAPTAIN EATS PINOCCHIO *AND* THE WHALE.

My mouth falls open. My stomach sinks. I immediately type back: **I'm not doing this.**

It doesn't take long for a response.

Private Number: to learn where our temple is, you'll have this picture making the rounds by noon.

Fuck. *Fuck.*

While still holding my phone, I slam my palm into the

side of my locker. Nearby students jolt at the noise, a few lifting their lips with snide disgust as they discover the source of the sound, then go about their day.

I'm not punching wood because I'm at a crossroads and can't figure out the right move—I'm doing it because there is no other current recourse to expel the furious energy running through my veins.

"Callie?"

The tentative use of my name draws my head up. "Not now, Ivy."

"I ... you're mad. That's okay. But I was hoping we could maybe talk at lunch and—?"

New target.

I whirl, punching the air with my phone as I lurch it into Ivy's view. "*I am not doing this.*"

Ivy pulls her books into her chest. "That's—omigod."

"You know who this came from." It's not a question.

She stutters out, "Yes."

"*This* is how the big bad society wants to initiate me?" I point at my screen with my free hand. "By doing ninth grade, social media bullying bullshit? After having me swim for my life under a goddamned *boat dock*?"

"I..." Ivy shakes her head. "It all depends on who's in charge of your initiation."

"Falyn?" My question contains more spit than air. "Why her? Shouldn't it be you? You excelled at duping me this entire semester. You'd think you'd be rewarded by being put in charge of my *worthiness*."

Every syllable I utter is filled with vitriol—poison I couldn't contain when I was freezing to death, and anger that was stifled by hurt when Chase visited me Saturday night. Now, though, oh, *now*, I am ready to unleash.

And Ivy, a person who I thought was my friend, will be my carnage.

Ivy flinches. "I don't agree with any of this, and you may not believe me, but I was never fake with you. I'm your friend."

"Are you?" I give Ivy the once-over, but all I can see is her swimming beside me, her hair rippling in the water as she allowed Falyn to take control. "What about Eden? Huh? What will this do to her? It rehashes the exact trauma she had to endure freshman year, and she barely made it out. She lost everything, Ivy. Her passion for swimming, her body, her mind, her *friends*. Everything was taken from her. And I'm expected to do that to her again?"

"She came back to us, asking to be initiated, offering us those missing pages of Piper's diary. But then Addisyn was arrested because of those very pages. Eden betrayed us. If she'd stayed away, she wouldn't be a target. But she wants this, Callie. Eden made it clear in one of our meetings how much she was willing to endure—"

"What kind of fucked up shit are you into?"

Ivy jerks back as if I slapped her. "You put your life on the line to see what crap I'm into. Now suddenly, you can't stomach it? We're not nice, Callie. The Virtues aren't *kind*. They prey on weakness and test our limits to the greatest extent, so we can come out better. Stronger. We're given the ability to leave this school and enter men's playgrounds with the exact weapons required to get what we want."

I stumble back with each breath she takes. "Stop saying those things. This isn't you."

"Isn't me?" Ivy echoes. "Everything you've seen up until this point is who I am. But we've only known each other a few months. I couldn't give you every facet, especially when you started your quest to reveal secret societies on campus. How would you have reacted if I told you I was a member from the beginning?"

"But you're the one who gave me the Nobles' name in the first place." I stare at her, searching for the friend she promised was still in there. "Did you do it on purpose? To test me?"

Ivy's eyes dart to the side, then come back to mine. "The minute your name popped up as a Briarcliff enrollee, you were considered as a possible initiate."

"What? That's not possible. I can't..." Can't believe my best friend introduced herself to me with the intention of planting a seed in my mind to prove my worthiness. Can't comprehend that the instant I stepped on Briarcliff soil, I was societal fair game.

"It can't be true," I manage to say. "How could they be interested in me? I'm nothing. No one. Just a girl from the Lower East Side."

My grip clenches on my phone, and I work to bring our conversation back to Eden. "And I'm still not doing this. Consider me unworthy."

"Come on, Callie." Ivy cocks a hip. "You're willing to give up everything, even after the gaslighting you went through to get to the Virtues' door? Don't be like this. You're so close."

"Shaming another girl isn't something I'll ever take pride in," I say. "I'm really disappointed that you think it's a weapon that will positively shape your future."

I push past her.

"They won't stop, Callie. And whatever task they substitute for this one, it'll be worse. Please. Do as they say."

Ignoring her, I turn into the hallway.

"I'm trying to help you!" she calls. "Please, let me…"

But her voice becomes softer, then fades away entirely, as I put more distance between me and the one person at this school who had my trust.

6

———————

*L*unch hour is safer in my dorm room.

After the last morning bell tolls, I bypass my peers jumping up from their desks and grouping into cliques, ducking from the classroom well before my exit is noticed by Chase or Falyn.

It's not that much of a feat. Their attention was so focused on the professor during class, I could've put a Mentos in a coke bottle, and they wouldn't have turned. When it comes to my presence, Falyn must've decided against threatening me in public, and Chase seems to be intent on keeping up his unconcerned veneer.

That kind of self-control, after the weekend I endured at their orchestration, actually scares the shit out of me.

It shows just how serious they take their positions in Briarcliff's secret societies.

When I arrive at Thorne House, there isn't much activity. Most students take their lunch in the dining hall where they can catch up with their friends, crushes, and latest gossip. My heart pangs at the thought.

Any normalcy I craved when coming to Briarcliff left with Ivy once she jumped into the lake and dragged me out.

Upon entering my apartment, I expect to see Emma at our small kitchen counter, hunched over her food and eating quietly and alone—how she prefers it, and lately, how I'm coming to like it, too.

What I don't expect, once I shed my jacket and dump my bag, is Eden to be eating with her.

"Oh. Hi," I say.

All I can see when I look at Eden is the picture stored in my phone.

Their heads snap up at my voice, and both straighten from their conspiratorial positions on the couch.

Emma speaks first. "Hey." She puts down her chopsticks. "Didn't expect you back so early."

I open the fridge. "I lost my appetite for the dining hall."

Eden says, "I would've brought you some pho, had I known you were coming."

I shrug, preferring to bury my face in the cold icebox of the inner fridge than make eye contact. I'm a terrible liar. If they see my face, they'll know.

"I think there's some jelly back there," Emma says, her voice light as air. "Make yourself a pb and j, then come sit with us."

I do what she suggests. After slathering peanut butter and strawberry jelly between two pieces of bread, I join Emma and Eden on the couch.

Emma finishes her bite of noodles, her attention

straying to the sandwich, remaining untouched, on my lap, before snapping back to my face. "I told Eden what you went through over the weekend."

I swallow, my saliva thick and unyielding. "I figured you would."

Eden makes a low sound in her throat. "They think up the most fucked-up things, don't they?"

My traitorous mind flies back to her naked picture on my phone, burning my retinas. I blink against my dry eyes. "I wasn't prepared for that kind of initiation. I wish you would've let me in on your plans after Addisyn was arrested."

Eden shrugs, as if tossing me into a frigid lake was the least of what could've happened. "We weren't sure it was going to work. Yes, betraying you in Addisyn's room was believable, but it wasn't just Addisyn we had to convince. We had to lower the Virtues' guards enough to get them to allow us to be the ones to collect Piper's diary pages from you. That was the easy part, since we had a closer relationship to you than any of them. It was exposing Addisyn and having her arrested before they found out what we really did with the diary pages that was difficult."

"You put yourselves in so much danger," I say.

"Exactly," Emma says simply. "We knew there would be punishment and didn't want to involve you so soon. Not until..."

"I took Addisyn's vacant seat in the Virtues," I finish, then glance between the two of them. "The Virtues are so pissed at the both of you."

"They're biding their time to retaliate." Emma shrugs,

but her eyes burn bright. "What's worse than what they've done to us before?"

I lean forward on my elbows. My phone, stuffed in my jacket near the door, blares a Siren's call only I can hear, but not yet. Not yet. "Explain to me what happened to you, Emma. I can't be left in the dark anymore."

Emma sets her bowl of pho on the coffee table while Eden huddles deeper into the couch cushions, bringing her noodle bowl closer to her chest like its warmth can replace what's missing in her chest.

"Don't I deserve to know?" I ask. "After you two colluded—"

"Successfully, I might add," Eden cuts in.

I sigh. "Achievement or not, the three of us are in a whole bunch of shit because of it. I need to know what I'm working with if I'm to take this ruse any further."

And put your entire life back into misery, I silently add, but internally shake myself out of it and push on, saying to Emma, "I can maybe understand why the Virtues believed Eden and that she wanted to prove herself by stealing Piper's diary pages from me the instant I found them, but you? You burned down a library. Why would the Virtues think you would still be on their side?"

Emma's brows jump before her lips turn down. "You may know I set the fire, but you have no idea what's been done to me these last two years."

"Then help me understand."

"My father is the king of the Nobles. My brother, the prince. They've spent their lives working themselves to the bone to keep the Nobles a secret, and because of that, they have to work to keep the Virtues a secret, too."

"And you put all that in jeopardy by drawing national attention to Briarcliff Academy by setting that fire," I surmise.

Emma's chin dips low in agreement.

I set my sandwich down beside her bowl. Emma watches the maneuver.

"My father spent these past two years indoctrinating me back into the Virtuous mindset. He used therapists that were Nobles, trauma counselors that were Virtues, and I spent months being told the societies weren't the problem. I was."

I think of the three days I spent in a psychiatric hold after physically attacking my stepdad, and the pills I swallowed along with the words from doctors and nurses that I was experiencing a break with reality due to the trauma of losing my mother.

If only you'd listen to us and take your medication like a good girl, then you'll be back to normal in no time. Your father isn't a murderer. Cocaine and Oxy and a hard-partying lifestyle are what fuel your paranoid delusions. Your mother isn't coming back.

I was in that suffocating, nauseating fugue for seventy-two hours. Did Emma have to endure it for two years?

"Chase allowed that?" I whisper.

Emma shakes her head. "Not even close. But he was forced to watch it happen."

I wait for her to continue.

"My brother ... I had to make him understand we were

playing the long game. Instant retaliation doesn't work. I set the Virtues' temple on fire and look where that got me. The only consequence of my efforts was that they had to build a new one."

I choke on Emma's revelation, wishing I'd grabbed some water. "The Virtues' secret meeting grounds was hidden in the old library?"

Emma responds with a droll look. "Contrary to popular belief, I'm not a pyro who sets revenge fires just because a mysterious masked man who jumped me there was still running free."

"So, it was the Virtues who attacked you."

Emma cants her head in partial agreement. "It was their way of permanently severing me from the Virtues. Fracturing my face..." Her words hit a rough patch, and Emma clears her throat. I take that as a clue that all of us are in need of water, so I hop up and pour three glasses.

"An edict of being Virtuous," Emma says as I return, placing the drinks on the coffee table before reoccupying my seat, "is that you have to be beautiful. If you don't have beauty, you're no use to them."

Eden drops her head, her long, black hair swishing against her cheeks, obscuring her profile. My chest tightens as I glance between them, their minds more battered and disfigured from the existence of the Virtues than their bodies ever will be.

I hate them, I think with ferocious venom. *I hate these societies.*

"So, you tried to destroy the Virtues' property as payback," I say, thinking this through as delicately as I can. "Except, you were somehow trapped inside while doing it."

Eden nudges Emma. "Might as well tell her everything."

Emma watches me for a moment, then parts her lips. "I wasn't trapped. I was locked in."

I stare at her. "What?"

"It wasn't my intention to destroy the whole building," Emma says. "I only wanted the underground temple to burn for what they did. But the queen caught me, and instead of screaming at me to get out, she shut and locked the door in my face."

I hold a hand to my neck, my stomach lurching. "But you managed to escape. You survived."

"Because my brother saved me."

The mention of Chase's name holds the same power it always does, my heart cleaving in two at the thought of him running into flames to save his sister, and the lies he had to weave to ensure both his and his sister's survival at this academy.

And I told him I couldn't trust him.

"Do you see, Callie?" Eden asks, shuffling closer to Emma and putting her arm around her shoulders. "Can you understand why we duped you? We need someone on the inside, to get to the Virtues' written recordings, to collect evidence against them, to expose them for who they really are." Eden waits a beat, both of them watching the information they imparted slip under my skin, erode my bones, and turn my insides to ash. "Are you with us?"

I lick my lips. Take a long, cold gulp of water.

Piper was their inside girl before me. And now she's dead.

So is my mother.

So is the carefree, beguiling, cheerful Callie Ryan that I used to be.

I raise my head, including both Emma and Eden when I say, "Yeah. I'm in."

"I have a confession to make," I say to Emma and Eden, threading my fingers together on my lap. "The Virtues contacted me this morning."

Emma's brows lower. "What did they say?"

I lock my jaw, my gaze sliding over to my bag, slumped innocently beside the door. "It's ... well, let's be real. It's Falyn, and she's teed me up for another screwed up test."

Eden nods. "That's usually how it goes."

"How many?" I ask, mild desperation lacing my tone. "How many will it take before I'm robed?"

Emma answers. "Hard to say. Each girl is different. You're not a legacy, you're a BU freshman and they're letting you into the society because you've basically strong-armed them."

"*And* Falyn's in charge of your initiation," Eden adds.

"Gee. Anything else?"

"I'm betting on a pretty brutal future for you," Eden

says, her eyes as flat as her voice. "But if you can take it, I'll have mad respect for you."

"God." I rub my eyes.

"Sack up," Emma says. "You can do this."

I nod with forced vigor, because I'm not looking forward to what I'm about to say. "Eden, what they're asking me to do is about—"

A hard knock sounds against our door, making all three of us jump. Eden's pho splashes on her white button-up shirt, and she curses.

Ivy's voice floats through the gaps. "Callie? Are you there?"

Emma mumbles something close to an insult then leans back and crosses her arms. She says to me, "Your move. I'm not letting her in."

My attention flits between Emma and Eden—two people on my side, but who've proven their willingness to throw me under the bus if it suits their larger plan—and Ivy, the girl who saved me from drowning, yet disillusioned our friendship to the point that I'm questioning if it ever existed in the first place.

Are these my choices?

Standing, I sigh. "I'll get it."

Emma frowns. Eden's expression becomes unreadable, but she watches the door.

I stride over and unlock the deadbolt, revealing Ivy, unkempt, windblown, and bringing in the scent of a chilled forest with her. Her shoulders sag at the sight of me. "I wasn't sure you were going to answer."

"I debated it."

She nods, her gaze falling to the floor as she wrings her hands. "Can I come in?"

"No," Eden calls behind me.

"Yes," I say, and step aside. "But if it isn't obvious, I'm not alone."

Ivy tiptoes in, her focus centering on Emma and Eden, both rigid and watchful. Neither have resumed eating.

"Hi, guys," Ivy says to them quietly.

Emma levels her chin. Eden glares.

"I'm glad you're all here," Ivy says. With the way she stands in the center of our room, leaving her coat on and her bag strapped on her shoulders, it's clear she doesn't think she'll be staying long.

My heart aches at the sight. Just a few days ago, Ivy was bursting in here, her jacket, shoes, and books flying everywhere before she splayed on my bed and asked me how I felt about binge-watching baking shows.

"We know about last weekend," Eden supplies. "And what was done to Callie."

The memories get the best of me. I blurt out in defense, "Ivy saved me. When I was in the water, she jumped in and swam me to the docks."

Eden's brows hike up. Emma's lips thin.

Ivy turns to me, her blue eyes lighting up with a familiar smile. "Obviously, Callie. I couldn't leave you to drown."

Eden makes a sound of disgust. "I can't with this drama. The water's like, ten feet deep under the docks. It's not like Callie couldn't—"

"I can't swim," I say.

Eden's mouth falls open.

"Wait a second," Emma says. "You can't swim, and you managed to find the Virtues' key under the docks?"

"Badass," Eden says, her expression turning to one of admiration.

Ivy ignores them both. "Callie, you may think less of me because I hid my membership, but if you keep up your initiation, you'll understand why. The society doesn't play around. I *couldn't* tell you, even though I really wanted to. I tried to leave clues…"

"Like telling me about the Nobles when I first came to Briarcliff," I say. "Then denying you ever said anything."

Ivy slumps. "This world we're in, it's a gift and a curse. With the Virtues, our future is pure gold."

Emma snorts. But Eden's stare becomes almost feverish as she listens to Ivy.

"But the curse…" Ivy continues, "the curse is to sign away your soul."

My eyes narrow at the sudden turn. I study Ivy harder. "We're talking real life here. They can't possibly own your *soul*."

"I didn't come over to convince you to be one of us. I'm here to—I'm here…" Ivy trails off, one hand massaging her throat as she glances at Eden, but lands on Emma. "Eden was humiliated, you were hurt, and Piper died. The Virtues aren't who I thought they were when I pledged in eighth grade. I've seen things, I've—I've *done* things, I—"

"You're the new princess, aren't you?"

Emma asks it so softly; the sound barely travels to my ears. But her head is cocked, her eyes carrying the louder message. Suspicion. Warning.

"Yes," Ivy admits, but she twists and clings to my arms. "Please look at me, Callie."

I do, but the movement's stiff, my muscles slower to catch up than my mind at the word *princess*.

"I don't want this anymore." Her sudden whisper is ferocious, her eyes glistening with tears.

My hands move to cup her elbows, but in my periphery, Emma rises. She comes over to us, and with the gentleness of stroking a caged bird, she lays her hand on Ivy's shoulder.

It's all Ivy needs.

She releases me and folds into Emma, sobbing into her shirt. Emma tilts her chin, not in confusion, but to rest her head against Ivy's, to hold her closer and make the hug more complete. Emma's hand rubs Ivy's back, and I stand there, a sudden stranger to my friend as Emma, the person who's sacrificed the least emotion in this room, opens herself up to provide comfort.

Emma's eyes flick to mine over the pale silk of Ivy's hair. "I was a princess, too, once."

I give a minute shake of my head, figuring I'm comprehending about a quarter of what's really going on. Looking to Eden, I ask, "Are you aware of what a Virtue princess is?"

Eden's expression is the closest to mine. She shakes her head. "I never got that far in their initiation. But if the Nobles have a prince, it makes sense the Virtues would create a princess."

"We don't have to talk about it. Not now." Emma says it to Ivy, continuing to rub Ivy's shuddering back. "That's not why Ivy's here."

"What, suddenly you're on her side?" Eden stands. "She's one of them. She could be setting us up."

"I'm not," Ivy says, gulping air as she lifts her head. The fair skin of her cheeks is splotched in sections, her hair sticking to her tear-slicked face. "I came for some understanding. I've felt so alone since Piper died and thought there was no one. Then Callie and I got close and you came back," Ivy says to Emma. "And Addisyn was arrested for Piper's murder. After that, Callie was tapped for the Virtues. It's too much. This isn't how it was supposed to be. Callie, I didn't want to bring you into this. I wanted you so, so far away, but now it looks like I betrayed you, but I swear ... I swear I only want what's good. I became a member under Rose Briar's teachings, but it's been twisted and broken, and ... and ... when I was asked to step in as princess, I couldn't say no. But it's a pretend power. It wasn't enough to stop them from coming for you, from getting you to that dock, even though I said nothing. I promise you I didn't tell them you couldn't sw—"

It's too much. Watching my friend fall apart is too damned wrenching, and I fly forward and wrap my arms around her.

She doesn't break down in tears again, but Ivy clings so tight, it's like she's asking for my intact soul to become hers, too.

"I had no idea you were so empty inside," I say close to her ear.

"Please forgive me," she whispers into my neck.

My grip tightens around her shoulders. "The Virtues take so much. I don't want them to take our friendship, too."

Ivy nods, sniffling into her sleeve, then slips a tissue out of her pocket.

"Are you saying you're a part of our..." Eden trails off. "What are we? A team? Special ops? Cat burglars?"

"We're the girls the Virtues crossed," Emma says, her expression hewn from stone. "Ivy, if you're to be a part of this, you have to prove you're on our side."

"I am." Ivy nods sharply. "I'll do whatever it takes to help you." She looks between all of us. "What are you doing, exactly?"

Three of us stand in the center of the room. Eden makes it four when she draws nearer, a suspicious gaze cast on Ivy, but somewhat amenable to a new member, nonetheless. She mutters, "All for one, I guess."

Emma takes a breath. "Okay, then. First test. Callie, what were you saying about your next task?"

My stomach sinks. But under Ivy's sympathetic eye, I pick up my bag and pull out my phone. "This," I say, though I keep the screen black.

"We need a little more than the big reveal of your phone," Emma says.

Although I'd prefer to stare at the floor while unveiling the terrible details, I don't. My mother didn't raise me that way. Instead, I stare directly at Eden, and include only her.

"They have pictures of you. New ones. In the locker room. You're changing out of your gym clothes and..."

I can't make myself continue when Eden's eyes die out.

Emma hisses out a curse. "*Fuck* them."

"I agree," I say, leveling my shoulders. "I refused to send it to the entire school like they wanted."

"I'm worried they'll ask for something worse," Ivy says, her voice treading carefully. "I'm fairly convinced they were behind your mom's photos, Callie. The ones of the crime scene."

My focus zeroes in on her, but I blink out of it before my heart can crash to my throat. This isn't about me right now, and I can't say I'm surprised the Virtues were behind that terrible prank.

Ivy says, "They dig into your past, figure out your worst history, then throw it in your face. The things they could do with your most guarded secrets…"

I swallow. "Then I'll have to grin and bear it, because I'm not putting her"—I point at Eden—"I'm not putting *you* through that again."

Eden, her expression dulled, doesn't even blink in reaction. Emma worries her lips as she squints at her friend, but with the way she keeps involving me in her stare, I can tell her thoughts are whirling toward—

"Do it."

I stiffen, at first convinced the directive came from Emma, but she's just as shocked as I am. Ivy folds her arms in on herself, appearing too gaunt and thin to unleash such a command.

That only leaves one other person.

"Are you serious?" I ask Eden.

She sets her jaw and nods. "This is my punishment for betraying them. I expected it. And if you don't do this, they'll come after you harder, and Emma and Ivy can both attest to the fact that it won't be Falyn behind the next idea. Just do what that bitch wants and be done with it."

"But ... but last time—"

Eden cuts me off. "Last time, I was unprepared. And I—had no friends. None that stuck with me after the photos went out, anyway." She lowers her head, hiding behind her hair.

"Eden," Emma tries.

"Do it, Callie. Before I lose my nerve."

I hold up my phone but shake my head. "I'll take whatever they have coming next. I'm not going to—"

With the grace and speed of cutting through water, Eden darts close and snatches my phone from my grip.

"Eden!" I cry, but I'm the only one who does.

Emma and Ivy both look on, awed and horrified as they watch Eden thumb through my screen. The second she sees her photo, her face spasms before she smooths it into a hardened mask of hatred.

A few minutes later, she tosses the phone back at me. I fumble to catch it, clutching it to my chest.

Eden takes a deep breath. "It's done. I've sent it out through a fake account."

I'm going to be sick. "Eden, you didn't have to do that."

"Forget about it," she says, then swivels to grab her things. "It's nothing they haven't seen before."

My lips tremble. Ivy holds back tears. Emma lifts her hand as Eden walks through our tiny group and toward the door.

"Go home, Eden," Emma says. "*Home* home. By the time Thanksgiving is over, something else will draw their attention."

"That's the thing," Eden says, her hand on the doorknob. She doesn't turn around. "*I* don't forget. But I'll be better, I'll feel whole again, if you bring me their heads. Even if you have to betray Chase, Callie, show me it was worth it, and I'll learn to forgive."

"You have my word," I say softly, but Eden doesn't catch it, because she's already thrown herself into a hallway of laughing, howling wolves.

I spend Thanksgiving in full-on Hates-giving mode.

I don't let it show, to my dad or Lynda. I'm docile, accepting the catered turkey feast and the extravagant holiday party with the smile of a perfect daughter.

To be honest, my relationship with Dad and Lynda moved by leaps and bounds in just one week. I arrive on their doorstep the morning of Thanksgiving, and Dad envelops me in a huge, hard hug. We're both still dealing with our grief over Mom in different ways—he was able to grapple with the consequences of her affair with Paul Harrington for over a year, while I've just found out, and I'm still having trouble with the imperfect image of Mom—but I haven't enjoyed the smell of his cologne this much since I was nine. I haven't let myself look forward to a baby sister this much since I was a kid, wishing for a sibling. And I haven't gotten to know Lynda this much since ... ever.

It's enough to put my anger on simmer instead of boil, but the back of my mind crawls with thoughts of Eden and how she's coping. She didn't show up to any of her classes for the rest of the shortened week. My multiple texts to her go ignored. My calls are declined. Because she won't talk to me directly, I focus on backdoor ways to help her out, like reporting the Instagram posts and sending an anonymous email to Chancellor Marron about the harassment.

It will never be enough.

That slithering thought, with a rattlesnake tail, refuses to uncoil, and I live with it for four days before I can reenter Briarcliff Academy turf and begin my take-down of the Virtues' secret society.

Because that, for Eden, *will* be enough.

After the holidays, the train into Briarcliff arrives on time. I'm saddened to see another driver waiting to chauffer me to campus. I was hoping that my favorite guy, Yael, also Eden's dad, would meet me, so I could poke around regarding Eden's welfare.

Then again, he's probably at home with his wife and Briarcliff custodian, Moira, deciding if this is the instance where they'll override their daughter and send her some-where else to complete her college years.

I can't blame them, and I'm sick at being part of their reason, not their cure.

That has to change.

I'm not about to become the Virtues' vessel for getting petty, terrible shit done.

In fact, I'm so consumed by thoughts of Eden, Chase

doesn't enter my mind until I'm practically on top of him once I reach the academy's outdoor pavilion.

"H-Hey," I hedge, when he turns around from his group of friends, a hot drink in hand.

Chase doesn't nod. He won't shift. Just stands in my path, his lids lowered, concealing the depth of his eyes.

I lift my chin, despite his attention turning my insides to mush. I'm thankful the weaker parts of me are surrounded by hard, emotionless bone. I ask, with as little care as possible, "How was your Thanksgiving?"

His lips part. "Move along."

"*Possum,*" James adds behind Chase, snickering. "You got some naked pics for us, too?"

I give him a sidelong look, though inside, that slow simmer of mine is hitting a dangerous boiling point. I guess it didn't take Chase long to forgive his buddy for helping to orchestrate my deep-dive into the Briarcliff lake.

Chase steps aside, his movement carrying a cold wind. I chance another look—just one *sign*—that this is an act, and there will come a moment where we can share our true emotions in private, or that James will receive another face-punch, but I receive nothing in return. Not even a ripple of emotion in those river-rock eyes.

He's let James get away with it. Again.

"See you around," I say, keeping strong, staying level, until I'm inside, out of sight, and I can slouch my shoulders without being watched.

I plan to hit my locker and dump the books I'd brought home before walking to the dorms, where I'm hoping

Emma will be, and we can have a late dinner together, far from the dining hall.

Maybe Eden will be there, too. Maybe *something* can go right for once, and the three of us can have a quiet evening with noodles instead of rumors coming between us.

As always, unlocking the padlock to my locker causes my spine to stiffen and my feet to brace on the floor. I'm torn between flinging the door open and getting any nasty surprises over with or creaking it ajar with my fingers and peering over the wood.

"Glad I caught you!"

The jarring trill makes me jump, almost into my locker.

"Jesus," I say, heart pounding as I spin around.

"Sorry," Ivy says. "I probably should know by now to approach you with caution."

"I almost used these textbooks on you," I say after catching my breath.

Ivy loops her thumbs in the front pockets of her jeans, sporting a simple white T-shirt on top. "How was your—?"

"Fine," I say, cutting off what will inevitably be the most basic, polite question ever after coming back from Thanksgiving. Our cobbled-together friendship deserves better than that. *And I just used it on Chase.*

I cringe.

Ivy takes my expression another way. "Shoot—sorry, again. I didn't mean to pry. I know you and your dad have problems, and I wasn't—"

"It's fine," I assure. "Better than fine, actually. Dad and I are on the mend."

"Really?" Ivy's raises her brows with pleasure. "Callie, that's awesome."

The genuine warmth in her voice relaxes the tight cords in my chest. "Yours was good, too?"

"Sure." Ivy shrugs. "If you count eating a goose instead of a turkey. Loved seeing Mum and Dad, though."

"I'm glad." Then I cringe again. This is *not* how we usually are with each other.

"Um, so..." Ivy peers over her shoulder. No one else hangs around the lockers. Not surprising, since it's late Sunday night, and students don't normally run straight into the main building after arriving from vacation.

I dump my books in the locker, then bend to grab my duffel and slide it back on my shoulder. "What's up?"

"I mean..." Ivy's cheeks puff out with held-in breath. "We're on such fragile ground, you and I..."

Another cord loses tension inside my chest. "You sense it, too."

Ivy widens her eyes in a *hell yeah* gesture, then digs her thumbs harder into her pockets. "And I'm about to make it worse."

There we go. Knots upon knots behind my ribs. "Don't prolong the torture. Out with it."

"I'm a—ugh." Ivy sighs. "I've been sent as an emissary, and I *hate* that they've chosen me to do this, but Falyn flaunts being in charge of your recruitment so *freaking* much, and I'm seriously about to lose it on her—"

"Ivy. Get back on track."

"Yes. Okay. You need to come with me."

"I'm to what?"

"Right now."

I point to my duffel bag. "I was planning to—"

"Stuff it in your locker."

Ivy's flicked some sort of inner switch, her expression falling as flat as her voice.

"Ivy…"

"Please." For a second, her brows furrow. "Don't make this harder than it has to be."

My hand comes up in surrender. "Okay. Fine. Whatever."

I squish my duffel, and then my winter coat, into my locker, then shut and click the padlock before following Ivy into the hall.

We walk in silence, something we've never done before, and without anything to fidget with, I resort to rubbing the hem of my hoodie between my thumb and index finger.

Once at the back of the building, Ivy pushes the heavy wooden doors open, a counteracting winter wind rushing through the cracks.

I grimace. "I should've brought my coat."

"We won't be long." Ivy points to the adjacent building beyond the howling wolf fountain.

My gaze travels past the roaring snout, and I sigh. "Should've known."

"Come on."

Following her brisk steps, I navigate around the stone fountain (thankfully turned off and thus avoiding a freezing, spraying mist of water) and toward the new library, or, what it's officially called: the M.B.S. Library of Studies, built by

Chase's family and constructed over the ashy bones of Emma's revenge gone wrong.

That kind of awareness causes enough heebie-jeebies when stepping through the sleek, chrome-lined sliding doors. Add in the Virtues' hidden temple and … yeah. I'm not looking forward to my final destination.

They've recruited you because they think they can control you. Don't let them be right.

I reply to my mom's quiet voice: *I won't.*

The lights are dim to non-existent once we step through the turnstiles with Ivy's keycard, and the librarian is nowhere in sight.

Usually, the natural hush of a library is soothing, soft voices and rustling pages some of the only sounds breaking through a quiet solitude. This time, however, my back is up, my eyes alert, and my hands clenched.

We head to the back, single file, until we reach a wall of books. Long, rolling ladders are on either side of us, and what seems like unending stacks of books are behind us. The furniture is magnified, somehow, with just Ivy and me here. The aisles growing smaller in the swallowing darkness, the shelves looming larger over my head.

I shake off the fear, because I've never been afraid of the dark, and I'm not about to start now. I watch as Ivy crouches to the ground and lifts a floorboard, the movement smooth and quiet.

I swear, if an owl hoots outside, I might jump out of my skin.

Crossing my arms, I say, "Is this how you usually enter the temple?"

Ivy looks up. "There's an outside entrance, but it's not used much in winter."

I make a sound of agreement, if only for something to do, as Ivy reveals a small coding panel in the floor and types in a pin. I recall what Chase said to me. "So, I guess the ancient key I snorkeled for is more of a symbol."

"It belonged to the old temple, built when Rose Briar was in charge. With this new construction, we were able to update a lot of things."

Eyeing the wall of books, I step away once the pin pad flashes green. Lately, I've had a lot of back walls move to reveal secret chambers and figure I should keep clear.

Nothing happens.

"Aren't these books supposed to move?"

Ivy rises beside me. She points to the left. "Over there."

When she shifts, I mimic her movement, wary of what will open and how..

A large, person-sized panel in the floor unlocks and lifts with invisible hands. During its slow rise, I glance behind us in automatic caution to ensure we're alone.

When I turn forward again, a rectangular blackness awaits.

"I'll go first," Ivy says with quirked lips, likely understanding that there's no way in hell I'm stepping into a dark hole before she does.

Ivy's covered in complete darkness within two steps, her long legs eating up space faster than mine do, but I keep close to her heels, blinded in both sight and mind. I have no idea where we're going, where to step, or what staircase I'll topple down next.

"Here," she says, and takes my arm, gently guiding me to her side. We inch along a few steps before Ivy does something to cause a ring of sconces to light up around our forms.

My breath hitches as a single room illuminates, the ceiling door we entered through long shut with its silent, ghostly slither.

Gray, flat stone encircles us on all sides, the massive engraving of *altum vultaire in tenebres* carved in classic cursive directly at my eye-line.

"We rise high in the dark," I translate. "You and the Nobles have the same motto."

"Kind of. We interpret it in different ways."

I'm about to ask how the Virtues differentiate such an ominous sentence, but Ivy moves us into the center of the room.

"Holy..." is all I can get out when what I thought was our ceiling lights up with another row of second-floor candelabras, revealing a circular balcony with long, Roman-style columns dividing the circumference into four sections.

Robed figures appear from the shadows, stepping up to the stone balustrade. Their cloaks shimmer gold in the fire-dappled light, but their faces remain darkly obscured beneath their hoods.

Pomp and circumstance.

I think of that pretentious phrase and picture them puffing out their chests as they take their places between the columns, until the eight of them surround us, instead of the sick terror worming its way through my gut.

"Welcome to our temple," a soothing, feminine voice chimes, directly above the carved motto.

It's not a voice I'm familiar with. Not Falyn, or Willow, or even the whispery Violet...

"If you manage to achieve a coveted position in our ranks, this will become your sanctuary."

My throat spasms with a swallow that echoes in the cavernous silence. "I'd hope a sanctuary would contain some comfortable couches. Or maybe some curtains? Except, there are no windows..."

"*Quiet*," the female voice hisses.

Crap. I'm rambling. I'm not comfortable revealing such a nervous aspect of myself, but with hooded, concealed stares beaming down on my head, remembrances of being stuck in the black, freezing depths of the lake come to the forefront. My near-death becomes real when I think of my face forever contorted with the spasms of lost breaths.

And they watched it happen.

"Calla Lily Ryan," the mysterious voice continues, "you've been summoned here so you may have your curiosity satisfied. What gave you the impression that you could reveal our existence without consequence?"

It's as if she's reading my mind, parting the mists of my thoughts and zoning in on my fear of further reprisal—of something *worse* than drowning happening to me in this place.

"I admit..." I clear my throat when my voice comes out as a warble. "I admit I wasn't careful, or conscious of what I was seeking. My roommate died, and I wasn't satisfied with the simplicity her fall was given. There had to be more truth than she was so drunk, she lost her balance and fell, or—"

"Therein, you found Rose Briar's original writings," the woman cuts in. "And concluded—falsely—that we Virtues had a hand in her murder."

"I didn't ... I wasn't sure what I was uncovering. It was her diary I discovered first. A diary planted by Addisyn. A girl who *was* a current member of yours, until she was arrested a little over a week ago. A girl who murdered her sister, also a member of the Virtues. How could I not conclude you had something to do with it?"

"I assure you, young one..." The woman's tone takes on a dangerous edge. "We are not behind Piper Harrington's death. You would have exposed us for nothing, had we not intervened."

My brows furrow. "Every clue I uncovered led me to your doorstep. Every paper I read, from Rose, to Piper, to Howard Mason breaking into the Nobles' tomb—"

"Planted."

I shake my head. "Not all of it was stashed with bad intentions. Rose Briar's letter was hidden by Piper to protect it, not use it as bait."

"Piper relied on misguided notions rather than coming to us first."

"Piper was killed for her involvement—"

"*Enough.*" The woman's voice crackles against the stone, but the only one who shivers from the electric charge is me. Every other person remains still, serene, and targeted on the girl in the center of the room below them.

"Your grave errors, your rampant mouth, your

unfounded theories have brought you to this point, Calla Lily. Remember that, the next time you are given the honor to address the Virtuous Queen."

I glance back at the woman. She lifts her hands, the heavy, golden fabric falling down her forearms and creasing at her elbows as she hooks her hood and pulls it back.

The sconces seem to flicker with exposed power as silky brunette hair cascades down her shoulders, and she dips her poreless face until her features come into the light.

My knees snap together. My nails dig into my palms. My lips fuse into one line as I put a name to that face.

Sabine.

Sabine Harrington is the Virtues' queen.

"Mrs. Harrington," I breathe out.

Piper and Addisyn's mother.

I don't need to see her eyes to recognize the dangerous feel of them crawling across my skin, judging mercilessly..

I reach out to grab Ivy's hand but end up clutching air. She's gone, slipping away during the distracting reveal of the queen.

The back of my throat itches at the thought of being left alone, but my eyes scrape up from the floor, scanning the circular balcony for a ninth Cloak.

I find it to the left of Mrs. Harrington. Ivy may not have asked to be their princess, but she's up there, donning her title and casting a hooded gaze in my direction.

I turn my attention back to Mrs. Harrington. "I'm so sorry for causing you pain. You've lost two daughters, and I never intended to make it worse. And as for my mom and what she did to your family, I—"

"Silence." Mrs. Harrington's voice cracks through the cavernous chamber. "I haven't asked for an apology and don't require one. Talk of my daughters is no longer welcome on your tongue. I've summoned you here not to get to know you—you ruined any chance of a bond due to your unfortunate DNA and your insolent involvement in my daughters' affairs—but due to a development that cannot be ignored."

I shove my hands into my hoodie's front pocket so I can fist them together without anyone noticing. "You don't have to make some grandiose speech to make your disdain clear. I'm partially responsible for your loss of your youngest daughter. The only one you had left. And my mother never took your feelings into account when she—"

"*Enough.*"

Mrs. Harrington's expression is so frozen in time, her frost expands to me, but I grit my teeth and push on. "Why am I here? Why did you choose me to become a Virtue when I so clearly don't belong?"

Mrs. Harrington's eye tics at my questions, but she otherwise maintains her blank, flawless state. "You may have passed our first level of recruitment, but two steps remain before you're invited into our ranks. Are you willing to continue?"

"Do you *want* me to continue?"

Mrs. Harrington's upper lip twitches, the second fracture in her façade. She says, with slow, deathly cadence, "I will ask you this once. Deny us, and you may turn around and leave our temple, so long as you promise never to speak of the Virtues again. However, accept your next two tasks, and the rewards will be everlasting, but once passed, you will *never* be permitted to leave our ranks without severe repercussions. Have I made myself clear?"

"*Altum vultaire in tenebres.*"

The girls' voices combine into a flat lull, but that one note circles the room and prickles against my ears.

Ivy. Where's Ivy? Why won't she let me see her face?

Piper's face swims in my mind's eye instead, transforming into my mother's in a blink. Both expressions are twisted in fear, shriveling my lungs and taking my breath. I lower my head and close my eyes until a vision of Chase takes hold, his lips softened from my kisses, his eyes in vivid, brilliant relief.

I want you to feel me inside you, as much as I feel you inside me...

I search for him now.

Multiple wrongs surround this group and his—wrongs Chase wants to change, suffering I'll expose.

Eden. Emma. Ivy. They've been mutilated by these women, too. What I've experienced is but a quarter of what they've endured.

Their combined hope, directed at me, to infiltrate the Virtues and assist in taking them down, makes my answer come out easy, despite my heart pounding at my mind's door, begging me to say the opposite.

My voice echoes with a strong, sure, "Yes."

A few beats of silence pass, where only the *thump, thump, thump* of my heart is heard in my ears.

"Very well," Mrs. Harrington says, and raises her chin, a power move that ensures she can peer down her regal nose.

Her eyes glitter with refractive, ominous light. "Your second task is simple. Confess to us your worst sin, and let it fall on Virtuous ears."

My mouth goes dry. I once again scour the nearest Cloak for Ivy's familiar face but can't find her in all the gold fabric.

"My patience wears thin, Initiate," Mrs. Harrington says.

"Okay, uh..." I search the floor beneath my feet for answers. The memory that floats to the surface makes me squirm. "My best friend. Back in the city. It's because of me she experimented with drugs. At first it was just weed. Then coke. By the end, she ... she took it further. To Molly and LSD, but she wasn't getting it clean. It was laced with other things, like baby powder, and..."

I can't escape the microscopic effect of Mrs. Harrington's stare. She alone regards me without a hood, her expression filled with both judgment and indifference.

"And Fentanyl," I finish. "Sylvie overdosed and almost couldn't be saved. It was my fault. My fault she got into drugs in the first place."

Mrs. Harrington cants her head. The ring of girls surrounding us keep still and silent.

At last, she speaks. "This sounds more like your friend's weakness than yours."

I shudder at the remembrance of my careless peer pressure. "She didn't even want to try a blunt. I had to cajole her, guilt her, into doing one with me. I used my mom's death as a weapon. Sylvie couldn't deny me. I should've kept it at weed. I shouldn't've forced coke on her, too."

"Mm." Sabine gives a slow, bored blink. "I'm unconvinced this overdose is the worst part of yourself. Tell me more about your mother."

My stomach revolts at the word *mother* crossing Mrs. Harrington's scarlet lips. What kind of mother is *she*? Both her girls are—

No. No, I can't fling blame where more than enough resides within my soul. Mrs. Harrington has every right to hate my mother. Meredith Ryan wasn't just a hard worker, superhero mom, and a caring friend. She was a mistress. A homewrecker. A liar.

I squeeze my eyes shut, queasy inside the spiral of my mom's shame. *Human. She was human, and I miss her.*

I exhale. Breathe.

"My mom was brutally murdered," I say, my voice going quiet. "In her bedroom. Her killer has never been found." I look Mrs. Harrington dead in the eyes. "I'm sure we can agree that's punishment enough for her mistakes."

She ignores my goading as easily as a nearby gnat. "But you had a killer in mind, didn't you?"

I flinch. "My stepfather. I blamed him, had him taken into custody, but..."

"You were wrong."

I nod. Forming my costly mistake into words is still too painful to emit.

"Your mother also had an affair."

My gaze snaps up. Will Mrs. Harrington confirm I'm her ex-husband's daughter? Now that she's lost both of hers?

Mrs. Harrington's mouth curves at my expression. "I'm aware, Initiate, as are the rest of my Virtues, of your mother's transgressions, and of whom she had them with.

Perhaps another time, we can discuss the sexual relations between her and my ex-husband, but again, her DNA is not the worst part of you, now, is it?"

"Am I his child?"

The question comes out sharp, and I bite my lower lip at the eagerness it exudes, like I'm desperate for the answer.

Mrs. Harrington's eyes grow small, but the power filtering through them doesn't flicker. "You read what my late daughter had to say about it in her diary. What do you think?"

"Piper could've been misled." *I hope she was wrong.* "I don't think I'm related to your daughters. I don't think Paul Harrington is—"

"You don't *want*, is the correction I must make. You're disgusted at the thought of being a Harrington, aren't you?"

I hesitate.

Mrs. Harrington pounces. "What makes you interested in the Virtues, then, if you cannot stand the leaders within it?"

There are no Harringtons left, except for you, I almost bite out. But I'm outnumbered, and while they may all be on a balcony well away from me, I'm not an idiot.

"My mother would've told me." I find more strength as I let the truth flow. "There's no reason she would've kept his name from me all this time. I wouldn't—*she* never—came after you for any kind of support. We were fine. Proudly independent. Best friends." My voice breaks.

Mrs. Harrington pounces on my hesitation. "Maybe she concealed his name in order to protect you. Have you thought of that?"

My breath stalls.

She chuckles. "Enough idle talk, my dear. You're correct. Paul is not your missing father. Your paternity is, yet again, *not* your darkest secret. Your poorly construed accusation against your stepfather is also not among your top transgressions, though you're certainly collecting a stack of them." Mrs. Harrington folds her arms. "I'll give you one last chance. What remains to be confessed to the Virtues?"

My eyes flit around the room, catching upon featureless, obscured faces.

Sylvie overdosing from my drugs was bad. Sending my stepdad to jail was terrible. The possibility of having Mr. Harrington as my real father is a nightmare.

...what's left?

"Tell me, Calla Lily." Mrs. Harrington leans her forearms against the railing, tilting seductively in my direction. "What have you done while at Briarcliff Academy?"

I rack my brain for details. "You mean, other than have a roommate die, accuse a teacher of murder, break into a secret society tomb, and sleep with—"

Oh my God.

Sleep with Chase?

"Dr. Luke," I divert in a scratchy voice. "I accused him, too."

Mrs. Harrington clucks her tongue through a Cheshire smile. "Is that what your new sisters need to hear?"

"What do you want? What are you digging for?"

Mrs. Harrington laughs. "Don't be obtuse, dear. Confess to us who you care for, despite what he did to you. Who you're loyal to, regardless of his cruel intentions. Who you cannot help but follow, despite him not being yours."

Chase.

I step back, but as I'm in the middle of a circle, it brings me to no safer distance. "What's so important about him? He's far from the worst thing I've done."

"Ah." Mrs. Harrington holds up a finger, her nail, painted blood red, visible from my vantage point. "Was I not clear to you before? I asked you to tell me your vilest secret." Mrs. Harrington's red-lined, menacing lips peel into a smile. "I didn't say whose secret it had to belong to."

My brows draw in. I take another step back, toward a nonexistent door. I'm trapped in this corrupt stone temple. "Chase has never made me aware of the secrets he keeps."

"Hasn't he?"

My mind works backward, even as the denial crosses the threshold of my lips. It catalogues and highlights the pieces of knowledge Chase gave me, then comes to an abrupt, alarming halt at his latest confession: *I don't want to end the Nobles. I want to control them.*

Shit shit *shit*.

Chase's dad is the head of the Nobles. Their king. He's engaged to be married to Mrs. Harrington. The last thing this twisted couple wants is Chase toppling them like two chess pieces.

What level of betrayal do I have inside my head?

"He's closed off," I say, keeping my voice level. "We never get that deep with each other."

"Are you saying you only have surface-level fucks with him?"

Such profanity, coming from a Briarcliff parent, is off-putting and creepy. But the girls around her merely sway, their robes fluttering but their shoulders as stiff as the Roman columns framing their forms.

I grit my teeth. "Not that it's any of your business, but yes."

"The truth, Callie," Mrs. Harrington warns, "the *truth* is the only way you will leave this temple one step closer to becoming a Virtue."

"I don't want—"

But you do, my whirring mind slows down to remind. *Think of what Eden is going through this very second. What more will happen to her or to Emma if you don't pretend the Virtues have control?*

Ivy. Where's Ivy?

I pinpoint her when her hood ripples as she turns her head to the side. As a ribbon of light hits her cheekbone and reflects the blue of her eyes.

Her stare is pleading, her lips pulled in. As if she's telling me, *do what Mrs. Harrington wants.*

"Fine," I say. Mrs. Harrington cocks her ear, feigning deafness.

I yell, "*Fine.* I have feelings for him. Does that please you? I care for Chase Stone in a way I've never cared for anyone. I crave him despite the malice he's inflicted and the apathy he gives me, except for when we're in bed. I like him, okay?"

"Like?"

"*Love.*" My voice goes hoarse, gritting with sound. "I'm falling in love with him. *That* is the worst part of myself I can give you. I love a boy who's cruel, who was never mine to begin with, who belonged to your daughter first." I breathe out a few breaths. "And I've destined myself for heartbreak."

"Sweet girl, I can somewhat believe your confession, with your large doe eyes and your thick, pathetic tears splashing over our pristine marble floors. But I can't say the same for Chase Stone. He's slept with you, he's protected you, and he claimed you as his soulmate not two weeks ago."

"That was in retaliation to Falyn's hazing. I would've died from hypothermia had he not put a stop to it."

Mrs. Harrington laughs, and a shiver shoots up my spine at the image of a wolf, with ferocious fangs, chasing a vulnerable girl through a forest.

"Secret societies live and die by their rules, do they not?" I ask. "He invoked the soulmate rite to stop her abuse of power."

A Cloak hisses. Falyn. I flip her the my middle finger, overjoyed that she actually gets to *see* the disgust written all over my face.

"Soulmate protection provides so much more than a shield against your fellow sisters," Mrs. Harrington says. "As you're about to find out. You must admit, after all the hurdles he's defended you from, despite being explicitly told to isolate and humiliate you, that Chase cares for you."

"He might," I say, but my tone is unsure. I have the dizziest feeling that I'm walking into a trap. "You'll have to ask him."

"He does."

My back goes up. "So what? So what if he cares for me despite your stupid threats and orders? If that's all you want, then you have it. Let me leave."

"You've given me exactly what I need, my dear. That is his worst secret you bear." After a slow, satiated smile, Mrs. Harrington pulls her hood over her head and retreats from the railing. "You are that boy's greatest weakness to exploit."

10

One by one, the golden Cloaks draw back from the balcony and disappear into the ether upstairs.

When I'm alone, the hidden door to the temple opens. I dash up the stairs and burst into the library, my breaths heaving.

The blue hue of sleeping computers guides me through the stacks and to the main doors, and when they hiss open softly, I sprint out, glad to be rid of that place.

Mrs. Harrington didn't have to say it, but I hear her implications echoing in my ears. *Chase is your greatest weakness.*

When did that happen? I'm trying to recall the moment when Chase and I pivoted from enemies, to fuck buddies, to ... whatever we are now.

The foreboding swirl in my gut has me sprinting faster to my dorm, a place where I can find some semblance of peace, of order.

"Callie!"

The familiar call slows my steps, but not my resolve. I don't turn around.

"Callie! Wait up!"

I walk faster.

"Hey." Ivy grips my shoulder, twisting me over my feet. "Couldn't you hear me?"

I regain my balance and wrench out of her hold. "What are you expecting me to say to you right now?"

Ivy's breath puffs next to mine as she trots to keep pace next to me. "It was necessary."

"*Necessary?*" I echo, halting and facing her in the middle of the night-shadowed pathway. "I had to pour my heart out to that witch. With *everyone* watching. Do you know what kind of ammo I gave them? What kind of trigger Falyn's going to pull when classes start tomorrow?"

"She won't. Falyn can't," Ivy assures. "What occurs in the Virtues' temple is sacred. For us alone. Falyn isn't allowed to use any of that against you."

"Like she was forbidden from pushing me off the dock? Or sending me nude photos of Eden? C'mon, Ivy, you can't be so innocent as to—"

"I'm not innocent." Ivy's eyes shine white in the dark.

"Then why allow this to happen?"

"There hasn't been anyone to successfully go against them in years. The Virtues have grown in power, Callie. After Emma, no one was willing to rebel against Sabine. Until..."

I throw my hands up. "Until what?"

"You."

The one syllable strikes my heart like a fist. "Don't put so much faith in me. I'm far from your perfect savior, and Mrs. Harrington proved that tonight. Even my *worst* traits weren't enough for her. She wanted my weaknesses, too. Now she has them. And that *terrifies* me."

"Please." Ivy doesn't have to get on her knees to beg. Her lower lip trembles. "You're not alone."

I catch her eye. Hold it. Even as my heart hurts, it sings. *You are not alone, Calla.*

"Okay." I bite my lower lip. "I'll do the third and final trial. But Ivy?"

"Yeah?"

"If anyone else gets hurt..."

Ivy pulls me into a hug. Her comforting, wildflower fragrance mixes with the bite of winter air, and my shoulders relax in her embrace. "It's not easy, but you're lowering her guard by being honest."

"Uh-huh," I mutter into Ivy's shoulder.

Ivy pulls away. "And hey—that whole Mr. Harrington possibly being your dad was an unexpected twist, huh?"

I give her the side-eye. "Was it?"

"Well." Ivy lets out a laugh, keeping one arm around my shoulders as we resume walking. "Then celebrate that he's not. She wouldn't lie about that."

I turn to look behind us, down the pristine, paved walkway and back toward the library. "I'm not so sure."

"The queen only imparts truth. That's a requirement of leading us."

I scan Ivy's profile, my back tensing under the weight of her arm. She says *queen* like it means something. Talks about her belief in truth like Mrs. Harrington has to abide by it. Really, Sabine Harrington can do whatever the fuck she wants—*that's* one of the requirements of being human.

A flicker of distrust grows its flame in my chest. I sigh, wishing for the Ivy I once knew, not the one who's become the Virtue in my head.

We reach the dorms. Before I go in, I ask, "Are you sure you want to help with the downfall of your sisterhood?"

"I'm wishing for the Virtues of yesteryear. The ones my grandmother spoke of. If that's not possible anymore, then I'm okay if they're disbanded and exposed." She pauses. "Annihilated."

I distance from her when we reach the doors to Thorne House. "You're a legacy?"

"Yeah." Her ice-blond brows lower. "My grandma, and then my dad, were students at Briarcliff."

I wait for Ivy to say more.

"He was kicked out before he could graduate," she says. "And he said it was the Nobles' fault."

"Holy shit, Ivy."

Ivy offers a waning smile. "You and I haven't known each other for long, but you agree we connected right away, right?"

"Sure."

"It's why I stupidly mentioned the Nobles to you so early. The Nobles were told to keep watch on you. They've been interested in you from the very beginning, and I felt so, so bad for how you were treated."

Ivy's not asking a question, but I nod under her scope. I

have the distinct feeling that's what she needs right now, even though it's far too late to rewind our choices.

"I'm not just a scholarship kid," Ivy says. "I haven't been the most upfront with you, but you're an initiate now, and I can tell you what my dad did."

I answer hesitantly. "Okay."

"He did some things that got him expelled, and during one of his rants with Mom, I overheard a conversation I wasn't supposed to."

"Go on."

"It's not much, but ... Dad only freaked out once our lives started falling apart. He said it all came back to betraying the Nobles in university, that he shouldn't have done it, and if he could go back and be a 'good little preparatory prick,' we'd still have our money."

"What did he do?"

"He stole a Stone's girlfriend. Chase's uncle."

I breathe out a gust of air. "Whoa."

"That girlfriend is my mom."

My mouth hangs open.

"Thing is..." Ivy lifts her hands in an empty gesture. "He tried to get back into their good graces by pleading with me to accept the Virtues' invitation to become one of them. That maybe, if I become Virtuous, the perks would stretch to my parents again and he'd no longer be blacklisted from top companies."

It all makes sense. Ivy's hesitation in telling me the truth. Her excuses and lies. "You're trying to save your family."

Ivy wilts. "I'm desperate to. Mom and Dad have scraped

by for so long. When I received a scholarship here, my dad became my *dad*. Loving. Attentive and present. I'd never felt anything like it before. He put so much hope in me, in my ability to get our reputation back. I'm sorry you're caught in the middle. I try to do what the Virtues want, but when Piper died, and I took her place beside Sabine—Callie, I—" Ivy's mouth seals shut, her jaw hard but her eyes shining with tears. "There's more to the Virtues than my parents know. My mother was never one of them. I can't be Virtuous anymore. Not after what I—what Sabine made me—"

"Shh," I soothe, drawing Ivy to my side. "It's okay. Let's just go home, get warm."

"I'm sorry for lying to you."

I rest my head against hers. "You don't have to apologize anymore."

Ivy glares in the direction of Thorne House, her forehead creasing. "I'm not finished telling you everything."

I hold Ivy in a light, but secure, hug. "Then we'll sleep on it. To be honest, I need a break from all these big reveals."

Ivy's soft laugh flutters my hair. "Deal. I'll see you tomorrow?"

We separate, and I nod. I back up a few steps, waving goodbye, then swivel to walk through the doors and step into the waiting elevator. When I turn to face the front, Ivy's still standing on the path, her stare unwavering on mine until the elevator door slides shut.

I'm dressed and ready for class well before Emma wakes up, and I pour myself a thermos of coffee before quietly departing our room.

The day dawns bright and frigid, and I huddle into my winter coat as I walk, backpack-free, to the academy. I left most of my things in my locker before my summons last night, and had no urge to run back into the deserted academy afterward to get my things—lest I stumble upon a Nobles' meeting, too.

Only one secret society per night, please.

Gray skies cloud the horizon, and as my breaths puff sharp, white clouds, I wonder when it will snow. In the city, we either received white-out blizzards or blackened sludge piled up on curbs. I've never experienced the true, Christmas effect of blanketing snow on open fields and weighing down thick branches, unmarred and sparkling under the sun's white-washed winter lens.

I'm so distracted by my unexpected Christmas wish that it takes me a moment to connect the dots when I see a cluster of students outside, their neutral-hued winter coats and parkas blending into the cobbled stone of the pavilion and academy.

Heads start popping out of collars and hoods like turtles the closer I get, and the harsh connection of voices and wild gestures slow my steps.

"Fuckin' fight club," a guy murmurs as he passes me by.

He's young, pimply, and thin, likely a freshman, and when I catch his eye, I ask automatically, "What's going on?"

He turns at my question, walking backward, his hands

stuffed in his coat pockets. "More elitist bullshit. Looks like there's an opening in their ranks."

I raise a brow. "Huh?"

But he spins around, bypassing the gathering crowd and skipping up the school's steps without a second look.

Me, not so much. I creep to the outskirts of the growing ring of students, too indoctrinated into Briarcliff Academy's clandestine violence to ever turn a blind eye.

I peer above shoulders and through the spaces of arms until I can get a better view. Jeers mixed with encouragement become easier to decipher, and what I hear makes my breath quicken.

"Can you believe this?"

"What'd he do?"

"Who'd he fuck?"

"It's fucking happening, man. Chase Stone. Look what they're doing to him!"

Chase.

His name catches fire in my mind, and I shove through bodies, and ignoring the resulting "hey!" "fuck off, possum," and "rude, much?" I break through the wall of students, finding myself a few feet too exposed in a makeshift circle.

Guttural laughter flows into the spaces around me, as well as its deep, familiar tone. With a sickening *click*, my eyes hit on the spectacle in the center.

Chase stands between his two friends, Riordan and Tempest, with James facing them.

James's lips peel back from his teeth. "It sucks to be on the bottom rung, doesn't it, man?"

My gaze pings over to Chase, searching his face for any clue, any reaction, to tell me what's going on. But he's steadfast, staring James down without the slightest tic or tell of emotion.

Until his eyes wince shut and a grunt sounds out from his tightly shut lips.

Chase's knees buckle, but he keeps his balance.

I step closer, enough to see Tempest draw back his fist to aim another punch at Chase's lower back. His kidneys.

"Wha—" the last letter meant to complete that word doesn't have sound on my tongue.

Chase isn't standing between his two friends. They're *holding* him by his arms.

"Tempest!" I run forward, the primordial part of my brain wanting to catch Riordan by his ear and tear him to bits. But his hand shoots out at the last second, sending me stumbling back with a surprised rush of air exiting my lungs.

Chase reacts to my voice, his eyes flicking up to mine, then darting to Riordan.

But not before I see his flash of warning, the pain at registering my presence.

He roars, fighting against his restraints with sudden vigor, tendons popping out from his neck, his jaw becoming rigid on a scream.

Chase is outnumbered, but he struggles with untapped fury, his once docile, stoic acceptance of being restrained by two buddies bursting into ash.

"Don't you *fucking* touch her again!" Chase roars at Riordan, his voice rough and guttural.

James, who watches the show with thinly veiled pleasure, mutters, "Keep doing it."

"Let him go!" I cry at the same time, but don't risk running up against Riordan again. Not if it will turn Chase feral and reckless.

"Callie, get out of here!" Chase demands between his ragged breaths.

I jump on Tempest instead, clawing at his arms and trying to draw them away from Chase.

But he's Chase's second. They row crew together six out of seven days a week. He's stronger—so much stronger —than me.

His hurricane-green eyes meet mine right when I'm about to use my teeth, and they're direct and bright with warning. "*Leave*," he whispers. "*Before you*—"

I smack Tempest in the bicep, pissed as all hell that I can't do more harm. "What are you doing to him? Let him go!"

Chase cranes his neck to glance at me. "This is none of your concern," he pants between clenched teeth. This close, I register the beads of sweat on his forehead, the tears in his blazer's seams at his shoulders.

How long has this been going on?

"I'm not going anywhere." I clench my hands into fists, and I direct my caustic tone to Riordan and Tempest. "You're supposed to be his friends!"

"I said *do it*!" James roars above us, and, despite Chase's valiant, stronger-than-most, efforts, Riordan lands his foot against the back of Chase's leg, bringing him to his knees.

No! I race to the front, falling to my knees in front of

Chase and holding his face. "What's going on?" I whisper furiously. "Make this stop!"

Chase's lids lower to half-mast. Droplets of blood fall from his lower lip onto my thumbs. "This ... this has to finish."

I agree whole-heartedly. "Stand up. I'll help you out of here." I glare up at Tempest and Riordan, who continue to hold Chase's arms back, pushing his torso forward by wrenching his shoulders.

Their faces ... I blink them into focus. They're like soldiers in battle. Blank, determined, and forced into blindness. That way, no color can infiltrate their feelings until the task is done.

"Stop," I plead with them. "You're hurting him."

Pain sears into my shoulders when strong, angry hands clamp down, flinging me aside as if I weigh nothing.

Chase's roar sears my eardrums as I'm thrown, my palms scraping rough asphalt, and my stockinged knees taking the brunt.

James's body blots out the sky as he stands over me, his fair skin blotchy, color riding high in his cheeks. But it's not simply the winter wind that's making his blood swirl. "Quit getting in the way of things, stupid possum, then maybe your boyfriend won't have to pay your dues."

"Chase hasn't done anything," I seethe. When I stand, the torn skin on my palms and knees scream, but my voice doesn't transmit the pain. "And don't you fucking call me vermin. Haven't you heard? I'm an initiate."

James smiles. From a distance, most would see it as his usual goofy, lopsided grin.

But maybe it's because he's facing only me. Maybe this smile shows his canines because his friends can't see, and James is allowing his true self to come out and say hi before he buries it under a joking, *sorry dude, but I gotta beat up your boyfriend* shrug.

As if in confirmation of the creature he hides, James winks at me before twisting around.

"He's my soulmate," I grit out, loud enough for James to hear, but not many others.

James stills.

"Chase announced it at the docks last weekend, and I'm confirming it," I say. Frantically, I scroll through recent flashbacks to find Chase's exact words. "We can invoke protection. Does the mutual rulebook not say that if a Noble member attacks a Noble prince's soulmate, the prince may exact any punishment he wishes?"

James cracks another smile. "That only goes one way, *possum*. You can't invoke shit. And Chase? Chase agreed to these fun times."

The ground drops from beneath my feet. "He wouldn't."

"He refused the Nobles' edict, as confirmed by *your* testimony last night. And he's paying the price." James spits out the last word: "*Willingly.*"

I step around James, but fury quickly overrides any logic in my head. "By what? Making him endure a public lashing in the Town Square? Where's your whip, you sick bastard? Why not tear his shirt from his body and lash him until he bleeds? Or wait—I forgot." I throw my hands on my hips and glare. "It's probably because we're no longer in the *seventeenth fucking century*. Let him go, you turd, before I—"

"Before you what?" James's voice takes on a needling tone, and he scrunches his hands under his eyes and fakes a baby crying. "You'll tell the teacher on us?"

I stare at him, my eyes narrowing as his antics draw in giggles and laughter from the crowd. He drops his hands and chuckles, shaking his head in amused disdain. "Go back to your ignorant hole, you rabies infected—"

I spit in his face.

James rears back, color draining from his face until it becomes white with ominous fury.

"Callie!" Chase rasps behind me. I hear a *thump* and Chase's resulting grunt. One of them hit him again. They're beating him up.

With adept slowness, James wipes my saliva from his cheek, his hands shaking with fury and his eyes darkened by it.

I brace for his counterattack, whether it be a hit or a shove—as long as he doesn't direct it at Chase.

What I hear instead is, "Take her. Take her before she does something epically stupid, like put me in a position to knock her the fuck out."

Gentle hands envelop my arm, but my gut reaction is to swing out.

"It's me," Ivy says into my ear. I never heard her come up behind me. "Let's go. Now."

"But—"

"Chase is doing what he has to," she says. "And now so are you."

"Like leave him here to be humiliated? For his friends to use his blood to paint the asphalt?"

Ivy forces up my chin until I meet her eyes. My tumultuous heartbeat must be thrumming into her fingers. "This is the way it is," she murmurs. "You knew it the instant you left our temple last night."

I search her eyes, but I'm not seeing the blue. I'm thinking back. "That I'm his weakness? That's why they're doing this?"

Ivy's eyes soften. "You confirmed Chase refused his orders. The Nobles wanted him to get close to you for their purposes only. To watch you, manipulate you. *Never* to care about you. For that, he has to be punished."

I shake my head, unable to tear my gaze from hers. "We've got to do something. As Virtues, can't we—as his soulmate, can't I—?"

"No. I'm sorry, but we don't meddle with internal problems. This is for the Nobles to figure out."

"But it's my fault."

My heart sinks as Ivy tries to lead me away, but I keep hearing the thumps, the punches, the swallowed, enduring cries of pain.

I tear out of her hold.

Ivy whirls. "Callie—"

Backing away from her, I say, "I won't get in the middle of it. But I'm not going to leave him here, either. I'll watch. I'll watch all of it, to make sure he knows I'm here."

Ivy's mouth falls into an *O*. She re-hinges her jaw enough to say, "That's not how we..."

"I don't care about your traditions. And I'm not going to desert him because of Mrs. Harrington's manipulations. I'm not going to turn my back to preserve more Virtuous and Noble lies."

"You're risking the queen's wrath."

"Our plan to make me a Virtue is still in place," I assure. "She can't do anything if I just stand and watch."

"But will you be able to? They're hurting him pretty bad. Chancellor Marron is a Noble, and he won't intervene."

"I know," I say, then turn away from her, toward the crowd, squeezing through for space until I'm back at the front.

Tempest's frown has grown deeper, Riordan's back stiffer, as they continue to hold Chase down. But James … James goes in for a kick to Chase's gut, and some students cheer, while most gasp.

A girl with a long braid whispers to her friend beside me, "James is having too much fun. These guys follow Chase Stone's every order. Why isn't Chase fighting back?"

Her friend responds, "I dunno, but whatever Chase did, it's three against one. Even our Briarcliff prince can't fight those odds."

"What'd he do, though?"

"Something terrible," her friend mutters. "Something really, really bad to deserve this kind of treatment."

"Where are the teachers?" Braid Girl asks.

I pull my lower lip in, biting down hard enough to pierce skin, but keep my eyes forward. Chase lowers his chin, covering his wince and grunting at James's kicks, but raising his head after each blow, ensuring James meets his eye between the hits.

Chase's glare could destroy cities.

And James's hesitating blink before he raises his fist tells me all I need to know.

"Grab the back of his head," James snarls to Riordan. "Expose his neck to me."

Riordan stalls.

"I *mean* it!" James bellows.

After a heartbeat, where Riordan and Tempest stare at each other over Chase's slumped form, Riordan grabs a fistful of Chase's hair and pulls until Chase's face is almost tilted to the sky.

James's lips curve. "Not so fun, is it? To be nailed in the face by someone you thought was your buddy. This is for your smackdown at Piper's memorial."

Chase doesn't respond, instead dragging his eyes to the side, where he catches mine.

Stay with me, I mouth, unshed tears building in my eyes.

And with each punch thrown, with each of James's cackles and kicks, we don't look away from one another.

Not until Tempest lays down a final, merciful blow, and Chase is sent into the black.

I've never made myself bleed before.

Yet here I am, pacing back and forth outside Chase's dorm room, chewing my thumb off to the first knuckle.

A metallic, bitter tang coats my tongue, but I swallow it as if it were wine. The bittersweet taste is a telling reminder of where I am, who I've become, and what I'm waiting for.

It's second period, and Rose House is pretty much deserted, everyone heading for class after the violent theatrics were over. It ended when, at last, a sole teacher ran down the academy's steps, ordering James to halt at once.

He did, but not before kissing his knuckles for doing such a good job, and winking at Chase, half-conscious on the ground, and sauntering away.

God. And Chase took it. He submitted to James's cowardly brawl, all but inviting his friend to inflict permanent physical damage. And for what?

My back stiffens when I hear footsteps thudding up the staircase and the low murmur of deep voices.

"Why'd he take it so far?" I hear Riordan ask.

"Deep down, James is a sick fuck," Tempest responds.

"You would know," Riordan says, trying for a joke, but it falls flat. "I mean, I always thought you to be the sociopath, not our fucking comic ginger top."

I wait for the fire exit to open.

Three bodies fill the frame, piling through with Chase's head hanging in the center.

"Fuck," I whisper, my throat growing hot.

I run over, bending to peer into Chase's half-closed eyes. "Shouldn't he be with the nurse?"

"He refuses," Tempest says, grunting as he takes more of his friend's weight.

Riordan digs in his pocket for his keycard and holds it out to me. "Mind?"

I grab it without question and beep us into Riordan and Chase's dorm room, holding the door open for them to drag Chase in.

I've never been in Chase's room before, my mind taking cursory stock of the dark wood and brown leather furnishings, a large flat-screen TV with various gaming consoles, and a lot of black, sleek appliances, before Riordan tells me to take a left into Chase's bedroom.

A calming, grayish-blue interior greets my vision when I step in, surprisingly clean for a boy, though there is a faint, locker room smell emanating from all the sports-gear piled up in the corners.

Riordan is the first to duck under Chase's arm and toss

him on the bed in a heap, Tempest being slightly more delicate.

Chase groans at the movement.

"Ice," I mutter to myself. "I'll get some ice."

Riordan stops me with a clear, "Better yet, possum, you should scat."

My eyes narrow. "I'm not going anywhere while he's like this."

Riordan retorts, "It's because of *you* he's here."

"Guys," Tempest warns.

"Oh really?" I put my hands on my hips. "Was I the one holding his arms back so he couldn't defend himself? Was it me who gave James over fifteen minutes with a human punching bag?"

Riordan's face grows dark. He stalks over, pointing his finger. "You have no fucking clue, you stupid cu—"

Tempest attempts to come between us, but Chase's guttural mutter stops all of us cold.

"What'd you say, man?" Tempest asks.

Chase's throat bobs. His eyes stay closed. "She stays."

Riordan curses, spinning away and dragging a hand over his short crop of brown hair. "You're gonna be the end of us."

"I'm not trying to be," I say, and cut around both boys to perch on the side of Chase's bed. "I'll stay with him today."

"It's a bad idea," Riordan says, but not to me. He's talking to Tempest.

Tempest takes a long moment to study me, but I only half see him when I grab Chase's hand and squeeze. "I'm here."

"Might as well give Chase what he wants," Tempest says to Riordan. "We can get to class, make a show of being present and unaffected by what we just did."

I swallow, stroking Chase's pale cheek, but keep my ears open.

"Should we leave *her* here, though?" Riordan asks. "Chase wants it, but our king's made it clear—"

"Who's gonna say something?"

Thick silence blooms.

"It ain't gonna be me," Tempest continues. "We may've been ordered to put Chase on his knees, but nothing was said about the after. We did what was directed."

"Yeah, but..."

Tempest's voice grows ominous. "And now, we leave him be. Whatever occurs after we toss him on his bed is his business. And he says Callie stays."

Riordan sighs. "Fine. *Fine.* But I don't fucking like this."

Tempest says, "You're not going to fucking say anything, either."

I jump when Riordan says, close to my ear, "If we're told to hold him down again, it's on you, Callie. You hear me?"

"I snuck up here without anyone seeing," I say. "I won't be obvious."

"Or do anything stupid," Tempest warns.

I nod.

Riordan stomps out of the room, but I feel more than see Tempest lingering at the door.

In a quiet voice, Tempest says, "You know what would be best for him."

I lower my head. "I do."

"Good. So, take this moment, talk it out, whatever, but then leave. Leave for good."

My answering nod is heavy, my neck unable to hold the weight.

Tempest shuts the door with a soft click.

I stare down at Chase, the black crescents of his eyelashes soft against his alabaster skin, normally so golden and flushed with the rush of endless activity.

Despite my attempt to stay strong, my throat swells, thick and hot, and incoming tears prick the backs of my eyes. I sniff back the threatening sob.

Chase's hand twitches in mine. His pale, rose-colored lips tilt into a smile. "You're not actually crying over my broken body, are you, sweet possum?"

His eyes open, and I'm hit with polished, shining bronze.

"So what if I am?" I mumble, rubbing the heel of my hand over one eye.

Chase's lids lower, softening his intensity. He murmurs, "I'm not brutalized enough to deserve tears."

"No? Because after what I saw…"

"James is a pussy." Chase grunts while pushing himself to lean on the headrest. "He thinks he can wail on me and have me down and out for good, but I'll be fine in a few hours."

My brows spike. "He must've punched you a few too many times in the head, because you were barely hanging on out there."

Chase's lips quirk with a wry smile, but his expression is weighed down and tired. "I know how to take punches.

And James doesn't know how to tell I'm softening his blows."

I think back on the way Chase curved his body every time James came after him, his muscles relaxed, his head hanging low.

"It was all an act? The whole unconscious, suffering thing?" I resist the urge to stand and tower over him, but holy *hell*, my heart cracked open when each fist landed on his body.

"I had to keep up pretenses. Make them think they're winning. Not gonna lie, though." Chase grimaces as he pulls his hand from mine and rubs his chest. "He got in a few good ones."

I ask softly, "Why'd you let them do it?"

Chase lifts his gaze. "I had to. If I don't take punishment like the rest of them, what kind of leader will I make?"

"This is all my fault."

He shakes his head, his fingers finding mine. "They would've found out another way."

I flip my hand, so the pads of his fingers trace the sensitive skin of my palm. "Was I..."

"Were you what, sweet possum?" Chase's voice contains a tinge of amusement.

I swallow. "Was I right? Was what I said to Mrs. Harrington ... to Sabine ... true?"

The room becomes so silent, I'm afraid to look up at him. But I force my gaze to meet his. Unwavering. Curious.

He answers with a simple, steady, "Yes."

"I'm your weakness," I whisper.

Chase leans forward to cup my face, cringing momentarily at the movement. "The Virtues have been looking for one for a long time. I've been masking my emotions, pretending I don't have any preferences, for exactly this reason. But I'm human. I was bound to break. And I'm glad I broke with you."

"No." I clasp his wrist, welcoming the warmth against the chilling consequences of his words. "Not like this. We can't care for each other when the Virtues are our enemies. Because that's what they are. The Nobles, too, aren't they?"

Chase sighs. "Piper died. That's widened an already fractured divide. Sabine is the Virtuous Queen, and my father is the Noble King. Engaged to be married. Sabine lost it on my father. Accused him of not doing enough to find Piper's killer, of not interrogating the Noble members. It was all of us at the cliff that night. Nobles and Virtues partying. One of us had to be responsible."

"But it was Addisyn. Sabine's other daughter was responsible."

"Yeah. How'd that go?"

I cringe. "Sabine discovered Addisyn was the killer, and she protected her daughter. Made Addisyn a Virtue to keep her quiet and shield her from investigation."

"Sabine blames you. For destroying Addisyn. For almost revealing our societies to the school, the Briarcliff PD, fuck, the NYPD, too, with your relationship with that detective guy."

"Then why did she accept me?"

"Same reason she accepted Addisyn. She keeps her liabilities close, makes her enemies her friends. She'd do anything to keep her position as queen." Chase tucks a strand of hair behind my ear, watching me closely. "You need to be careful. You're not safe."

"Neither are you." I study his wrinkled uniform, the blooming bruises along his collarbone. James was smart enough to keep the most damage away from Chase's face. "This morning proves that."

"I've been dealing with this my whole life. That little show-and-tell they had in the pavilion is nothing. I can handle it."

I frown. "Whose instruction were James, Riordan, and Tempest following? Your father's or Sabine's?"

Chase's touch strokes down my chin to my collarbone. I hide the little tremble under my skin that follows. "Both."

"But ... I thought..."

He traces lower, until the tips of his fingers rest against the open collar of my shirt. I work to control my breaths. "We shouldn't."

Chase gives a sage nod. "We *definitely* shouldn't."

He pops open the button.

"You're coming off a severe punishment because you went against your orders to manipulate me."

Chase pauses at my second button, but the heat of his fingers, the promise of *him*, scores into my skin like a welcome burn. "You watched it. The whole time, you didn't run. Does that mean you forgive me for ignoring you this past week?"

"I have to believe..." I say in a hushed voice, then close my eyes as he flicks open another button and then another, exposing my bra. "I have to believe that our sex was real. That you didn't use it as a weapon."

Chase's hand goes into one side of my bra, cupping my breast and stroking my nipple. I suck in a burst of air. "Our first time, I wanted it to be about my control over you. And it was."

I open my eyes, seeing his face for the first time since he started touching me, his brown sugar gaze, his tightened lips. His short breaths.

"You did that to me," I whisper.

"Not in the way I hoped." His thumb circles my nipple, then he flicks it. I flinch in the best way, tingles traveling from my breasts to my core. "I told myself I fucked you out of Noble duty. Made you come the same way I make tons of other chicks come. But your body fit against mine in a way I didn't expect. Your moans made me hard during a time I wasn't predicting. And those lips..." Chase leans forward and traces his tongue across my lower lip, my nose brushing against his cheek as I tilt toward him for more. "What comes out of your perfect, prissy mouth pissed me off and turned me on. And your pussy?"

Chase uses his other hand to spread my thighs, and when he meets my underwear, I feel his grin on my lips.

I'm already wet for him. Swollen and throbbing with need.

"It tasted sweet, and I kept wanting to suck my fingers to keep tasting you, long after I'd fucked you."

My breaths barely fill my lungs. I'm hot and struggling all over—to be strong, to be timid, to have him despite being warned away from him—but his hands lead the dance. I'm bending and twisting in tandem to his seductive choreography, and I can't stop.

"You don't want to do this," I say against his lips, putting space between us when he tries to win me over with one of his world-tilting kisses. "You're hurt, despite avoiding the worst of it. You're still bruised."

"Then I guess you'll have to be on top."

My core flutters open like butterfly wings as he sneaks past my underwear and dips into my folds, curving his fingers in orgasmic perfection.

"I … oh." I curse, then push his shoulders, sending him smacking against the headboard.

He growls, "What the—"

But my movements are faster, and he quickly shuts up, choosing interest over yelling as I scramble with opening his belt, then his pants, practically panting over what I'm about to reveal.

"My sweet possum," he purrs.

"Shut up."

It takes both of my hands to cup his entire shaft, and I twist, massage, and play with his balls until he throws back his head and groans.

When a bead of wetness shines on his tip, I bend and lap up the salt.

His chin falls forward. "Fuuuuuck."

I flick his tip with my tongue, my eyes trained on his. "If we're going to do this, this is how I want you."

"Fine. Yes. Anything. Just don't stop. Don't you dare…"

I grin, then shift on the bed until I can better take him in my mouth.

Chase has never allowed this type of closeness—eating

me out and fucking me with ease, but never wanting me to see *him* vulnerable and exposed.

But this is my moment. My time to make him mine in the same way he's made me his.

Am I forcing his hand at his weakest point? Maybe. But with the way he supplicates, grinding his hips and fisting my hair ... I doubt he'll regret it later.

Especially when I...

"Oh. My. Fucking. Hell." Chase's mouth falls open as I suction my lips around him, then take him deeper, and deeper, and deeper still, until he hits the back of my throat.

His breaths grow harsh, and I rear up before I gag, but I think I got my point across.

"Where in the hell did you learn that trick?" he asks, his voice hoarse with lust.

"I've been waiting to try it out," I say, lining him up to my mouth again. "Only with you."

One side of his mouth tilts. "Do it again."

I do.

When Chase is clinging for control, when sweat dots his forehead, and he clenches his fists with restraint, I grab a condom from his nightstand, slide my underwear off, and, keeping the rest of my clothes on, straddle him while I suit him up.

I don't make us wait. I *can't*, as I'm about to orgasm simply from losing my underwear and hitting air.

He slides inside me easily, perfectly.

Chase's hands grip my waist, and I smile at his attempt at control, but this is my ride. I throw his hands off, and lift my own to tangle in my hair, arching my back so my unbuttoned blouse spreads further. "Watch. Just watch me."

He does.

With every circle and bounce, Chase keeps his hands to himself, though it pains him sincerely. I ride him exactly the way my body demands, clenching around his dick and making sure my clit is rubbed and pleasured with the same satisfying strokes I'm giving to him.

"I'm gonna come," I whisper.

Chase's expression is tight, his jaw locked. "F ... I can't ... I can't fucking hold on..."

I bend down, pressing my lips onto his. "Don't."

It's here he loses control, gripping my ass, spreading my cheeks, and thrusting so hard and deep, my eyes pop wide.

The orgasm hits me at the perfect angle, and I groan into his mouth, flashes of red and white sparks spreading across the backs of my eyelids and bursting fireworks down to my core. Chase rides the gunpowder fire with me, and we cling to each other's clothes until every firework, every second of our spark, burns down into languid smoke.

12

The rest of the week goes by with innocuous boredom, which can only mean one thing.

Something sinister waits along the fringes of this pretend normalcy.

But as the days wear on, I manage to ignore the uneasy goosebumps pimpling my flesh, gaining enough distraction from the everyday people in my life, when they're not wearing their cloaks.

Emma and I go about our dorm room business as we usually do, with short bursts of conversation, mostly over our morning cup of coffee, before departing to our various classes.

Not much can be done regarding our infiltration into the Virtues until I pass the trials, and each initiate's tests are tailored to the queen's preferences. Added to that, I'm a BU freshman and most indoctrinations occur in ninth grade.

A shudder caresses my shoulders at the memory of

what I witnessed in the Nobles' hidden ritual room in the Wolf's Den. Grown women and young boys...

I shake my head, dislodging the image. But it serves as a necessary reminder that while the Virtues are more outwardly vicious, the Nobles' quiet acts are just as dangerous.

Chase is the hardest to ignore, even though he avoided the academy for two days, nursing his injuries—or so he told his friends. We left a lot unsaid after I departed his room that night, on what we are, or how far we're willing to bend the rules. But I used the thought of Chase to keep me company while I couldn't see him, the glimmering remembrance of being on top of him, kissing and clinging to him. It's a gravity I'm more than willing to fall into, so different from the sinking, sickly feeling of being sucked into the dark abyss of the Virtues.

And when I finally ran into Chase in real life on Thursday, the hot scrape of his attention over my body and the light, almost invisible graze of his fingers on the back of my hand as we passed each other in the hallway, told me he'd been thinking of me, too.

That happy Thursday ending is why, on Friday morning, when Ivy bursts into my dorm room, I'm convinced my sinister intuition has come to fruition.

"We need to talk," Ivy gasps, out of breath, like she'd sprinted up the three flights of stairs rather than take the elevator.

I freeze with a carton of cream half-tipped over my coffee. "Is there news of my final trial?"

"Not that. I mean—no." She smacks her palms on the counter, and I jump, splashing cream. "Winter Formal."

"I—huh?"

"I know what you're going to say. With all this secret society stuff, what's the point of a school dance?"

"Since you figured out my question, you'll have my answer, too." I finish sloshing cream into my mug, then turn to her.

"Yeah, but this is our *freshman year*." Ivy says it like she's whispering a prophecy. "And so far, it's *sucked*."

I cast my gaze to the ceiling and sigh, but I catch Ivy's sunburst smile along the way.

"Think about it," she says. "You and me in some gorgeous dresses, sipping spiked punch and dancing under the lights, forgetting about our problems for just one night. One *night*. That's all I ask."

I lift my mug to my lips to disguise the wavering curve of a smile. "There's no telling what the Virtues have in store for me, Ivy. It might not be smart to flaunt my freedom."

"You should go."

Both Ivy and I swivel at the sound of Emma's voice as she exits her room.

"Are you serious?" I ask. "But it's so public. So exposed. So ... normal."

Emma shrugs. "It's a good way to put face-time in and signal to the Virtues that you're participating in school activities and making an effort to support Briarcliff."

My upper lip curls. "Really? But they're evil. Without morals. Callous and cruel. Why would they ever be interested in a dance?"

"You forget," Emma says, heading to the coffee machine, "The Nobles and Virtues were created from Briarcliff. They may not be recognized extensions of the school and more of an underlying cancer, but they show respect where it's due. All the other Nobles and Virtues will be there."

Chase.

His name hits my tongue one second before I speak it, and I hide behind my mug again.

Chase will be there. We'll keep our feelings private, but our thoughts can be unprovoked. Perhaps I'll catch him across the dance floor, parting the crowd and holding out his hand for a dance...

I cringe at the daydream, my teeth clanking against the ceramic. There's no way we can do any of that. And there's never been a time I've hit any dance floor sober. It was always a sweaty, tangled mess, with rushed highs and pulses of music—my eyes shut and blind to my surroundings.

Setting down my mug, I say, "It's not a good idea. I'm sorry, Ivy."

"Please?" Ivy bounces on the balls of her feet. "It'll be harmless. I swear."

I send a wary look Emma's way. "Uh-huh. And what usually happens after someone makes that kind of promise?"

"Goddammit, Callie, I'm the *princess*."

I jolt at Ivy's rare curse.

"I'll ask the queen's permission. Order the other Virtues to stand down. We deserve this." Ivy's gaze includes Emma. "All of us."

Emma barks out with laughter. "You two have fun."

"If I'm going," I say, crossing my arms, "you are, too."

Emma doesn't bother to answer as she fixes her cup of coffee, turns around, and goes back to her room.

"There's safety in numbers!" I call after her.

She glares at me over the rim of her mug before shutting her door.

"Well. She didn't say no. I think that was positive," Ivy says to me. "Don't you?"

My last class of the day is biology, and I sit through Professor Dawson's lecture with half-glazed vision, science always being my toughest subject. I'd resolved myself to doing better and achieving the grades I used to, but it's becoming remarkably harder when I get so little sleep, my thoughts churning day in and day out.

Unlike me, Dawson is working hard today, calling on students at random, so after a final, firm blink, I straighten in my seat and stare at the whiteboard as he writes about osmosis.

"Miss Ryan?"

Crap. My instincts were spot-on, but I've only skimmed the numbers on the board.

"Um. Yes, Professor?"

Dawson glances over his shoulder, still writing about cell division. "It wasn't me who called on you, Miss Ryan, but proving your utter inattention in my class is always lovely. Look toward the door."

Everyone turns to look at me, including Chase, Falyn,

and Emma. Cheeks hot, I pretend not to feel their stares as I glance at the classroom door.

Miss Maisy, the guidance counselor, stands there wringing her hands. "You're needed in the Chancellor's office, dear."

Brows pushing low, I stand and walk toward her, but Miss Maisy stops me with a flutter of her fingers. "Bring your stuff as well. You won't be coming back to class."

My stomach pitches, a natural reaction at being called to the principal's office, but the depth of nausea is on a whole other level when that principal is also one of the echelons in a secret society.

Emma goes back to scrawling in her notebook, feigning disinterest, but the redness on the tip of her ear tells me she's piqued. Falyn leans back with folded arms and a smarmy expression.

And Chase ... Chase eyes me the entire time I pack up my things, and unable to help myself, I throw quick glances at him throughout, attempting to decipher any clue as to why I'm being singled out in the middle of class.

It's not for comfort. That's what I tell myself as I keep meeting his eyes, searching for softness in his features. For safety and warmth.

Nothing but burnished bronze meets me at the end of my path.

I throw my backpack on and clutch my biology textbook to my chest as I cross the aisles of desks and follow Miss Maisy out of class.

"Be sure to grab notes from someone, if you feel like

passing final exams," Professor Dawson calls before Miss Maisy shuts the door.

"Come, dear," she says, her eyes kind but her expression blank.

"Am I in trouble?" I ask as I follow her down the cavernous hallway.

"I don't know, honey." Her heels hit the parquet tiles at a brisk clip, and I rush to keep up with her.

"Is this related to my meetings with you?" I ask with tentative fear.

I thought I'd been doing so well with her, easing everyone's—including my dad's—minds about my ability to handle the Briarcliff courseload and not fly *off* the handle like so many were worried about.

"Not at all, dear."

We reach the main foyer, where Miss Maisy pauses and sweeps out her hand. "I trust you can get to his office?"

I don't miss the underlying *you've been there a few times before* in her tone.

"Sure," I say, hitching my bag up higher and heading into the west wing.

The hallway of trophies and faculty paintings is silent and yawning as I turn into it, the arched ceilings creating a dome of entrapment I always seem to feel whenever I tread into this side of the school.

Chancellor Marron's heavy wooden door is closed when I come up to it, and after another glance at the hidden iron crest in one of the displays—the forging of a raven, with the Nobles' and Virtues' maxim in curved script underneath—I knock lightly.

"Come in."

I jolt at the tone. That's not Marron's voice. Nor is it male.

My hand hovers over the doorknob, confusion blotting over the foreboding weight in my chest after being called out of class.

It finally hits me—why kids are pulled from their classrooms in the middle of the day. Is this about Dad or Lynda's pregnancy? Is anyone hurt? Is there a policewoman on the other side?

Breaths hitching, I twist the knob, desperate to get to the part where I'm blindsided, when terrible news is etched into the air, carved down my throat, and pouring blood into my chest, over with before I lose all capability to breathe.

I throw the door open, but my knuckles are white against the frame.

"What is it?" I gasp out. "Is it the baby?"

But I'm met with shadows.

The thick, velvet curtains behind Marron's wide desk are pulled shut, their golden tapestries swinging as if they were recently used. His various knick-knacks and bookshelves are darkly illuminated, a single lamp shining within the gloom.

It's disconcerting, meeting such interior gloom while the winter sun shines bright against the skeletal trees and dying grass outside.

"Take a seat, Initiate."

A shiver barrels down my spine at the voice, recognizable and pristine.

"Sab—I mean, Mrs. Harrington," I breathe out as I round one of the visitor's chairs and sit.

"You may call me your queen."

Her form is carved out in the shadows, lamplight and darkness playing across her features as she reclines in Marron's seat.

The loudest sound is my bag thumping to the floor.

Despite my bones going rigid, I say, "Is there something wrong, my queen?"

The question sits on my teeth like sour candy, too sweet and too cloying to be good for me.

"There might be," Sabine muses. "Considering how you are enduring voicing my title like you would swallowing a rat's tail."

Double crap. I press my palms into my legs, forcing poise into my posture and my voice. "I mean no offense. It takes some getting used to, this..."

"Indeed. Most students exceptional enough to receive our invitation would do anything, say anything, to be in your position. Yet here you are, wondering if my power over you is merely a joke."

"I don't mean to come across that way." Ivy's words come to the forefront. *Your honesty makes her trust you.* I clear my throat. "But I'm confused. I was called out of class and thought something was wrong, with either my enrollment at Briarcliff or my family. I'm surprised to be meeting you in Marron's office."

Sabine pauses for a beat, and a shiver skitters over my skin, as if her view of me is so much clearer than what I see of her. "You'll come to learn, dear girl, that I enjoy throwing my girls off-balance during an interrogation."

I latch onto the word. "Interrogation?"

Sabine cants her head. "Are you honestly surprised, Calla Lily?"

Inclining my head in the other direction, I ask, "I don't think I'm reaching when I say the last time you saw me, I was more open with you than I've been since—" I stop myself, but the maneuver is useless when I see Sabine's teeth flash in the dark.

"Your mother." Sabine leans forward, her elbows poking against the desk's wood. "To be a good mother is a great responsibility. To be a good daughter, even more so. You no longer have yours, and I no longer have mine. We're on similar paths. More kindred than you'll ever come to realize."

I wish for light. For some kind of strobe to land on Sabine, so I can read the grief on her face and see if it matches mine. Because all I hear from her is ... cold.

"It's what I'm asking of you, as my newest initiate. I'm asking you to see me as a mother figure—never to replace yours, mind you, but as someone you can come to and trust. In return, I'd like to treat you like a daughter. Like all my girls."

Bile sloshes deep in my belly. "I'm not sure I need that."

"Maybe 'ask' is too loose of a word," Sabine continues, her voice nothing but languid charm. "If you want the privilege of Virtuous protection, the marker of prestige, you will listen to me."

I force down the growing thorns in my throat. "I've

submitted to your trials, done everything you've wanted so far."

"Yes, but have you bent to my will? I do not think so. Chase Stone." Sabine murmurs his name with a serpentine tongue. "You are not to see him. Under any circumstance. Not for academic reasons, or extracurriculars, and certainly not in bed."

My back smacks against the chair. "I haven't spoken to him. Since our meeting in the temple, I haven't—"

"Do not lie to me, dear girl."

Sabine's tone is soft, almost soothing in its allure—if you're not the prey meant for a feline predator.

An exhale whistles through my lips. "He was beaten up and humiliated for going against the Noble rule. I watched it. I'm not about to make him go through that again."

"No?" I feel more than see Sabine arch a sculpted brow. "Then why were you in his room after such an obvious message was delivered to you? Why did you spend hours there? And why, dear, were you moaning and crying out his name?"

I stop breathing. My heart slams against the walls of my chest.

"Here is where you need to listen closely, Initiate. I have eyes where you will never see. Ears where you will always be deaf. Feet and hands where yours have been amputated. I am everywhere in this school."

Then why did your eldest daughter die under your nose? I almost retort, but better judgment catches my tongue. "I understand."

"I hope you do, dear, because this is my last warning.

You do not want to put me in a position where I'll punish rather than impart motherly advice. Say it."

I suck in a long breath, my voice carrying more wind than sound when I say what she wants to hear. "I'll break it off with Chase. For good."

Sabine leans back, her forearms gliding down to the desk in soft repose.

"I'd like to ask one thing," I say.

Her shoulders go rigid. "How daring. Go on."

"Why don't you want me to see him anymore?" I bend forward in my chair, inching closer despite every instinct telling me to run far away from this woman. "I thought the linking of a Noble and Virtue was encouraged. Relied upon, even. Isn't it better for the Virtues if the Noble prince were with one of us?"

The room falls into such deep silence, I'm doubting if Sabine will ever answer.

I stand, lifting my bag, and turn to the door.

"You are not one of us yet." Sabine's whisper tickles my ear like the long, furred leg of a tarantula. "And if you ever wish to attain Virtuous status, you will not even lock *eyes* with my daughter's soulmate. Do you understand?"

I rest my hand on the doorknob, my back rigid, my body still. It makes sense, what she's guarding, despite the very real fact that Piper is never coming back. I did it for my mother, and I do it for her still. Yet, the matter remaining unspoken, the one involving Chase and his father, Sabine's fiancé, is what comes to the forefront.

What would Daniel Stone want for his son? Certainly not to be forever linked to a girl in her grave. There is no power play in that, no maneuvers in which he can properly control his son. How long will Daniel let his future wife's wish be fulfilled before his selfish motives become more important?

If I continue to flout their rules, I may be putting Chase in more danger than he's already in.

I look over my shoulder at Sabine, thankful all my questions are masked by her makeshift shadows. "I understand."

"Good." That one syllable is a musical trill throughout the room. "The next time I see you, my dear, will be in better circumstances, I'm sure. I've left a gift for you at the foot of your bed. It's my greatest wish that you enjoy it."

My shoulder blades push into my spine, but I force my body steady. "Oh?"

"You're dismissed," Sabine says airily.

I don't hesitate.

And once I enter the cool expanse of the hallway and shut the Chancellor's door behind me, I can finally breathe properly again.

13

I stare at the gossamer fabric, its silky, white skirts flashing a rainbow prism of color each time I pace back and forth at the foot of my bed.

Not quite mustering the courage to lift the white rose perched on top, I've been circling the unwelcome dress like one of those cleaning fishes on a shark, staring at it like at any moment, the ivory silk will form into fangs and take a chunk out of me.

But within its gauzy material lies a thick, cream envelope tied to the rose's stem, which, if I stop gaping at it like a dummy, might give me more context.

Tentatively, I untie the black ribbon and slide the envelope out, opening it and reading the simple cream postcard inside.

Dear Initiate,

Wear this beauty with grace, respect its folds with delicacy, and stand within its silk with pride. You are to become a Virtue, and in time, you must prove purity and worth.

Attend the Winter Formal at the princess's behest and the queen's command.

And as a gentle reminder, this invitation is not to be declined. At any cost.

"Damn it, Ivy, I thought the formal was supposed to be *normal*," I mutter, the letter slipping through my fingers and fluttering to the ground. Leaving it there, I grab the long-stemmed rose and dump it in the kitchen trash.

"Another letter from your secret admirers?" Emma asks as she reclines on the couch, her laptop propped on her thighs.

I acknowledge her with a grunt. "I suppose we never should've thought the Winter Formal was optional."

"There's no *we* about it," she responds, before resuming typing.

"Right," I mumble, then stride into my room, figuring I'll be like Emma and try to get schoolwork done in the gaps of time where secret societies and their princes aren't taking up all my mental space.

I grab my stack of textbooks on my desk, and they land on my bed with a *thump*. I climb aboard as well, deliberately avoiding the dress and crossing my legs while dragging my laptop along with me.

Just as I'm opening my computer, my phone I'd stuffed

in my hoodie pocket vibrates and lets out a tiny ping of sound.

I try to ignore it, sliding my calc textbook closer and fanning the pages until I find the section we've been assigned.

My phone pings again.

There's the option of silencing it. Or hell, turning it off. But with what I've discovered, been told, and witnessed these last several months, I'm positive I can do neither.

Casting my gaze to the ceiling, I pull it out, then grit my teeth, drop my chin, and read.

Chase: we need to meet.

Breath whistles through my teeth as I contemplate the meaning behind his words. Has he heard of Sabine's visit? Does he know that's why I left class today?

Me: we can't. queen's orders.

Chase: King's orders too, but I enjoy finding loopholes.

He may get off on defying the societies' rules, getting a public beating for it, then learning nothing and returning to his old ways like slipping on a comfy sweater, but I don't have the same liberties.

Me: it's not smart right now. I've been told to stay away from you. And for the good of everyone involved, I should probably do as Sabine asks.

A solid five minutes pass, my text window blank. Thinking I've won, I go back to focusing on math problems.

Until—

Chase: Lover's Leap. Nobody goes there anymore. Meet me at midnight. I'll make sure we're not followed.

Does this boy not understand what it's like to have such a fragile foothold even while treading on solid ground?

Even as my mind whirrs with the potential consequences, my heart is figuring out ways it can be done.

I can see him one more time. Just once. Face to face, I'll lay down the law with firm conviction, and explain to Chase that there's more at stake than our relationship. That I'm working for Emma and Eden ... Ivy, too.

Chase: Don't make me beg, sweet possum. There's something I need to explain to you.

. . .

I bring a hand up to massage my temple. My other thumb hovers over the phone's keyboard.

Me: okay. But ten minutes max.

Chase: You're the boss. See you soon.

Instead of texting back, I choke on a frustrated breath. I hope Chase knows what he's doing. And I pray I'm doing it right.

A few hours later, the biology homework is completed, but barely.

My bedside clock tells me it's eleven, so I close my books, rationalizing that I can complete the rest of my homework tomorrow.

I slide off my bed, setting the books in a pile on my desk, then pad into the main room, noting Emma's laptop and notes laid out on the couch and coffee table, but not Emma. I assume she's gone to bed, since her door is shut, and the light is off.

As quietly as I can, I shower off the remnants of the day, allowing the hard, hot spray of water to massage my shoulders and the back of my neck, but keep my hair tied up and dry. After, I slip into the warmest clothing I have, with thermal underwear under my jeans and a long shirt, hoodie, winter coat, hat, scarf, and gloves.

Briarcliff has yet to experience the full effects of snow, but Jack Frost seems to be giving me the finger wherever I go these days, and if Chase wants to meet me outside at night, I'm going fully prepared for an Arctic trek and not a secret meet-up between the gnarled trees at the base of Lover's Leap fifteen minutes away.

Thinking to warm my insides as much as out, I also craft a decaf latte to stick into a thermos for my walk.

Now that I'm fully loaded and have nothing left to procrastinate over, I creak the front door open and make the softest sounds before clicking it shut behind me.

The dorm's hallway is at its dimmest light setting, but I take a hard left into the neighboring staircase, allowing the red, emergency exit signs to guide me to the main floor.

After that, it's a matter of utilizing the best time to slip out the side exit and avoid the security guard's rounds. I peer around the corner, and as I suspected, the two guards are chatting over their mugs of coffee at the lobby desk before they make their switch.

I slip from the building without anyone noticing, and with one mittened hand clutching my thermos and a knitted scarf covering half my face, I cut through the front of Thorne House and through the backwoods of Rose House, finding the trampled path to the cliffs with the careful use of my phone's flashlight.

It's only when I arrive at the barbed-wire gate blocking students' entry to the edge of the cliff that I take in the forest's stillness, its eerie winter silence sinking into my bones and settling its cold, frost-dampened fingers around my ribcage.

I'd been making so much noise trampling through the brush and kicking aside dead branches and rocks, that once I stopped moving, the frigid December presence made itself known, freezing the air and strangling everything that was once vivid, green, and bright, icing the ground beneath my feet.

Chase isn't here yet, making the nightmare of this forest and the dark creatures lurking within it too imminent to bear. To give myself something to do, I prop my phone, flashlight on, against a blackened, twisted tree root, then uncap my thermos and drink some warmth back into my bones.

I won't retreat. A simple swatch of forest, monitored by a security guard in a golf cart every twenty minutes, isn't going to be the thing that takes me down.

There are far more vicious creatures in my daylight hours.

A low, motoring sound gets my attention, and I inhale icy air into my lungs, shoving the lid on my thermos and shutting off my flashlight before security finds me.

Crouching low, as headlights illuminate my spot, I curse Chase and his assurances that he had the times of security rotation on lock. These guards prowl our campus at all hours these days, December cold or not.

Branches crack and mounds of frozen ground fracture

beneath tires, the engine growing closer and the beam of light becoming wider.

Shit. *Shit.* There's still time to escape if I leap up and run *now.* I balance on the balls of my feet and lunge to the side, avoiding the outer edges of the pale, yellow spotlight cutting through stripped-down trees.

"Scampering somewhere, sweet possum?"

Halting with one foot high in the air, I pivot to the golf cart with a sigh. "Should've figured."

"That I'd borrow a cart with heated vents instead of force us to negotiate ourselves into a deep freeze? Bet your ass you should've figured."

"Define *borrow,*" I say, but move toward the vehicle, drawn to his words of 'heat' and 'vents.'

As I sidle up to the cart, Chase meets my half-covered face with a closed-lipped grin. "There's nothing money can't buy. Even a slice of time."

"How long do we have?" I ask as I take a seat, leaning close to the hot spurts of air in the console.

"Enough." Chase slides his leather-clad hands from the wheel, puffed-out and comfortable in his black Canada Goose parka.

It's a standard, open concept golf cart, so I'm not holding out much hope for a sauna-like experience.

"Won't these headlights be obvious through the trees?"

"Callie." Chase gently pries the thermos from my hands. "We're fine for as long as we need."

Chase uncaps the lid and tips it to his mouth. "No alcohol," he says. "Disappointing."

"Take this seriously. Please. Sabine pulled me out of

class this afternoon for the sole purpose of telling me to stay away from you. Her entire aura *screams* danger, yet here I am." I stare at the dark spots around the twin circles of light coming from Chase's cart. "I've figured it out. I have a death wish."

After a hard exhale, Chase sets down my thermos between us. "I'm taking this seriously. We're meeting here, in the fucking cold, so nobody will see us together."

I slide my gaze back to him. "Do you have any idea why Sabine doesn't want us together? She made it sound like you still belong to Piper, but there's got to be more to it. Your dad, her fiancé, wouldn't want you attached to a—" I almost say *to a ghost*, but catch myself.

Chase stares at me for a long time. I blink uncomfortably under his study, my eyes feeling like cold, hard marbles shoved inside my skull.

Instead of answering, he murmurs, "If you were to have more control over the Virtues, would you take it?"

I press back into the seat. "I've never thought about gaining control over them. I've only ever wanted to dismantle them."

Chase nods, clouds of air billowing out of his nose. "What if I gave you the chance to do either?"

I squint at him, the movement difficult with my fast-freezing cheek muscles. "What are you getting at?"

Chase twists to face me, holding my mittened hands in his. "I'm tired of my father commanding my life and ruining my sister's. I don't want to fucking stand down to his edicts. Not this time."

"Chase." I lean in closer, our clouds of breaths mixing

and mingling in a way we can't anymore. "I'm furious with your dad and Sabine, too, expecting us not to be together simply because they forbid us. But we have to be smart about this. You can't thwart his rules with such obvious disregard and be beaten for it again."

Again, Chase searches my face. I pull my hand from his grip and place it on his cheek. "What is it? What are you not telling me?"

He surprises me by diving in for a kiss, my cold lips melting under his, Chase's hot tongue doing more for me than warmed coffee in a thermos ever could.

Instead of fighting him, I grip his shoulders and angle my head to bring the kiss deeper. I thought we couldn't do this anymore. I was prepared to stand back and watch him from afar for the greater good, but the moment he lays his lips on mine, the second his arm comes around my waist and makes me a part of him, my plan to remain calm and collected shatters.

We burst apart, our clouded exhales wider and opaquer.

"I shouldn't have done that," he rasps.

I glance around us, licking my lips, tasting him. "Like you said, we're safe for the moment."

"Ah, sweet possum, we have so much more to do before we can find safe harbor."

"I know," I murmur, looking down at my hands.

"We can meet in secret, in places they'll never find. I'm not about to give you up with a snap of their fingers."

Rather than argue the point, especially when my lips still tingle from his stubble, I say, "We'll figure it out."

Chase catches my chin and tips it toward him. "We'll do more than that. We'll thwart them in the shadows."

I sag underneath his touch but tell myself not to lose my spine. "Not if it means witnessing you get hurt again. I'll endure whatever Sabine has planned for me, but if she uses you again, like she promised she will, I can't prove her right. I can't give her my weakness on a golden platter."

His cold, leather thumb strokes my jaw while his eyes catch the luminescence of our only source of light. "I can't bend to their will. I don't have it in me, and I'd rather James break my arm and Rio kick me in the nuts than forfeit my time with you."

I pull out of his caress, though every ounce of heat remaining in my body begs to draw closer to his flames. Instead, I change the subject from one of pain to tactics. "The Winter Formal. Sabine's ordered me to go."

"It's a mandatory event for us. We dress up, make good face on behalf of Briarcliff Academy, and then attend the real ball underground."

My brows squish together.

Chase smiles indulgently. "The dance continues in the Nobles' ritual room, sweet possum. That's what you're being ordered to attend, and you can't do that until you show your face at the formal."

"And what's the point of it?"

Chase tips his head, his brows furrowing with over-dramatic contemplation. "Elitism? Privilege? Entitlement? All the things the rich and powerful do to separate themselves from the commoners. It's one of the only functions we have together as Nobles and Virtues."

"I wonder why Ivy didn't tell me that when she begged me to go?"

"Probably because her mouth is claimed by the queen, and Ivy bends to Sabine's rules because she's afraid to break them."

Chase says it like it's a bad thing. "She's scared. Ivy doesn't have any sort of fallback like you do if she betrays the societies. Her dad's a disgraced member, her family's broke because you Nobles love your payback."

"Is that what you think?" Chase's tone grows hard. "That I'm only doing this because I have a cushioned life for my ass to land on if things go south? I assure you, if I'm caught, there will be more hell to pay than landing in Hell itself. I'm not doing this for kicks."

"That's not what I meant." I squeeze his bicep. "I'm not trying to lessen your risk. God, Chase, I'm just so scared. I *don't* want you hurt. I don't want Ivy punished."

Chase leans in for another kiss, this one tender and slow. He pulls away once, twice, stroking the escaped hairs from my hat off my face, then pressing his lips to mine again. After one final stroke of his tongue, he draws away, but keeps his hand on the back of my neck. "Trust me."

"I want to."

"Allow me to earn it, then. The Virtues' temple will be deserted during the Winter Formal, and the dance itself will be crowded, all of us, even faculty, wearing masks. If we can time it right and have enough decoys, we can slip into the temple and find the documents relating to Rose Briar that Piper was trying to uncover for my sister."

My heart swings like a pendulum. "Will it work?"

"It has to. This is the only chance we have before school ends for the holidays."

A reminder flickers in the back of my head, remembering my time in the chem lab when I thought it was deserted. "Aren't there cameras? Motion detectors? Something to alert them?"

Chase sets his jaw, staring off over my shoulder.

"Chase. What is it?"

His eyes scrape back to mine. "Tempest. I've given him my father's passwords. He'll log on and put a video of the empty tomb on a loop."

"You brought *Tempest* into this?"

Chase clamps a hand over my mouth. "While I said we were safe here, I didn't mean we were safe if you shouted."

My response comes out muffled, but I make sure the features he can see are carved with a stony glare. "Sorry."

He removes his hand. "How'd you say it last time? Our 'Bonnie and Clyde shit' can't work. We need more people."

"Eden, Emma, and Ivy are more than enough."

"Can any of them mess with a top-notch security system?"

"I didn't know Tempest could."

"How do you think Eden's photos got buried so quickly?"

My skin tingles despite the numbing cold. "I assumed it was Briarcliff's fickle rumor mill. Eden was horribly humiliated by the same tactic years ago. I figured the lack of originality bored most students and they forgot about it."

"Think again." Chase settles back in his seat, interlacing his fingers between his thighs. "We're like vultures. We'll pick at dead meat until it's nothing but old bones. Tempest got in the way of that by intercepting your dummy account, deleting the pictures, and doing other techie stuff I can't even begin to describe to scrub the photos from the internet."

I pause. "He did all that? For Eden?" Then I frown. "Why? He hates people."

"He did it for me. My boy's temperamental, but his loyalty is unmatched."

My voice is soft. "Thank you. For asking him."

"Don't thank me or make assumptions about every member of the societies when you've been part of our fun, secret club for all but a few weeks."

"It's hard not to, with the types of members I've been lucky enough to meet." I turn forward, sucking on my teeth. On the night my dorm room was broken into, the photos of Piper's diary were deleted off my laptop and my cloud without my knowledge.

Was Tempest the Cloak that did it?

Chase speaks before I voice my thoughts. "My beat-down was Tempest putting on the same act I did, assuring the Nobles that his loyalty is intact. But he has his own reasons to bring them to heel and force my father out."

"And Riordan and James? How about them?"

The line of his jaw almost cuts through his skin. "They're loyal to my father. There's no act about it, although Rio less so."

I pull my scarf over my nose and mouth, staring into the dense copse of trees. "My trust is wearing thin."

"Mine, too." He grabs my hand, and though we're both gloved, his grip is firm and stable.

It's nice, a pocket of peace in an otherwise unyielding amount of stress, and while I'm stiffened with cold, I wish I could find more moments like these with him.

As if he can read my thoughts, Chase gives my hand one last squeeze before switching to the steering wheel.

"We'd better go," he says. "I'll drive you closer to the dorms."

Nodding, I cross my arms, reclaiming warmth where it's been lost. Soon, we're rocking and bouncing over the uneven forest path, the golf cart's quiet motor thrumming beneath us.

Chase pulls to a stop near the back exit of Rose House. "It's safe for you to walk from here. Any closer, and we'll be caught."

We spend a long moment staring at each other. I find the courage to say, "We can do this."

Chase cups the back of my head, bringing my forehead to his. "Do whatever they ask. Keep calm. I support you, regardless of how I act during the day. We'll win and take them down. For Piper. For my sister and Eden. For us."

I pull my scarf away from my face and risk another sweet, icy kiss. When I pull away, my lips brushing against his, I say, "That question you asked, about me trusting you."

He nudges my nose with his. "Yeah?"

"I do."

Smiling, Chase kisses me again.

I leave him in the dense thicket of trees, my boots crunching against half-frozen, decayed leaves and branches, peering over my shoulder a few times before I round the corner of Rose House and cross over to Thorne.

At each pivot, he's in the same spot, his eyes brilliant but his lips grim, and I find myself hoping that my white lie will eventually turn into the truth.

That I can trust him with my life.

The Virtues leave me alone for thirteen days.

Whether or not that number will end in an unlucky consequence remains uncertain.

I'm not about to sit around and wonder, instead focusing on my neglected schoolwork as well as our plans to enter the Virtues' temple on the night of Winter Formal. Emma was the first to agree after I outlined my meeting with Chase —out of everyone, she'd be the person to keep my continued association with her brother to herself. Then, we folded Eden into the idea, without mentioning Chase. Once we included Ivy, the only aspect I explained to her was the threat of Sabine, and what she said to me after she pulled me out of class. Sadly, I wasn't sure I could trust my best friend with my secret meet-up with Chase. Ivy has her own bonds to fight against, without enduring mine, too.

With all the piecemeal information I'm feeding to each friend and the different sized holes I'm leaving behind, on the afternoon of day thirteen, I feel more like Swiss cheese than a person. That is why I take the time to sit with Ivy, Eden, and Emma at lunch—Emma, who we coaxed out of our dorm with the assurance that nothing has gone wrong for almost two weeks, and she'd be safe with us.

Famous last words, right?

"Has anybody had time to think of finals?" Ivy asks, pushing her bibimbap rice dish around her bowl with her chopsticks. "Amid all this ... stuff?"

"Ugh. Don't remind me." I press my fingers into my temples, not so much feigning a headache as preventing one. "I don't think I've had a worse semester. Ever."

"Isn't it easy to get A's in public school?" Eden asks. I search her face for sarcasm, but surprisingly find none.

"Not always," I say, but I'm distracted by commenting on her sheltered Briarcliff-living when there's motion at the front of the dining hall, Falyn, Willow, and Violet waltzing into lunch late.

The room transforms into a stuffy, cloying environment as they wander through the tables and to the buffet at the back. These girls command the dining hall in a fashion entirely opposite to their male counterparts.

When Chase and his crew walk in, students go quiet, but not out of intimidation. Every move of those boys' is watched by admiring, heart-filled eyes and unrequited hearts. It's hard not to when Chase, Tempest, Riordan, and heck, even James, are carved from beauty, their movie star faces mixing with pro-athlete bodies.

In most schools—including public—there's usually

only one guy who claims those kinds of looks. Here? There's at least ten, with Chase Stone being at the top.

Falyn, however ... she and her besties shush the room through fear of reprisal, stealing their throne through opportunity and deceit. Falyn reminds us all of that fact as her gaze sweeps through the room, grazing over heads and landing on nothing, until she reaches me.

"Incoming," Emma mutters. With a few flicks of her fingers, she's holding her chopsticks like weapons. "I knew there was a reason I didn't want to come down here. I thought you said they were independently training?"

Ivy shrugs at the question. "Independent being the buzz word. We don't always have to train at lunch."

Emma curses the closer Falyn looms, and I don't blame her. Here I was, hoping for a predictable, average lunch after almost two weeks of being ignored.

Falyn must've sensed the weakening of my walls. I meet her eye, and her lips slink into a smile.

"So nice to see you all out in public," she simpers when she draws near. "I'd thought you'd have claimed your own misfit island by now."

"It's our school as much as it is yours," Eden retorts.

My eyes flare at her unexpected retort, but I shouldn't be surprised. With the release of her photos and the lack of torture that followed, she regained a small amount of confidence. One side of her hair is even tucked behind her ears, as if she's half-willing to show her face around school again.

I switch my focus to Falyn, watching her carefully, ready to strike if she so much as bats an insult Eden's way.

Falyn laughs at Eden's remark, full and throaty. "My

memories at this academy are going to be *so* much sweeter than yours, since I don't have lard coating my fat, pimply ass—"

"Those are big words coming out of a mouth so recently filled with an extra-large, silicone cock."

My gaze pings to Emma. Ivy's breath squeaks with sound.

Emma cants her head. "Wasn't it you in that sex video James circulated last year? Yep. It definitely was. Those lips of yours blowing a fake dick while James stuck his up your ass was verified by Riordan, since he was the one holding the dildo for you."

Falyn sucks on air.

"You're such a wasted bitch," Falyn says, tipping her chin up as she stares at Emma down her nose. "Did you rub one out to the video when your daddy had you locked up in the basement? Was it conversion therapy? Were you so obsessed with Piper, your daddy had to show you amateur videos with dildos and James to make you horny and straight?"

"Enough," I say, rising from my seat. "We were eating our lunch in peace before you came along. It's time for you to leave."

Ivy nods, standing with me. "The public spectacle isn't worth it, Falyn."

I note the attention cast in our direction, some mouths gaping, most whispering, and a *lot* holding up their phones to record. Their interest doesn't capture me the way Ivy's does, though. She's staring at Falyn like she's imparting a silent message, one I'm coming to decipher as *retribution*.

These girls can't do anything without Sabine hearing about it, and either punishing or rewarding them.

With that thought, I wonder how Piper's cornering me in this same dining hall went over with her mother, accusing me of stealing her boyfriend, then ending up dead that night.

It was Addisyn who killed her, I remind myself. *Case closed.*

In a rush of memory, a few of Piper's last words encircle my mind. *I'm doing you a kindness…*

Was Piper warning me away from the Virtues? Or was it really about stealing Dr. Luke from her?

"Did you hear me, possum?"

Ivy elbows me, and I glance up from the section of table I'd been vacantly staring at, lost in thought. I say to Falyn, "No, what?"

"I'm not leaving until you come with me."

I recoil. "Why?"

Falyn smiles but hides her teeth. "You sit with us now."

"But Ivy never has to." I gesture to Ivy, who gives a minuscule shake of her head, like I shouldn't have said that.

"*She* isn't starting at the beginning like you are," Falyn says. "Come join our crew, Callie."

Ivy's whisper touches my ears. "Do it."

"But—"

"Go," Emma says from across the table. "I don't want this table further stunk up with Falyn's presence, anyway. Good luck trying to be popular, possum."

I gape at her, but my brain makes up for my stunned body, assuring me that this is part of Emma's act, that no one can know we've teamed up for anything.

It's better if we look like enemies forced into proximity, nothing more.

"Okay..." I say, and tentatively pick up my tray. My stomach sinks at the obvious answer to my next question. "Is this a permanent thing?"

"More permanent than a tattoo," Falyn says with a succulent, dire undertone.

"Great," I mumble, but after a last, entreating look to my friends, who subtly nod with encouragement, I follow the Wicked Witch of Briarcliff to her lunch table.

Willow and Violet are seated with their food when I arrive. Willow undercuts me with a glance, but Violet pulls out the chair next to her and gestures for me to sit, the cerulean blue of her eyes vulnerable and friendly.

"Welcome," she says.

I perch at the very edge of the chair, ready to bolt if a piece of Falyn's lunch so much as lands on my side of the table.

"Is this really necessary?" I ask the group. "You guys don't like me. I'm not sure why we all have to endure this quality time."

"Coach's orders," Willow says, the hue of her eyes matching the auburn of her tied-back hair. "Like with any new trainee, we have to make them part of the team. Even the ones we think suck."

I lick my lips, parsing through her clues until I reach the conclusion that their rowing team and the title of coach is public code for the Virtues. It has to be, because there is *no* way I'd ever join—

"You guessed it." Falyn's lips stretch wide as her

searching gaze centers on my face. "As part of this bullshit charade, you have to join our rowing team."

I blurt out my response without thinking, "No way."

Violet frowns, her small voice somehow coming through the white noise of the crowded dining hall. "It's not that bad. You can join me as the other half of the bow pair."

"Addisyn's absence has to be filled," Falyn barks. "In more ways than one. Stop being so fucking difficult, Callie."

I jolt at her venom but keep my expression calm. I could figure out a way around this. There's no immediate need to be out on a boat, in the middle of bottomless water, without a life jacket or a clue. They're no longer training on water—it's winter, so a lot of their practice is in their weight room or that crazy hydraulic thing they have in the boathouse that simulates a race. I could handle that.

I think. Better to change the subject.

"So, Winter Formal," I segue, stretching my smile until it's sincere. "Are you guys excited?"

Falyn makes a sound of disgust, then picks at her rice bowl. Willow rolls her eyes, but Violet bounces in her seat.

"Absolutely," she says. "Falyn chose the theme this year. Well, it was meant to be Piper, but ... um, you know. We're honoring her with the theme of Snow White."

I push my brows up, but they quickly come down when I recall the ending and the princess encased in a glass coffin, for all the world to see, beckoning her prince with her cold, waiting corpse...

I find my voice again. "That's ... a heck of a way to remember her."

"Relax," Falyn says. "It's not like we can display her. She

fell off a damn cliff. We want to remember the *idea* of her, so we'll put a glass case out, fill it with her favorite flowers, and have the rest of the ballroom be winter-themed, including our outfits. Get it?" Falyn waits for my nod. "She'll be the only bright, spring center point in a room full of snow." Falyn settles back in her seat. "I'm a fucking genius for thinking of this."

"You are," Willow assures, but her gaze slides to mine with an eerie, practiced movement. Her red-painted lips curl with a grin. "Everyone will love it, *especially* after the last dance, when Chase opens the case, picks a flower, and makes a speech as the Winter Court King, pledging his everlasting love to Piper."

It's as if my throat picks up the icicles outside and nestles them against my vocal cords. I force out a platitude. "What a beautiful way to honor your friend."

"You won't mind," Falyn says, "since you broke it off with Chase. He's ours now, to do with as we please. Chase will always follow our instructions. Those boys may think they have control over the school, but they haven't for quite some time. Remember that when you're tempted to choose sides."

"Aw." Willow points to my untouched meal. "Lost your appetite, sweetie?"

Violet lays a delicate hand on my shoulder. "Do you need some water?"

"She needs a new life." Falyn snorts. "Because this one's about to get so *brutal* for her."

15

The forest must be listening, because as a complement to the incoming Winter Formal, Briarcliff is blanketed in snow for the first time this year.

I'm woken by the seeping cold through my window, as if Jack Frost has come through the cracks with his long, gnarled fingers, gripped my shoulder, and whispered in my ear to look outside.

Shivering, I sit up, wrapping my comforter around my shoulders and shuffling to my single window, the sun rising white and pale over the glittering, untouched snow of Thorne House's backyard.

The glass is hard, frigid ice beneath the pads of my fingers as I lean in closer to better see the snowdrops clinging to trees, weighing down the branches and stifling the morning bird calls.

My lips pull wide in a smile.

I've been waiting for this—for my first sight of snow. I

whirl from my window, padding around my room with eager feet as I dress in Briarcliff's winter uniform of thermal tights, a plaid skirt, and a long-sleeved, white button-down shirt, throw on my winter coat, and slip on my boots before grabbing a to-go coffee and skipping out into the silent hallway.

I didn't even check the time, but with the beginning sunrise, it must be close to 6:30 AM. No girlish titters can be heard from the other side of the closed, locked doors. I don't run into anyone during my trek down three floors, not even Moira, as I swing through the side exit and trek through virgin snow to the back of Thorne House.

Clouds of my breath and the crunch of my boots lead the way, until I pause next to a first floor window, cup my mittened hands close to my mouth, and sip my coffee while taking in the muted sounds and glaring white of Briarcliff Academy's winter makeover.

With nothing but an acre of thick snow at my horizon, sparkles winking with the rising sun, it's easy to fall into a meditative state, to close my eyes and breathe in the cold, unfiltered air of the nearby forest. I'm immersed in the brief pleasantries of a season that mainly brings blizzards, subzero temperatures, and gray, drab skies, and I'd much rather face the calm of an impending snowstorm than mull over the havoc Winter Formal could bring.

Or the disaster that my time here at Briarcliff has become.

I thought I'd have the upper hand by becoming one of them, but not *really* being one of them, yet the Virtues test me at every turn, hoping I'll fall, ensuring I'll prove my weakness.

Newly-formed icicles on the windowsill beside me crackle against the reflected sunlight, beginning to thaw, and I stare at the uneven spears, my cheeks frozen and my exhales heated, wondering if tonight will finally be the moment I can reduce the Virtues' hold on this beautiful, deadly campus, by finding enough proof in their temple to bring them to their knees.

Is it possible? Would the Virtues store such damning documents? Piper thought it was. She may have died for unrelated reasons, but she was on to something, hiding codes in her diary and planting founders' letters in obscure texts where only someone like her could follow the clues.

I could finally get answers, like why Ivy is looking so broken and sallow since becoming the Virtues' princess, or why Emma won't tell me what she did that warranted so much torture from a group meant to protect her.

If they won't—or can't—tell me, then I'll break into the temple while they're all at the dance.

With the sun glinting above the tallest evergreen trees, I turn my back on the majestic view and plod to the front of the dorms, December's morning bite gifting me with more energy and resolve than a cup of coffee.

✻

The week passes like a frostbitten dream, classes going on as usual, the dining hall—for once—uneventful. On Thursday afternoon, many of the girls leave campus at lunch to either drive into Providence for hair and makeup, or have a glam squad come to them in their dorm rooms.

I was so immersed in how to infiltrate the Virtues' temple without being caught that I neglected to plan for any sort of beauty regime, until my phone chirps in my locker. I set aside the textbooks I was switching out for my next class, reading the incoming text with a hesitant twist to my lips.

Lynda: Surprise, sweetie! I've sent NYC's best to glamify you for your first, amazing dance. We're so proud of you. Your dad sends his best and encourages you to skip your afternoon classes (I think he's experiencing a bit of pregnancy brain too, so let's take advantage!). He even says to invite some of your friends if they haven't already booked for hair and makeup. Oh yeah—my glam squad is waiting in your room!

I lean against the neighboring locker, rereading Lynda's text. I hadn't mentioned a word of the dance to them, and she thought of all this? Immediately, I'm filled with guilt. Guilt over not being a typical college kid excited for a winter dance. Guilt because I haven't asked Lynda about her pregnancy since I was dunked in the Briarcliff Lake, and she's ready to pop any second.

Me: You think of everything! Thank you. I'm leaving right now (but don't mention that to Dad. Hearing that my

ditching is actually happening might make him change his mind). How's my baby sister doing?

Lynda responds immediately: **She's enrolled herself in Krav Maga. Can't wait to get her out of the wrestling ring she's built in my stomach. We're still on track for a Christmas due date, so don't you worry yourself tonight. Just have fun and tell me all about it tomorrow.**

Smiling, I pocket my phone and cut through the academy's halls until I'm outside the pavilion and on the pathway to the dorms.

That freshly fallen snow I'd been marveling over this morning has rapidly overstayed its welcome, the plowed walkways turning into black-gray sludge under students' shoes and the wind making the sunny day seem like a lunchtime picnic in the Arctic.

I keep my head down and hood of my jacket up for that very reason, avoiding more icicles on my eyelashes. It's at that exact moment, with the blinders of my hood and the jerky movement of a light jog, that a hand grabs me at the elbow to twist me around.

I squeak, the soles of my shoes scraping over slippery sludge, but ball my free hand into a fist and swing.

"Jesus!"

Chase ducks just in time.

My breath billows out. I scan the walkway, wondering if we'll be noticed. "What are you doing here?"

"What am I—?" Chase collects himself. "You almost clocked me in the jaw."

"I'm jumpy."

"They won't schedule your third trial during the day." Chase shoves his hands in his coat's pockets. On him, the December day looks like he's just broken off from a passionate kiss, his golden skin flushed with rose, and his lips red slashes against the white of our backdrop.

"Tell that to the dead rats in my locker a few months ago," I say. "You shouldn't be talking to me."

Chase dips his chin. "All I'm doing is making sure you're ready for tonight."

"I think so." I sigh. "I hope so."

"Go with what we talked about. What Emma's run you through. We should be fine."

I haven't seen Chase in almost a week, and I'm praying my eagerness to see him, to trace every angle of him with my eyes, isn't obvious. He's been speaking through his sister, as they meet at their lake house most nights to discuss how best to break into the Virtues' tomb without notice. Evidently, Piper told Emma where she found Rose Briar's letter, and how there were many more, as well as other artifacts outlining the secret society's creation.

Piper. Helping Emma. I'm still trying to wrap my head around that.

I raise my brows. "You sure we have the right decoys?"

"Practically every chick will be in some sort of white dress and we'll be in tuxes. We're covered."

I gnaw my lower lip. "And the masks?"

Chase nods in the direction of our dorms. "Emma has them. You can thank Ivy for that."

"I will."

I've unintentionally mirrored his posture by stuffing my hands in my pockets and hunching over, when all I want to do is burrow into his warmth and beg him to take me away to his lake house. Somewhere safe. With him.

My nails dig into my palms as I fight the blooming frustration. "Is that all?"

Chase arches a brow. "You can run along, possum. We're done here."

"That's not..." Chase isn't asking for an apology for my snippiness, but I feel the need to explain. "I'm stressed. Worried. The Virtues keep coming at me with underlying threats, and I feel like the worst is yet to come."

Chase replies with a low undertone. "It probably is."

"Tonight, at the dance," I say quietly. I force myself to continue, though I've avoided asking him this question almost as much as I've tried not to run into him. "Falyn said you're going to make a speech."

His eyes grow shadows—difficult to do in such a pure, glaring landscape. But in a blink, they're gone.

Chase lifts his hand from his pocket, toward me, but thinks better of it and shoves it back in. He murmurs, "Your feelings are written all over your face."

I cast my gaze to the side. "It's okay if you talk about her. I'm not jealous."

Chase's voice is so soft, I only hear it because it's carried by the wind. "I'm not talking about jealousy."

I blurt out, "Are you making a speech about Piper because the Virtues told you to?"

"They have their reasons, but I have mine. I'm not their mindless toy, Callie, as much as they're trying to make you believe it. Whatever they've said to you, it's only the half-truth."

I search his eyes, amber encased in glass. "You're not doing it under duress? It's your choice?"

His breath comes in small clouds. "Tonight has to run smoothly. This is part of it."

"You're avoiding the question," I whisper. "They're forcing you. What do they have? What is *making* them so powerful around here?"

One side of Chase's lips tics up in a miserable smile. "That's what tonight's about, too. Answers for you and my sister. Let's not screw it up."

Chase spins on his heel, but turnabout is fair play. I grab him at the elbow. "Why do I feel less like a Virtue initiate and more like Howard Mason the longer I put up this charade? He broke into the Nobles' tomb and wrote about what he found. But then it stopped. His last written words were '*help me.*'"

Chase stares me down, rigid and unmoved. "What are you getting at?"

"You're meant to be on my side. I'm doing this stupid thing of staying away from you and being a good little initiate because you've assured me you want them taken down, too. But there's so much left unsaid. If you won't tell me everything, and neither will Emma, how am I supposed to trust that tonight will be okay?"

Chase rests a hand on mine. "Howard Mason is not dead. He's perfectly fine. And you will be, too. Take comfort that this has been going on long before you enrolled. Your presence at Briarcliff accelerated our plans but didn't create them."

I say, firmer, "I swear I'm not checking out."

"You're scared. Understandable. But we have your back." Chase smiles, and for the first time today, it feels like real emotion he's directing toward me. "I hear you have a room full of powders and gels and shit. Go and get ready. Have fun and try not to look so spooked. I'll see you at the dance."

He pries my fingers off gently, and I take a step back, lengthening the distance between us.

"For the record," he says over his shoulder, "I wish you were my date."

Hugging myself, I watch his retreat, his blond hair ruffling with the breeze. He strides unhindered through the flattened, slippery snow on the pathway to the academy. I turn in the opposite direction, holding on to the pretense that everything he's said to me is his honest truth.

16

I can smell them before I see them.

A waft of sweetened, chemical fumes hits me when I reach my floor. That sharp, nostril-singeing scent of baby powder and hairspray vapor that seems to have followed me from Meyer House in NYC.

It's not a terrible smell, exactly, but one I associate with Lynda's many summer gatherings when I stayed at her luxurious Upper West Side townhouse with Dad. I'd be holed up in my room, pretending deep interest in a paperback and *not* focusing on the fact that I was imprisoned, while down the hall, Lynda laughed as her stylists regaled her with hilarious stories, a full face, and gorgeous hair.

I unlock my door with blatant wariness.

"*Callie!*" a male voice booms in my direction, making me jump. Today, of all days, is not the one to approach me with a yell.

"H-hi," I stutter out, shutting the door behind me.

I'm immediately engulfed in a superheated room, filled with enough salon tools and foreign products to make an Upper East Side socialite melt.

"You've arrived!" The owner of the loud voice bursts forward, his round body, dressed all in black, bouncing toward me like an Addams's Family beach ball.

I say this affectionately, as whenever I crossed paths with Davide during my rare exits from Lynda's guest room, he'd greet me exactly this way, his small lips pursed between bronzed teddy-bear cheeks. "*Ça va?*"

"I'm doing well," I say, angling my head to accept his air-kisses. "Thank you for coming all this way."

"Anything for Lynda. And at Briarcliff, no less! Lucky girl. This is Suzanne." He points to a twenty-something blonde girl, laying out supplies on a fold-out table they must have brought with them. "She will help."

Davide leans closer, cupping a hand to my ear. "Is your, ah, how do you say, roommate, joining us? We met her, she let us in, but..."

I search Davide's face for signs of horror, or plain shock, upon meeting Emma, but see none. Instead, his dark eyes are alight with eagerness, his expression open and sweet. "I do not know if she wishes for us to touch her."

"I can ask," I say, more out of politeness than in hopes of a positive outcome. Knowing Emma, she'll have locked her bedroom door from the inside.

"Please do. We shall wait. You two can get ready together, yes? Friends love getting ready together."

"Sure." If you can call Emma and I friends.

After heeling off my boots, I head to Emma's side of the dorm, which is ominously quiet when I knock.

To my surprise, she opens her door almost immediately, but only enough to showcase her narrowed, brown eyes. "You have uninvited, very fragrant guests in the kitchen."

"My stepmother sent them over." I say the next part in a rush. "Would you like your hair and make-up done, too?"

Emma's lashes flutter. She purses her lips.

I try not to react to her visible hesitation or show any keenness whatsoever. "Would you like to? Lynda said she was more than happy to cover my friends."

"What about Ivy?"

"Ivy's meeting me here in fifteen minutes. Eden, too. They're happy to do all of us."

I hear Davide squeak behind me, but if I only ask for the basics, they'll totally have time for the others. It's *lunchtime*, for God's sake.

Emma's brows lower. "I don't. I mean…"

"I'd love to do this for you," I say.

It's the wrong thing to say. Glowering, Emma moves to shut her door, but I slam a hand on the wood before she can succeed.

"Alas, my little night-blooming cereus," Davide says to Emma as he comes up behind me, poking his face over my shoulder. "Come join us. You will be missing out on oh-so-much *fête*."

Emma nails him with a glare, but Davide doesn't so much as shudder. She says, "I'm not going to the stupid dance."

"I did not say that was a requirement, *ma chérie*. Half the fun is getting ready, yes? Drink champagne with your friends—I won't say a thing—make *bonne* memories while you still can. This is your freshmen year. While you may not dance to-and-fro, you will regret not having my hands upon your face." Davide grows serious. "I am the best in the business. There has never been a woman I haven't made into a goddess, and I shall not back away from this door until you step out of it."

Emma retreats farther into the shadows of her room. "Go away, French man."

"Hmm. A challenge, then." Davide lifts a canister of hairspray from his toolbelt. His eyes grow small. "I can spray you from here, *chérie*."

Emma looks to me for support, but I shrug. "Talk to the man with the weapon, not me."

Silence stretches between the three of us, until Davide, with an expression of stone, presses the pump in two warning bursts.

Emma winces, but I note the wavering tremor in her lips as she tries to fight off a smile. "Fine. But only because you're threatening me with aerosol poisoning."

Davide breaks into a wide, luminous grin while I step aside so she can come out.

Emma waltzes into the main room, her chin raised regally, but her eyes are hard and flat as marbles as she comes into the light, like she's expecting Davide and Suzanne to comment about her scars or *tsk* that there's not enough product in the world to make her beautiful.

My chest tightens, because the Emma I saw in old pictures, the one before the attack, and the fire, and the

Virtues, would've loved to be treated to a makeover before a dance.

Yet, Davide's expression is soft as Emma approaches, before he scampers to the center of the room. "Come. Sit. I have just the things for you."

Emma perches on a stool, and I slide onto one next to her, conscious of how Davide and Suzanne treat her, but soon, he has Emma cracking a smile, and then the both of them are commiserating about their favorite villages in France, and my shoulders relax and submit to Suzanne as she plucks, mumbles, and paints.

Half an hour later, Ivy and Eden join us. We take a quick break to drag the office chairs out of our rooms, but with the speed of stylist professionalism, Suzanne and Davide have us lined up like soldiers as they work on our faces and hair in sections.

While my eyes are closed, I feel Ivy's cold hand clasp mine on my lap. "You ready?"

"Sure." My mouth is so dry, it comes out as a rasp.

"And we are complete!" Davide backs away from Eden, his arms lifted in triumph. "Go, ladies, see how I've transformed you into Snow White beauties."

Eden cautiously tucks her curled hair behind her ears and lifts from her seat. Emma follows. Ivy and I are frozen in our stools as we watch them find the closest mirror in the bathroom and stare at their reflections.

They don't speak.

"Are they okay?" Ivy whispers to me. "I didn't get a good look before they ducked in there."

I shake my head. "Me neither."

Davide waits patiently nearby, steepling his fingers and primed for any movement or sound. Suzanne parts her bright red lips to say something, but Davide shushes her. "Art appreciation cannot be rushed."

Emma's the first to come out.

"Well?" Davide asks.

"It'll do." Emma clears her throat. "It suits our purposes. We'll blend in with everyone else around campus tonight."

Emma's voice may be toneless and unimpressed, but her eyes glitter like diamonds against a flawless application of correcting foundation.

I smile at the sight of her, Emma's brown eyes deeply lined, her cheeks apple-pink, and her lips full and defined. While I've become familiar with her scars, they're almost invisible beneath Davide's expert fingers, only a few indents here and there and a small pucker at her lips.

The same can be said for Eden when she steps out. Her ebony hair shines, and her green eyes pop with the pale, moss-colored eyeshadow Suzanne swept across, and her pock-marks are smoothed and blurred.

"Are you sure you guys don't want to come to the dance?" I ask. "I'm sure there's time to find a dress."

"No." Emma utters the denial with the tone of a girl who has long given up hope for sweet college memories.

"It's a nice thought," Eden says, "but not for us."

Davide pushes out his lower lip. "I'm sad to hear it, but my talents are never wasted. I see it in your eyes, my little night-blooming cereus, and that is compliment enough."

Emma smiles uncomfortably, and Ivy takes the cue to

redirect the conversation by sliding off her seat and pulling at my arm. "Come on. It's gown time!"

I allow myself to be pulled into my room, but gesture for Emma and Eden to follow.

Emma shakes her head. "We have last-minute preparation to do. We'll see you when you guys are done."

It doesn't sit right, leaving them, but then again, nothing has felt okay since becoming a Briarcliff student. Wearing two faces is exhausting—the Callie who enjoys the academy and attends the dances versus the one who has x-rayed through the blackness and sees the broken bones. I wish I could choose one girl to become, and it's with that wish that I allow Ivy to guide me into the gown chosen by the Virtues and don the white-feathered eye-mask gifted by my best friend.

Ivy twists me to face the mirror stuck to the back of my door.

Davide calls his goodbye, and I answer, but it sounds like an echo of my usual tone as I take in my transformation.

My brown, flyaway hair has been tamed into silk tresses drifting to my elbows. My lips are painted a delicate sheen of pink, my usually fair cheeks matching the same color. I lift the feathered, silvery mask to take in my hazel eyes, my lashes thick and black with strategically placed falsies.

Then there's my dress. Lightweight, white silk that reflects a prism of colors as I turn.

A smile creeps across my lips.

If tonight goes as planned, then maybe, just *maybe*, I can permanently slip into this Callie's skin.

"Fabulous," Ivy says. Her long blond hair is sleek-straight to her shoulders, and she wears a silvery cocktail dress.

"I can say the same for you."

She grins, then hooks her arm through mine. "Let's begin the madness."

Eden and Emma are waiting for us on the couch. When she spots us, Emma lifts her phone. "Guess what that tiny, rotund man was calling me? What 'little night-blooming cereus' means?"

Ivy and I shake our heads.

"He was calling me a night-blooming cactus."

A beat of silence follows.

Then, all of us burst into laughter.

Emma pouts, but can't maintain it for long. "Maybe he was *slightly* accurate."

I sweep my gaze over all my friends, caught in such a brief moment of glee, wishing we could feel this free and bright all the time.

Then make it happen, Calla.

"I will," I whisper to my mother, and my friends are still laughing so hard, they don't hear my quiet vow.

17

The Winter Formal is held on campus this year, due to Piper's death and the faculty's concern over students leaving the academy's property.

A lot of students found disappointment in the change of venue (apparently, a hotel ballroom in a ritzy part of Providence was rented out well in advance, and now, the thought of holding it in the academy's gym is heinous), but as I walk through the grand doors of Briarcliff's gymnasium—a whole separate *building*—I can't make out the difference between a five-star ballroom and this.

"Holy..." I say, taking in the transparent drifts of white and pale blue fabric and the multitude of fairy lights covering the ceiling.

"Haven't been to a school dance like this before, have you?" Ivy muses as we walk forward.

I think back on the plastic bowls of punch and party

store cut-outs of Santas and Reindeer with the scents of rubber, spilled beer, and sweat in the air. "Not even close."

Fake snow lines the dance floor and sparkling glass snowflakes hang down from the ceiling as we wander close to the center, theater spotlights moving back and forth above our heads.

Ivy says something close to my ear that I don't catch. I'm focused on the altar in the center of the room and the clear plexiglass coffin raised on a dais, containing hundreds of stemless pink, red, and white roses laid within its confines.

"Wow," I breathe.

Ivy commiserates, murmuring over the gold detail and the thick folds of white satin holding up the pretend coffin. "I hate to say it, but Falyn and her cohorts embraced the Snow White theme with grace. I thought it was the dumbest idea ever, but this?"

I take in the dance floor circling the altar. "Are we supposed to dance around Piper's spiritual casket?"

"There it is." Ivy snaps her fingers. "I was wondering where Falyn's signature repugnancy was in all this perfection. We're probably meant to be the dwarves dancing around Piper's grave."

"How lovely."

Ivy sidles close. "At least you won't be here for long. Look alive, Callie, and talk to as many people as you can so no one can say they didn't see you. But don't be obvious. Like, still be yourself. It'd probably be suspicious if you started chatting with a ton of students you don't normally talk to. Actually..." Ivy winces. "Have you spoken to anyone outside our circle?"

"Thanks," I say, giving her the side-eye. "I'll be subtle, don't worry."

"Okay. Me too. Oh!" Ivy latches onto my shoulder instead of leaving my side. "And stay away from Chase. Not even hungry eyes across the dance floor. Got it?"

I sigh, then wave a hand at the bed of roses. "It'll be hard to, considering Piper's smack in the middle of it."

Ivy gives me one last squeeze. "It's been hard for you, but Sabine's reasons usually aren't unfounded. I'll find you in a few minutes, see how you're doing."

"Sure." I wave her off, anxious to make nice and do a few meet-and-greets before scuttling out of here and getting the job done.

It's not difficult to toss a few waves and smiles, especially once I take off my mask and let the few people I've spoken to in class put a name to the quick greeting. Like Ivy said, I can't approach a group and just start gabbing. They'd stare at me like fishes shocked onto land, and Sabine is the circling shark sensing the rippling waters.

After making the rounds, I find a corner and fit my mask back on, but my lips have gone chapped with all the nervous licking and my throat dry with the reflexive swallows. I stare across the room at the bar of drinks, then shimmy my way over and ask for a sparkling water.

The bartender acknowledges my order and turns his back to find a glass. The moment he shifts out of view, Sabine appears on the other side, wearing a blood red, strapless dress.

My body stills. Everyone in my immediate vicinity starts

moving in slow motion and a white noise rush of blood flows through my ears.

"Miss? Miss."

The bartender's voice sounds hollow, like he's calling out from the curled depths of a conch shell.

I shake myself out of it and accept the glass of water, a thin lime floating forlornly on the top. "Thank you," I think I say, but it's hard to hear my voice.

Sabine smiles thinly and curls her hand in a wave before moving along the edges of the dance floor. Her eyes slide away. I exhale, my shoulders falling from my ears.

It's a wonder she's here as a chaperone. Neither of her girls attend Briarcliff.

Stupid me, I think. She's the queen of the Virtues. Of course, she's present and will always be considered a parent within these walls, whether or not she's the mother of a killer.

She's a queen of a lot worse, hisses that voice inside me. I sip my drink, the water cold and smooth, but the bubbles pop and burn all the way down.

A soft drift of skin brushes my free hand dangling at my side, and I curl my fingers, glancing down when it happens again.

Calloused, long fingers tickle against my own.

"Enjoying yourself?" Chase asks while staring directly ahead.

"I wish I could." *With you.*

Even though he stands a few feet behind me, I sense the heat rippling off him and crashing against my exposed back like white, frothy waves against a cliff. For a moment, I imagine him stepping up to me and lifting his hand, his head cocked in a silent question while his eyes glitter mischievously behind his black, raven-feathered mask. I would slide my hand into his warm palm, and he'd lead me onto the dance floor, gathering me at the waist and pushing me against his hard body, every plane, every inch of him, pressing against my softest parts, ending with our lips...

"You're doing fine," he says, his voice grounding and sure.

It forces me to remember where I am, what I'm doing, and why I can't be with him.

"I'm chomping at the bit to leap out of here. I feel watched in every direction."

As if I asked for it, a tingle skitters up my arm, unrelated to Chase because it has the creepy, measured *ticks* of spider legs climbing my skin.

Falyn stands nearby, flanked by Willow, Violet, and a few other girls I'm coming to recognize as Virtues. With their faces half-hidden by masks, it should be difficult to discern their eyes, but for me, they're all too targeted.

The three of them cast their wicked stares my way, the outer edges of their lips curling with derisive sneers. Violet's is the only one that trembles at the edges, and I file that away, as I've done all her moments of sympathy.

"How am I supposed to escape without notice?" I whisper.

"Leave that to me."

His thumb strokes the side of my pinky finger, and I curl it in hopes of catching him and proving my wishes right—

that Chase is here, wanting to touch me as much as I ache to lean into him.

Chase's finger hooks mine. It lasts for a second—not even—but it's enough.

We break apart.

"The crowning of the Winter Formal Court starts soon," he murmurs as he angles away. "Ivy will find you."

"Stay." But he's too far away to hear my whispered plea.

Heart in my throat, I escape the edges of the dance floor and work for farther distance from Falyn and the other Virtues—but then stop.

The Virtues are supposed to be my sisters. As an initiate, I'm expected to socialize.

Setting my shoulders, I backtrack to the group, summoning Eden's eagerness when she spoke of her efforts to become one of them. She did everything she could to belong. Hoped against all barriers that they'd accept her.

I'm my own worst enemy if I don't do the same. And I'd be nothing but a disappointment to Emma and Eden.

"Hey," I say once I reach them.

Violet speaks first. "Hi, Callie."

Willow purses her lips, then finds deep interest in something behind me—or through me, but Falyn says, "Ready for the crowning?"

I paste on a smile. "It's so important that we honor our fallen members, isn't it? Piper would be delighted with what you've done to the school's gymnasium."

Falyn's lips waver between a sarcastic smile and a frown, unsure whether or not I'm complimenting her.

But I'm supposed to be supplicating to these assholes,

not low-key insulting them. I force another smile and make sure to include their silvery, off-white gown, exactly like mine, when I say, "Love your dresses. Did the queen purchase yours, too?"

I wince. Even my compliments are turning into sideswipes. I can't seem to help it around these girls.

"It's a privilege to wear our colors," Willow seethes. "If only your pallor could handle it as well as mine."

I suppose I deserved that.

"Attention, students!"

The DJ cuts the music, and we all turn to Chancellor Marron taking the stage.

"The time you've all been anticipating has come," he says, accepting a wireless microphone from the DJ as he passes. "And I'm so proud of each and every one of you for choosing to honor one of our fallen."

I tilt my head to Falyn and smile. She glares at me in response.

"I won't take up too much time," Marron continues. "I'm sure you'd all prefer music to your Chancellor's voice this evening, but I'd like to introduce you to your Winter Court King, a boy I couldn't take more pride in, both with his decorum on school grounds and how he's conducted himself after our most heartbreaking tragedy this year. The death of Piper Harrington, a wonderful pupil who you've posthumously crowned Winter Court Queen."

Scattered applause sounds out across the room, but I'm busy trying to find a line of sight on Chase through the glittering headpieces and slicked back hair of all the students.

Falyn has the same idea, but gestures to Violet and

Willow to follow her as she carves a demanding path to the center of the room, where a spotlight shines on Piper's altar.

I follow their path, students twisting aside before they're nailed by one of the serrated edges of Falyn's elbows, until...

There.

Chase cuts into their path, acknowledging their presence with an absent nod, his face indiscernible beneath his mask. Yet, I'm taking in more of him than I did when he settled discreetly behind me, like the cut of his tuxedo and the breadth of his shoulders. His hair is windblown, curling into stylized waves at the top and falling into his ears, but there's nothing boyish about him. The raising of his chin commands the room as he takes the few steps needed to assume his position beside the plexiglass coffin and turn, sweeping his stare across the audience.

Marron rests a silver, opulent crown on his head. Chase is so tall, he has to bend to accept the prize.

When Chase straightens, I forget I'm in a school gym. I forget the surrounding students who attend Briarcliff Academy, and that the U.S. has long since shed a monarch rule.

Because we're faced with a king, and despite his face half-hidden in velvet and feathers, the line of Chase's jaw, his confident stance, and his rough voice, takes everyone under his thrall.

I'm staring at the true Noble King, I think, then school my face before anyone nearby can read the awe.

"All of you remember the day we lost Piper," he says. "And every single one of you can recall the days before. She was sharp, she was cutting, and she was mean. I knew her well enough to understand what she disguised: her guardedness, her vulnerabilities, and her easily wounded heart." Chase pauses, allowing the heavy atmosphere of the room to coat his words. "I'm sure you can all name a bully in your life, and many of you would say it was her."

The cavernous gym, while silent to my ears, seems to echo the names whispering into each student's head. A lot would agree on Piper. Many would mention Falyn. And most would be naming Chase, too.

I glance back at the platform when Chase continues.

"I don't think any of you would agree she should have died for her pettiness. I certainly don't. Or maybe you think she got what she deserved, killed by her own flesh and blood."

The gym doesn't breathe.

My attention scatters, pinpointing the furious gaze of Falyn as she twists to Willow and hisses words probably to the effect of, *What the fuck is he doing? He's meant to be mourning Piper, not pissing everyone off!* Then, I scan the sidelines, where a magnetic force draws me to a sleek, form-fitting scarlet dress.

Sabine's expression is so rigid, so frozen, it might fracture with the barest squint. Only the red slash of her lips, the gloss shimmering under the lights from each twitch, each tremor, showcases her carefully controlled fury.

A hand grasps my arm and pulls gently. "Come on," Ivy whispers behind me.

I follow Ivy, carefully disengaging from the crowd and using Chase's primed weapon of distraction to duck out the doors without anyone so much as turning their head— Sabine included.

18

---

*L*ifting my skirts, I rush down the gymnasium steps behind Ivy, my dress billowing behind me under the chilled night wind.

"How long can Chase keep up the distraction?" I ask, my voice coming out breathless as cold air shrinks my lungs.

"Long enough to have everybody talking even *after* he finishes his speech," Ivy says, but whirls to grab my hand, forcing my legs to pump faster. In heels.

"Ivy, hold on—*ugh*, I wish I could kick off these things and run in bare feet!"

"No time." Ivy's voice is also breathy, her exhales plumes of smoke near my face. "Chase can buy us about twenty minutes. We have to be long gone by then."

"And Eden? Emma?"

"Already there." Ivy swings left, and my toes scream at the constant impact in such narrow, designer shoes.

Soon, we hit the path to the library, and with the stars as

our only witnesses, creep inside the emergency exit that Eden propped open earlier with a stick.

A waft of heat hits me in the face when we shimmy through the door, the exposed skin of my arms thawing under goosebumps and melting snowflakes.

My chest rises and falls with deep, collected breaths as I stand beside Ivy and take in the dark recesses of the M.B.S. Library of Studies.

The stacks stand in the perfect alignment of Underworld soldiers. I instinctively brace for their silent onslaught.

"Let's go," Ivy whispers, though we should be the only ones here.

Everyone else is at the dance, I assure myself. *We're fine.*

Ivy kicks off her shoes then hooks them in her fingers as she sprints to the back, and I follow her lead.

Eden and Emma are waiting at the last column of books. We all nod in greeting, making as little sound as possible, just in case there's an unscheduled security guard belatedly completing his rounds.

Ivy crouches and exposes the keypad, but before she enters the pin and scans her finger, Eden stops her.

She asks, "You sure Tempest can scrub your time of entry?"

Ivy glances at Emma, who says, "He's been texting me. He's in the Nobles' system and found a workaround to the Virtues'. The cameras are off, and as soon as the system triggers Ivy's entry, he'll erase it."

Did I say we weren't *Mission Impossible* agents? Perhaps I stand corrected.

"Okay," Ivy says, then presses her finger on the pad and enters in a code.

The hidden door opens like a silent predator's jaws, but unlike the time before, I'm the first to step through.

A few sconces in the cylindrical room light up at my entrance, but not enough to fully spotlight us. With Eden staying behind as the lookout, the three of us creep along the curved lines of the room.

According to Ivy, there are more than three, maybe five, hidden doors on this floor, one being Sabine's office head-quarters.

Ivy stops at an elaborate stone carving directly beneath the spot where Sabine stood on the balcony. Stepping next to her, I study the statue of a sleeping raven, wings tucked in, its talons curved over a twisted branch engraved in the wall.

Ivy wraps her hand around its neck and pushes. As if unable to help herself, she whispers under her breath, "*Altum volare in tenebris.*"

The carving sinks into a perfect square in the wall before it breaks into two pieces and the stone divides horizontally.

I've stopped breathing. My heart thrashes wildly in its cage, and I press a hand to my chest.

We step over the threshold into a large space, stonework turning into brickwork. A fireplace that could engulf me whole is to my right, and a wide desk sits in the center of the room. More carvings decorate the walls, each one a raven in different stages of flight.

Black iron and gray decorate the space, with intricate splashes of red, almost like rivers of blood between bone.

I gulp. "Where do you figure she's stashed her files?"

"Not here," Ivy says.

I'm the only one who jolts in surprise. "But this is her office."

Emma and Ivy share a look I can't decipher, other than it's grim. Then, Emma jerks her chin, as if giving Ivy the okay.

Before I call them out, Ivy moves behind the desk to the back wall displaying a large, vivid painting of Sabine, sitting in the identical, elaborate red chair showcased in reality, but with Piper and Addisyn seated below her in Briarcliff uniform, their legs curled under and their hands demurely resting on their shins.

"This is *so* haunting and creepy," I mutter at the same time Emma tells me to hurry up.

I pry my gaze from the painting in time to see Ivy duck into the fireplace.

Throwing out a hand, I cry, "Wait, what—?"

"It's another passageway," Emma says. "Go with her. I'll stay here and make sure no one comes."

"Shit," I whisper, but the word comes out tight, because I am *so* utterly freaked out right now.

Luckily, when I head into the fireplace, there are no dwarf-sized spiraling stairs into a basement waiting for me on the other side. Ivy's already opened the back wall of the fireplace, and I duck into a beautifully arranged bedroom.

"Sabine sleeps here?" I ask.

A gorgeous four-poster bed with a lace canopy sprawls

out in the center, with two intricately carved wooden night-stands on each side.

Unlike Sabine's spine-chilling office space, this one is painted a calming sage green, with century pieces containing a dresser, a wardrobe, and a vanity mirror. The walls are adorned with watercolor paintings, all of white roses.

Ivy pinches her lips, staring pointedly at the paintings and nothing else. "Check the drawers."

I stay where I am. "Ivy, what is this? What am I missing here?"

Ivy's throat bobs, and she won't look at me. "I said you had to see it. So, here it is."

My lips form on *what* ... but can't give the question sound. Ivy's fists are clenched to her sides, her stance rigid and her lips pressed together so tightly, they're bone white.

With my head filled with more questions than answers, I bend to the first nightstand and rifle through the drawers. I sift through sleeping pills, a lavender scented sleep mask, some lace underwear, a box of opened condoms, and something hard and rubbery.

When I pull it out, I screech, then let it loose.

It bounces a few times before landing at Ivy's feet. "Is that a—?"

"Sex toy. Yes."

"But—" Again, I stop myself. Too often, I say things before thinking, and Ivy's stare is so wide and fused onto the watercolor above the bed, it's like she's begging that I come up with the answer myself.

There's a dildo in Sabine's secret bedroom, I think first.

But ... if we were hopping behind a fireplace and exploring Sabine's home-away-from-home, Ivy wouldn't be so stilted. I chance another look at her, wagering my thoughts against her cracking armor, and deciding she's more delicate than stiff. Ivy's so vulnerable that if I stood up and screamed, she'd buckle under the pressure and break.

The more I analyze the situation, the more it makes sense.

Ivy is the Virtues' princess.

I whisper, "Ivy, is this your room?"

Ever so slowly, she nods.

"And..." My empty stomach lurches as I continue, "was this Emma's room, too? Piper's?"

This time, her nod shakes loose a single tear that runs down her cheek.

Bile hurls into my throat, searing the back and making my tongue curl over the bitter, erosive acid. "Do you have other visitors in here?"

Ivy bobs her head, her lower lip spasming as more tears course down her cheeks.

"Visitors..." My voice thickens. My eyes turn hot. "Visitors Sabine chooses?"

"Yes."

"That you're forced to ... host?"

"Uh-huh."

Sleeping pills. Lace underwear. Sex toys. Condoms...

I fill in the horrendous blank, asking, "Men?"

"Y-yes."

"*Ivy*," rips from my throat before I shoot to my feet and envelop my friend in a hug.

Ivy digs her fingers into my arms and buries her head in my neck. I cling to her, absorbing her shakes, inhaling her sobs, my heart fracturing with each erratic beat.

"We can get out of here," I say into her hair.

Her chin digs into my neck. "This is our only chance. In a few weeks, I—I'm meant to return to this room. I don't want to come back here again."

I stroke her hair, exuding calm, though so many questions, so much *horror*, begs to pry open my lips. "Then let's move fast."

Ivy lifts her head and collects herself. "Sabine keeps her confidential papers in here."

After pulling the wardrobe from the wall, Ivy crouches and loosens one of the lower bricks. She stands, a thick, red binder clutched in her hands. "I saw her put this away one night, when she thought I was asleep ... over there." Ivy's gaze skirts to the bed, then away again. "It was my first night here. I was afraid to do anything but lie still ... after. Terrified there were cameras in here. I'm glad you're with me this time. You gave me the courage to show you. Sabine doesn't put anything like this on her computer. Too concerned with unauthorized access."

I take the binder from Ivy's stiff hands, using my side to push the wardrobe back in place. "By whom? Hackers?"

"You can call them that. The society is subject to quarterly reporting, like any other corporation, except it's not through the IRS. It's by the Nobles. Sabine hasn't disclosed the Virtues' true operations for a long, long time."

My grip slides on the leather-bound binder, sweat

slicking my fingertips. I cast a furtive glance toward the opening we came through, then open the flap.

"Callie, we don't have time. Someone will notice we're not at the dance soon."

"Just a few seconds."

Time is a gift, a mantra I've learned the hard way. If there is any free moment to glean more information, I'll steal that time away rather than wait for it to be handed to me like a privileged present.

I flip to a random section, using this brief access not to understand Sabine's operations in their entirety, but just a glimpse, a snapshot of worth, so I can be sure our efforts at breaking in haven't been wasted.

A faded, thin page flutters to the floor, and Ivy bends to pick it up.

"What is it?" I ask. "Another letter from Rose?"

Ivy's eyes move back and forth as she reads, holding the paper up to the light until it almost becomes transparent.

It's a newspaper clipping, one with a picture.

The paper trembles in her hand. "Oh no..."

"What? What is it?"

She opens and closes her mouth, continuing to read the fine print.

"Ivy, we have seconds, remember?" I snatch the clipping from her so I can read it myself. She squeaks but doesn't fight me.

Actually, she's very, very silent.

My fingers start to shake as I take in the photo. I realize why Ivy's gone so quiet.

It's a black-and-white photo of my mother, smiling while

angling her head, her eyes as lively and her hair just as crazy as if she were standing here today. Even without color, her beauty is startling.

And my heart cracks to pieces.

A vicious killing has rocked Manhattan's Lower East Side. 36-year-old Meredith Ryan, a respected crime scene photographer, primarily employed by the NYPD, was found slaughtered in her bedroom, her throat cut so deeply, she was almost decapitated. Her 15-year-old daughter discovered the horrendous scene mere hours after Ryan was killed. The motive remains a mystery, as does the killer. A spokesperson for the NYPD comments, "This is a tragedy of the worst kind. We don't yet know if this is related to any of the cases she worked on, but we will pull every file and study every page until we either find the perpetrator or rule them out. Meredith was one of our own, and we will work tirelessly to find out why a young mother, a valued crime scene photographer, and a wonderful person, has been taken from us so senselessly."

"Why?" I whisper, the article audibly rustling in my shaking hand. "Why would Sabine have this?"

I stare down at the open binder in my other hand, its weight making my wrist ache, but I stop feeling it as I find more grayish bits of paper poking out, like a goddamned scrapbook.

Flipping furiously, I find more articles about my mom. Journalists who, at first taking a vested interest, peter out as the dates go by and no killer is found. No motive.

Even my dad's arrest is in here. My accusations written for the nation to read. And his ultimate release.

Everything is in here.

"Why would she have these?" I'm screeching, vowels breaking apart in my mouth.

Ivy clutches my hand, then delicately pries the initial article from my grip and places it in the binder. "I'm being honest with you—I have no idea. But we can't stand here and wonder. We have to *leave*."

Her words knock a small amount of sense back into me, and I let her lead us out.

We rush to the fireplace and duck our heads under.

Ivy's gaze is sunken, hollow, as we descend into the shadows. "We'll read everything, and you'll—"

"Dearest Calla Lily, are you so bold as to think you could outsmart me?"

The voice wraps around my ears, tightening with the accuracy of a garrot, before I emerge from the ashy depths of the hearth.

Ivy's ice-cold fingers wrap around my bicep, digging hard. I feel the warm trickle of blood from the crescent-sized wounds she causes more than I do the petrified squeeze.

Reluctantly, I raise my eyes from the floor.

Sabine stands in the middle of the office, with her arms crossed, flanked by Emma, Eden ... and Chase.

19

"Nice to see you've taken yourself on a personal tour," Sabine says, her storm-blue eyes razoring into me.

I break through the ice of her stare and turn to Eden. Eden, who was supposed to keep watch in the library. I'm filled with swallowed confusion when she won't meet my eye as she stands to the right of Sabine, straight-backed and shaking.

Our backup guard, Emma, is wound so tightly behind Sabine, so pale and stone-still, she won't look at me, either. Her vacant, sightless stare goes past Sabine, through me, and dead ends against the wall.

My arm twitches to help her, but under Sabine's scrutiny, I don't dare react so soon. Not when that's exactly what she wants.

Chase is next to his sister, hands shoved into his pockets,

but his gaze on fire. He's targeting Sabine like he wants to kill her.

I do my damnedest to summon a calm exterior and ask the question most likely to throw Sabine off-balance. "Why do you have news articles about my mother?"

Sabine's blood-red lips peel back, but it's not directed at me. "Ivy may have introduced you to the Virtuous boudoir too soon. She most certainly spoke out of turn when you were in that room. Ivy—with me."

My gown billows with Ivy's strides as she takes her place next to Chase.

While I'm not surprised at Ivy's compliance, the pull in my belly at watching her resume her position next to Sabine and donning a regal, highborn expression is very, very real.

Chase moves to stare at me with such intensity, such enraged scrutiny, that my feigned, unaffected exterior will crumble once he matches his tone to that expression.

It's not real. It's not real. They're playing a part.

Sabine's voice severs the pulse that happens between Chase and me as we lock eyes—hope, warning, assurance, fear. "You have something that belongs to me." Sabine lifts her hand, her fingers drooped as if she were already bored with going through the motions of retrieving her binder. "Bring it here."

My fingers tighten on the binder. "You didn't answer my question. Why is my mom in here?"

Her answering smile is kind. Patient. "Why, child, I do a copious amount of research on all the girls who pledge to become a Virtue. All current Virtues are in that binder, and my first impression notes. It's why you can't have it, you see. They are thoughts not to be made public because they can come off as rather upsetting."

I hold my position. Something doesn't feel right. Sabine is much too calm.

"But the dates," I say. "You have articles printed over a year ago, before I ever thought to come to Briarcliff."

"It wasn't meant for your eyes," Sabine continues, but her smile wears thin. "Nor for anyone else's. Bring it here, Calla Lily. *Now.*"

I debate the pros and cons of holding the binder tight to my chest and sprinting out of here. My escape fantasy doesn't last long, however. I said before that Chase and Ivy were playing their parts. As those good soldiers, they would be told to stop me. Restrain me. Rip the binder from my hands.

There's no chance of fleeing this room without doing as Sabine says. I'll have to figure out another way of uncovering the truth behind Sabine's retention of these articles.

And why they matter to her.

Reluctantly, I step forward and push it into her hands.

For the first time, Emma peels her attention from the walls and finds me. Her brown eyes are bloodshot, her lashes trembling. She blinks, but in between those seconds of blindness, her chin quivers.

I take in her hunched stature and what her mind must be forcing her to endure the longer this confrontation plays out. The torture she went through under Sabine's direction. The punishment Sabine could inflict now.

How could I think Emma would be able to withstand this? *Why* didn't I listen to my gut?

"As an initiate." Sabine's voice forces attention back to her. "You have no right, no *business*, looking into such private documents. If it weren't for my dear princess, you may have gotten away with your petty, impulsive investigation, but thanks to her, instead you're about to endure a most painful final trial."

The tiny hairs on the back of my neck rise.

Ivy stares at the floor, her lips clamped between her teeth. Despite my silent prod at her to look up, her focus doesn't stray from the ground.

Sabine chuckles low in her throat. I spare another glance at Chase, but his focus is straight ahead, muscles spasming in his cheeks as his jawline protrudes with a hard, tongue-severing clench.

"You must be wondering, foolish girl, why I'm not exiling you for your disobedience."

At last, I meet her stare. "I'm not your show pony. You got your binder back. So, kick me out, or I'll walk out myself."

Sabine's cheeks tic with amusement. "You've accepted our invitation, meaning, there is no possible way for you to *walk* out. It is up to me whether to banish you, but I'm inclined to provide you with a choice. Since your acceptance here at Briarcliff, you've been consumed by us. Hungry for our history and societal formation. And now, I hold articles of your mother in my hands." Sabine lifts the binder, dangling the weight easily, despite her waif-like stature. "I doubt you're willing to leave it all behind."

I remain closed-lipped, but Sabine sees past it. She smiles. "Stay and prove this was all a misunderstanding, dear girl. Fall into our ranks and learn our history and all we have to offer. Or, attempt to sever your connection with us and see how far that gets you."

Her veiled threat doesn't hit its mark. *She won't kill me if I leave.*

Piper wasn't killed by the Virtues—it was Addisyn, her sister. Howard Mason is still alive, according to Chase, and after what I've seen in the bedroom behind the fireplace, Sabine likes her Virtues alive, well, and complacent.

Sabine could be calling my bluff.

But as I hold her cool, depthless stare, a tinned, inner voice asks, *Is she, though?*

"You have too many qualities that can't be ignored," Sabine explains. She passes the binder to Ivy, who moves to set it on her desk. "Curiosity, stubbornness, pride, determination, instinctive intelligence—the type of traits that cannot be taught, and which we Virtues covet. It is only your foolishness I must confront, and I can do that easily. So, I either ban you from our society, or I keep you as planned, and thus seal your lips from ever speaking of the Virtues. Or the Nobles, I suppose."

Sabine includes the Nobles with the reluctant tone of including a neglected, middle child.

I jump on the opening. "What is Chase doing here? If the punishment is for me and involves the Virtues, why keep everyone here at all?"

"Oh, child." Sabine gifts me with another serpentine

smile. "Breaking you will be so much sweeter than allowing you to cleave yourself from the Virtues."

The image of the adjacent room curdles into my mind, its implications turning those sickening bubbles into pops of acid. Sabine's using some of these girls by offering them out for sex.

I can't leave now. Not after discovering what Ivy is forced to do to keep her place as a Virtuous princess and save her family from poverty.

As if sensing my silent answer, Sabine grins. Gestures me forward. "Come."

Sabine's dress swishes against the stone floor as she spins, her gait over cobblestones unusually smooth as she leads us to the door to the inner temple.

I step toward Chase, but he stops me with a searing, bone-rattling look, then gives a minuscule shake of his head. *Don't.*

Then, as if he hadn't communicated with me at all, he stalks to his sister's side and grasps her outstretched, shaking hand, murmuring into her ear.

Emma relaxes under her brother's protection, her shudders visibly subsiding.

Sabine pauses at the doorway. "Are you coming, Calla Lily?"

There's pressure at my back, Eden nudging me forward. "Go," she whispers. "We have no choice."

I risk one more glance at Chase before tottering forward, wondering if Sabine's focus on me means the rest of them can get out unscathed.

Foolish girl is right. There's no way Sabine will let bygones be bygones.

The large door guarded by the stone raven slides open, and Sabine disappears into the temple. When I follow her out with my friends at my back, I pause mid-stride and look up at the gold cloaks surrounding the balcony, interspersed with the black velvet of the Nobles.

I gulp, scanning the faceless heads and shapeless cloaks. This can't be good.

They're all here.

20

*S*abine comes to a halt at the center of the temple, sweeping her arms out and raising her head to her audience. "My children, it seems as though we have a minor interlude before we continue our formal winter celebration in the Nobles' tomb. Calla Lily Ryan thinks she can thwart our rules and bring in outsiders to learn our secrets."

The room erupts in chants of *"altum volare in tenebris,"* masculine and feminine voices mixing into an eerie, unisex chant.

I lift my gaze to the rafters, at the mingling of black and gold velvet, for the first time becoming subjected to the Nobles' scrutiny. Up until now, it was always the Virtues who tested my boundaries and stripped my soul. Other than Chase, the Nobles were ignorant of my initiation, or so I thought.

Yet here they are, about to witness my final trial.

Sabine clucks her tongue, disapproval etched into the

thin lines of her face as she watches my hesitant and wary study of the room. "Come, dear girl." But her eyes sharpen. "Don't keep us from the night longer than you already have."

Fingers brush against mine, the same touch I beheld at the dance, identical callouses sending a reassuring stroke over my skin.

I feel Chase's knuckles against my palm before stepping forward and pretending nineteen sets of eyes aren't staring at the top of my head, salivating over my potential demise.

Was every member made aware of our plans tonight? Is Tempest up there somewhere? I risk another glance above. Which one of these Cloaks haunted my dorm room at night, taking what they wanted while I slept?

With every step I take, I curse my weakness for authority. My need for companionship. I should be sprinting for the door.

Yet, I walk forward, summoned by the crook of Sabine's finger, pushed by my dread over what will happen to Eden, Emma, Ivy—*Chase*—if I don't bow down and take my spanking like a good, chastised girl.

No wonder my mom and Ahmar always worked alone. Almost nothing could be used against them if an angry criminal decided to take revenge.

Except ... Mom's dead.

As I move closer to Sabine, I'm positive that putting trust in others is vastly becoming my greatest mistake.

A flash of black alerts me to motion at my periphery. I turn. Daniel Stone waltzes out of another hidden entrance, his hood flipped back, his red cloak floating from the breeze of his prowl. When his pale eyes find mine, cold, skeletal fingers wrap themselves around my neck.

Daniel Stone's footsteps echo throughout the temple until he comes to a stop beside Sabine. No sounds emanate from the balcony, no murmurs or shuffles. Complete, utter quiet has stifled all the bodies in this room, every single person, including me, choosing their senses over their motions as events unfold.

Sabine reaches out a hand, which Daniel clasps. "Just in time, Daniel. It seems our Calla Lily needs a lesson in loyalty."

Daniel casts his gaze—briefly—in my direction. "Do as you wish, my love."

An answering growl sounds from behind. It's Chase.

Sabine says, "I'm afraid you're faced with another choice, Initiate."

A litany of possibilities fan through my mind. Back to the boathouse? Falyn's unfettered access to me during school hours? Free reign on my dorm room and locker to plant additional rodent corpses?

I wonder where Marron is, and if he's up there with the others, closed-mouthed and his interest piqued.

I keep my voice level when I ask, "And that is?"

"It's obvious to me, and everyone else in this temple, that consequence to you is—well, of no consequence. It is only if someone else, a person close to you, suffers, that you deign to give obedience any attention at all." Sabine angles her head, adding, "Isn't that right?"

I cover up my wince, but not in time. Sabine's tongue runs along her lower lip at the sight. "The minute Ivy admitted your transgression, I started to wonder, should I punish your father? Your stepmother?" She arches a brow. "Your unborn sister?"

Horrible thumps rattle against my ribcage. I beg my body to stay calm. Don't satisfy her by freaking out.

"Sadly, they're not here." Sabine over-emphasizes a pout. "And I do enjoy a show. Therefore, I am putting your pathetic accomplices up for auction, instead."

A hollow feeling engulfs my center, and I fist my hands in an attempt to keep my hopes from drifting. "Don't do this. We didn't read anything. Discover anything."

"Oh, but I must. Eden, come up to me, please. And dear Emma, come join your former queen. It's been so long since we've been close."

Emma's eyelids fly shut, as if by falling into forced blindness, she can exit this nightmare.

"Don't make me bring out reinforcements," Sabine purrs, but it's the sound of a cat toying with a long-dead mouse.

Gently, Chase pushes at his sister's shoulder, ushering her forward. Yet, the look on his face, fury-born and relentless, leaves me to believe that Sabine thought of everything she could in order to get away with this. Otherwise, Chase would torch this moment and gladly drag his sister from the wreckage he wrought.

"And Chase, handsome prince of the Nobles, you too," Sabine says.

Daniel interjects before Chase can react. "That is not what we agreed."

"I promise you will be very amenable to these new

terms, my love," Sabine says, "when you discover that these two have not been keeping apart as ordered."

Silence descends in the room. Daniel's voice comes out as a quiet *whoosh* of steel. "Is this true, son?"

Chase cuts a look in my direction, but I keep my expression blank, my thoughts bland. They can't read it in my face. I will never let them see how I feel for him. Never again.

Chase shakes his head. "I haven't touched her since we got what we wanted, Father."

"Liar!" Sabine shrieks, and for the first time, her face twists to reflect the Medusa she harbors inside, the jealous, reckless, awful recluse of a woman who's lost both her daughters and only has this empty stone temple to show for it.

A lupine, toothless grin stretches across Chase's face. "Prove it. *Mom.*"

Sabine's cheeks blotch to a startling red. She opens her mouth—

"Enough." Daniel comes between them. "If my boy says he's been following orders, then I trust him. He's well aware of the penalty that will follow if he doesn't."

Sabine breathes, in and out, through her nose. "That may be the case, but he's still required to stand among these fools as one of Calla Lily's choices. *Then* we'll see if these two have severed their emotional ties."

Daniel studies his future wife. They share a long look. Then, to my disappointment, he says, "I'll allow it. Come over here, boy."

Chase's focus slides over me as he passes, but soon, I'm left with nothing but the freshwater scent of his wake.

No one's behind me anymore. I'm standing alone.

Sabine preens in the middle of the group, settling her stare on each and every prize, before barreling into mine. "Everyone has their greatest fear, don't you agree?"

I swallow. Nod. I'm so tense, my shoulder blades touch.

"I've yet to fully realize yours, but here are people you've gotten to know. Become friends with, even found a lover in one. With that comes the privilege of sensing their desires, their flaws, and the one thing that will bring them down."

My teeth clench so hard, my jaw shakes with effort, but I force my lips to relax. My stare to remain benign.

Sabine continues, "If you are to prove yourself as a Virtue—that you are worthy of the title—then you have one way to redeem yourself. Choose one of these three to endure your final trial by submitting them to their greatest fear." Sabine smiles, slow, full, and bright. "You are about to prove exactly why I'm keeping you as one of us. Because you've catalogued, with *certainty*, each and every one of their terrors. Emma. Eden. Chase. Haven't you?"

She can't be right.

But ... as if charming a cobra from its basket, my mind betrays me.

I know their fears.

My cheeks go numb. Sabine watches me so closely, her eyes burn when she notes the flicker of realization in my expression.

"Good girl," she murmurs. "Now tell us which one."

Unable to withstand looking at her anymore, I lock eyes with my friends. With Emma, exuding terror through her pores, her face so pale, every burn mark and scar can be mapped. Eden is next to her, head bowed, hair falling forward, but what she's endured is written all over her body —the baggy clothes, the full coverage of her arms, legs ... and face.

Lastly, I come upon Chase.

He meets my study, unwavering and sure. The bronze of his irises darken to a hellish degree and are as intense as black fire licking at my cheeks. His forehead smooths and his lips are one line, closed and silent, but I can read what he wants.

I could understand his wishes even with my eyes closed. *Choose me.*

I forget to breathe in those painful seconds of searching my friends.

His nostrils flare as if to say, *I can take it.*

My fingers ache to touch him. *No. You can't.*

Because I'm sure of what will kill him, what will make him suffer the most.

... and I don't think he has any idea of the fear I know lives inside him.

21

"My patience wears thin, child." Sabine folds her arms, and in the din of the temple, nothing but the cracks and pops of flaming sconces sound out between her words.

I don't want to choose. Eden and Emma have both endured so much, and Chase ... Chase's childhood sounds like an endless SEAL training camp ruled by his father.

How could I subject them to more?

"I choose me," I say.

Sabine chuckles, while Daniel Stone sighs. "My dear," he says, "as much as the books and movies make sacrifice such a bold delight to watch, that is not what we encourage within these societies, especially as a test of loyalty. We battle wills, we push emotions, and we force strength. Those are most encouraged through the sacrifice of *others*— while the one we test watches."

"What my love has failed to mention," Sabine adds, "is that we will choose for you if you do not."

Saliva coats my mouth, thick and bitter as venom. Scanning the faces, I keep thinking *no.* Emma: *no,* Eden: *no,* Chase—

His confidence settles into my center—steady, stable, and sure.

Chase is the one who can take it. Chase emulates the three traits the Nobles embrace: strong will, controlled emotion, incredible strength. But ... can I?

Chase won't back down. Even as my choice scrambles, stretching and fracturing among the three of them, he won't break.

I grasp at one last chance by focusing on Ivy, but her expression doesn't hold support or assistance. It can't.

I go back to Chase, holding his stare as I would the delicate petals of an ink-dipped rose.

"Chase," I say to him, my voice rough and uneven. "I choose Chase."

He nods, offering reassurance where there is none.

"How shocking," Sabine says as she glides forward. "And as our newest Virtuous initiate, tell me, what is his greatest fear?"

Sabine's body blocks my view of him, but I can predict what he's assuming I'll say. *His greatest fear is losing his sister ... or ... he's afraid he'll lose his leadership of the Nobles ... or ... he's afraid of his father.*

But those are all abstract fears, relating to the future, where time is always variable and risky. Those fears could be conquered through making one single, tailored change.

Deep in my soul, I know that's not what Sabine wants.

No, if I'm to prove myself as a Virtue, then… "Small spaces."

The room seems to sigh, each person's inhale mixing with their neighbors' until it fills the lungs of the entire temple.

Sabine tips her head, her lashes eclipsing over her eyes in careful consideration. Daniel frowns behind her, and Chase—I can't see Chase.

"Are you certain?" Sabine asks.

My lips are dry, seeming to crack open and bleed with each breath. "Yes. He's claustrophic."

Sabine turns her head to Daniel, her neck long and smooth. "Darling?"

The movement brings Chase into view, long enough to witness the surprise in his eyes and the color leeching from his face before he forces his features into such hardened determination, the remaining blood can't escape.

Look at me. I'm so sorry, Chase. I'm so—

But he no longer has eyes for me.

My stomach pitches, and I fist a hand under my ribcage.

"Then I have just the thing," Sabine says. "Don't you agree, Daniel?"

Daniel's lips are bloodless slashes in his angular face. "Yes. But I'll say this, Sabine. It is better for all of us if you exile the girl, not punish my son."

"Strong words coming from a man who dismissed the idea of self-sacrifice as concession stand fodder," Sabine purrs.

"I'm simply—"

"Are you questioning my authority?" Sabine asks him. "In the presence of our young members? Or is your hesitancy to offer up your son merely proving why the Virtues have become more powerful in recent years?"

Daniel sets his jaw. "Do not do this here."

"Do what?" Sabine asks, too innocently.

"Make me bring up your daughters."

In an instant, the air in the temple becomes thick, heavy. Ominous. But I use their bickering to try to catch Chase's eye, but he won't even toss a look in my direction. Or anywhere. He stands behind his father, staring at nothing, while his sister murmurs to him.

In the few seconds it took to state his fear, their roles have shifted, and all I can do is watch Chase's strength ebb, then flow, into Emma.

"I have doubled Briarcliff's grants and donations this year," Sabine growls at her fiancé. "And despite losing two children, my Virtues have blossomed, and the graduates have taken their places to resurrect change in the most powerful of chairs. Do *not* question my authority, my love, and how dare you subvert my claim on Calla Lily Ryan and all she holds dear. Including. Your. Son. If the situation were reversed, there's no doubt what your actions would be, or can you look me in the eye and protest any differently?"

Low voices circle above us but are shut silent with a raised look from Sabine. She doesn't direct it at any one Cloak, but she doesn't have to.

Daniel glances at his son. Then back to his fiancée. And it is with the blackest of stares and the worst of promises that he finally lands on me.

"As you wish," he says, his lips moving with barely enough space to emit sound.

Sabine spreads her arms, lifting her chin and radiating all the color she's leeched from the temple and into herself. "Then it is to the Nobles' tomb that Chase Stone will endure Calla Lily's punishment for the rest of tonight and long into tomorrow. In twenty-four hours, at midnight, he will be released."

Voices laced with confidence and eagerness float from the rafters and into our ears. The Nobles' code of honor is chanted, over and over: *We fly high in the dark.*

"Celebrations are allowed to ensue," Sabine concludes. "You may all reconvene in the Nobles' ritual room for the true celebration of winter, our strongest and most honored season."

Movement follows, the Cloaks filtering out.

"Calla Lily, you are to come with us," Sabine says, then includes Daniel and Chase. "As for the rest of you, back to your dorms." She stares at Emma. "You must understand by now that you are not welcome here, and if I catch you within these walls again, there will be more than your beauty at stake."

Emma's hand clenches around Chase's, but Chase urges her to the exit with assurances that he'll be all right. Eden stumbles forward and clasps Emma's arm, dragging her away, but Emma refuses to break her stare from her brother's until the stone walls force her to.

In a flash of emotion before she follows Eden and Emma, Ivy sheds her mask, her eyes vivid with sorrow and fury as we connect.

I use that moment to form my own mask, because my night is far from over. Chase will suffer, and it's because of me.

The temple empties within minutes, and Sabine directs me through another door, this one leading down a vast, stone staircase lined with electric sconces.

Daniel leads the way with Chase behind him. Sabine follows next, as if deliberately coming between Chase and I as we walk single file down the winding steps. As much as I wish to be close to Chase, I'm aware of the futileness. He won't linger with emotion, nor will he search for my hand.

If Ivy wore her emotionless, blank mask, then Chase has just donned one of iron.

I can't even use this time to mull over where we screwed up, or how Sabine got so ahead of us in such a small amount of time. I'm too afraid of the consequences—if Ivy really did confess our plans to Sabine. Of what Chase will endure and if he can handle it. His *father* wasn't even aware of his phobia.

A loud creak comes from darkness below, and as I hit the last step, I notice Daniel has traversed to the end of a dim corridor and opened a wide, wooden door.

The Briarcliff underground resembles more of the barracks of an ancient castle than a school, and I shudder under the thought of heading into some kind of windowless dungeon.

Chase's strides don't hitch as he follows his father, his gait sturdy and his head held high. I try to exude the same confidence, similar will power, but he's been in this world a lot longer than I.

Once through the door, I take quick stock of the brick walls, and the oil sconces lit by Daniel's hand. Large, dusty gray stone lines the floor, each large tile reminiscent of a honeycomb—if hornets made their nests underground. Chains are attached in the middle of a select few, rising to the ceiling, and stacked high in one corner are broken, splintered pieces of old, rotting wood.

I almost recoil when I follow the chain-link trail to Daniel. He pulls a lever mounted on the wall. Chains clink, and neglected, unoiled pulleys spin, until a cylindrical cage is pulled from the ground through a cloud of dust.

Once the bottom of the cage meets the stone floor, the screaming creaks and clangs stop, but not their horrendous echo.

Daniel stares at the contraption, unblinking. "We haven't used this for over fifty years. It was meant for the foulest of betrayals."

"Then I guess it's time to pop its modern cherry."

Those are the first words I've heard from Chase since this shitstorm began, and my eyes cut to him, noting the sarcasm but studying the trepidation.

The muscles in his neck pop out and strain. His eyes, while focused, count each bar on the cage, wide enough to fit one person.

Him.

"Step in," Sabine says. Out of the three of them, her voice is the loudest. "And dear Calla Lily. Watch."

Chase's Adam's apple bobs, but he takes one step. Then two. After four, he's through the open door of the cage and turns around, facing me.

I mouth his name, because that is the only word that has meaning, and my heart wants to speak.

His brows smooth. He sets his jaw and clasps his hands. But he's shaking. "Do what you've been waiting years for, Sabine. Drop me into a black hole and jerk off to it already."

"*Son*," Daniel snaps.

Chase's gaze slides to Daniel. "Stop pussy-footing around."

My fingers tremble. I take one step forward, then back. I've never been great at family dynamics, but this is another, twisted level. One I should rip Chase away from and run until we've climbed our way out of here, fingers bleeding but hearts intact.

With forced steps, Daniel comes to the cage's gate and swings it shut. He clicks the rusted lock closed. "You brought this on yourself, Chase. I warned you, several times, to keep your relationship with Callie at a superficial level."

Chase stares at his father through slitted eyes. "Then I'll deal with it."

"*Chase.*"

His name bursts from my mouth, filled with too much emotion. It opens a window to vulnerability, but I can't control it.

We lock eyes. He murmurs, "It'll be all right."

But Chase shouldn't be the one assuring me. *I* should be saving him. As Sabine commands Daniel to lower the cage into the ground—into the black—*I* should be protesting. Screaming. Asking them why this needs to happen.

I do none of it.

The Virtue I'm supposed to be takes control, whispering

and stroking my conscience until it slumbers under its soothing hand like a purring kitten. Chase can stand a full day in the dark. He'll take it like he endured the beating in the pavilion, the orders of his father, the trauma of his sister. Because he's doing it for the greater good.

I admit, as Chase's feet, then his knees, disappear into the ground by the slow crank of chains and pulleys, it's becoming harder to see the big picture.

"Chase," I try again, his name more rasp than sound.

He doesn't break our stare as he submits to be buried alive, but he can't hide the terror slithering behind the bronze, tarnishing his arrogance.

We are both so composed on the outside as he's lowered into the jaws of his deep-seated fear. But inside, we're destroyed.

The escaped strands of his smoothed-back blond hair go bone white as the sconces spotlight his descent, and I inch forward, my fingers twitching to grab onto the bars and pull him out of there through sheer willpower alone.

He raises his head, and the corners of his lips curve as he attempts a smile. But he doesn't make it all the way. Shadows pass over his face before the gleam in his eyes snuffs out, too.

With a loud *clank*, Chase is sealed in a tomb, the octagonal lines of the roof fitting in seamlessly with the other tiles.

Those borders are the only sign of him in the ground.

"You are to go directly to the underground dance," Sabine says to me, but her attention remains on that middle tile—the one containing Chase. "You are not to mention—not even once—what transpired in this tomb. You are not to return and try to free him, for if you do, my punishment will be ten-fold. Do you understand?"

I blink back unshed tears and nod.

"Lovely." Sabine smiles, her lips remarkably red and unblemished throughout this entire ordeal. "Darling, I believe we're missed at the Societal Ball as well."

Daniel blinks out of his trance, his expression so different from his fiancée's, so silently torn.

"Don't you feel one *ounce* of guilt?" I ask him, my voice ricocheting in the chamber. It's the first time I've truly spoken in this crypt.

Daniel's gaze centers on me, that infamous, Stone cold

stare. "My son chose his destiny the moment he decided to abandon his orders and protect you instead of use you."

"And might I add," Sabine says to me, "you are the one who chose to do this to him."

I'm about to scream at her that it wasn't my choice but stop myself. Of course, it was my choice. I said his name. I pointed to him as the recipient of punishment.

"After you, child," Sabine says, motioning to the door.

I can't tear my gaze from the floor. Is Chase screaming by now? Has he lowered to his knees and slammed his forehead to the ground, clutching his head?

The dude hates small spaces, Tempest had said to me in the library one day. *He never takes elevators.*

That seasick swill in my gut splashes into my throat. This is so much worse than an elevator. There's no light. No air.

Can he breathe?

"*Callie,*" Daniel bites out, and I jerk to attention, though it physically hurts to leave Chase's prison.

I'll be back, I silently vow. *I won't let them do this to you.*

I stride forward, the soft breeze from the motion chilling me to the bone. My arms are damp with sweat, my chest probably shining with it, and the silk wisps of my dress feel like wilted petals against my legs.

Out in the corridor, Daniel takes the lead.

As I follow Sabine and Daniel through more underground tunnels, ostensibly leading to the Societal Ball, neither of them looks back.

Not even once.

When our footsteps stop echoing off the walls, and instead are replaced by the pounding vibrations of music, we're far enough away to never hear Chase's screams.

Sabine and Daniel take me through a wide archway and into another chasm of space—this one governed over by the large, black wings of a raven crest.

Bodies twist and writhe in the middle, some shedding their cloaks, others pulling down their hoods, and the rest cloak-less and carefree, their gowns and tuxes more stained with sweat and drink than when they started their evening.

Enough light emits from the walls and carefully placed spotlights on the ground. On the opposite side, the staircase I descended one time before blinks in and out of shadow as the moving spotlights crest over and around.

"Callie!" Ivy cries through the music. Once she reaches me, her damp, cold hand clasps mine.

Emitting nothing but joy, Ivy grins at Sabine, lifts my hand to twirl under it, then drags me away.

Ivy spins me in time to witness Sabine's approving nod at her replacement princess, and Ivy doesn't stop until we're well on the other side, and she pushes a glass of champagne into my hands.

"Drink," she says.

Even though my mouth is as dry and barren as the corridors I've wandered through, I say, "I can't."

"You have to." Ivy presses the slim flute to my lips despite my choking protest. "Look like you're having fun."

I ask over the rim, "How am I supposed to do that? Eden

and Emma have been taken God knows where, and Chase is fucking *buried*—"

Ivy shushes me, then responds in a low voice. "Eden and Emma are safe in their dorms. Sabine promised only one would be punished. And you're safe now, too."

"You sold us out," I blurt. I've only had one, forced sip, but my cheeks are hot.

The meager light remaining in Ivy's eyes dies out. "I wasn't given a choice. Sabine has Chase *followed*, Callie. She tracked him and his sister to their lake house on multiple occasions, even has pictures of you and Chase secretly meeting up at Lover's Leap. If I wasn't honest with her, what happened a few minutes ago would've been worse. She would've caught you, either way, but with my input, I tried to make the repercussions less lethal."

I hiss, "You could've warned us!"

"You wouldn't have attempted the break-in had I warned you. You would've kept seeing Chase. I would never have gotten the opportunity to show you what she's doing to her princesses—"

"Do you think I wouldn't have believed you if you had just told me?" I ask her, appalled. "Ivy, you didn't have to show me a sick bedroom to prove you were being molested!"

Ivy shushes me, her features rippling with desperation. "You have to act like Sabine to outsmart her, and that's what I did. I'm not ashamed of it. I'm sorry Chase is suffering and you're mad at me, but I'm *glad* I did it, because you're standing here. Livid and *alive*."

My anger simmers down. "You honestly believe she'd kill me for continuing to see Chase?"

"For transpiring against her." She croaks out her answer, then takes a long sip of her champagne. "She'd kill her own daughters if it came to choosing between them or ruling the Virtues."

"What's that supposed to mean?"

"Nothing. Hate me all you want, but I did this to save you guys. Remember that."

"Instead of being expelled, or beaten, or set on fire, I'm standing here with you drinking fancy champagne in a secret ritual room. Tell me what part of that is supposed to make me feel safe."

Ivy cups her own glass. "Sabine manipulates. You've seen it. Expelling you, beating you, exposing you isn't what would've broken your spirit, like it did Emma and Eden. But putting Chase in a box? You *have* to prove to her that's not your kryptonite, either. Get yourself under control, because if she senses your fractures, she'll go in for the final stab."

"He's in the ground." I breathe, in and out, attempting to regain control. "And I put him there to save my own skin. I can't feel good about that. I can't drink this shit and dance like the rest of you while he suffers."

Ivy scans those around us and pulls me closer, ensuring privacy. "She's keeping you for a reason. We have to figure out why that is."

"The last time we thought of the perfect caper, we ended up as theater for the rest of these assholes."

"Exactly. It's all a show. Outwardly, at least. On the inside, she's poisoning us."

My gaze sweeps around the room, but it isn't calculating like Ivy's. It's furious.

"Listen, I'm all too aware of what it's like to be put on display," Ivy whispers near my ear.

I absorb her words. My shoulders slump. I can't stay mad at her with what she's being forced to endure. Blackmailed and manipulated into Sabine's control. How didn't I see how easily Ivy has to cave to Sabine's wishes when we were planning the break-in? "What you said back there, about being forced into sex..."

She shakes her head. "I don't want to talk about that. Now, it's all about making a happy face and pretending Sabine awarded you the greatest honor by keeping you a member."

"Ivy..."

"Do it." Ivy's expression dims. "It's how I've survived these past few months, and it's how you will, too."

Ivy darts a look over my shoulder then spins me around with deceptively strong arms. There's no time to marvel at her strength—both inside and out—because it's as if the three Furies from Greek Mythology descend on us.

Falyn, Willow, and Violet, their cloaks clasped but hoods down, form a half-circle around our forms.

"Quite a scheme you cocked up, Callie," Falyn says. In this light, her pale-colored eyes take on the yellowish hue of the underground ballroom. "What were you hoping to find, exactly?"

The hidden bedroom comes to mind, and I glance at Ivy. The image must be written all over my face, because in those few seconds of connection, Ivy pales, then jerks her head side-to-side. Falyn doesn't know.

Falyn doesn't know...?

Repeating the question doesn't help. Who are the girls Sabine puts in that bedroom? And how many are there, because so far, I can only count three. Ivy. Piper. Emma.

And only one of them stands in this room.

"I was hoping to discover more information on Piper's death," I answer Falyn.

She snorts.

Willow mutters, "Not this shit again..."

Violet cants her head sadly, like it's hard to believe I'm still on the investigative track.

Falyn says, "When are you going to understand that being a Virtue is a privilege? Acceptance into the Ivies is guaranteed. A job in the Forbes Top 100 is an easy option. Marrying a billionaire is less of a chance and more of a given. What part of that displeases you?"

"What's the price you pay for those riches?" I ask. "Have you ever thought on that?"

Falyn curls her lips. "So far, being me is pretty fabulous. To be you, though ... I fully understand why you'd rather fuck up than level up. You're not meant to be successful or admired. You're not one of us." Falyn's gaze rakes me up and down in an assessing, disgusted sweep. "Our queen may want to keep you around in order to contain your screw-ups and prevent them from being made public but understand this: none of us think you belong. Nobody wants you here."

I sigh, having heard this—and predicted it—well before she approached me.

Falyn's eyes grow small. "Then how about this, possum? Chase was once the most sought-after guy in school. Every guy wanted to be him. All girls wanted to do him. And he could choose whatever he wanted in life—who he fucked, where he went after graduation, what top ten company to work for or what billion-dollar start-up he wanted to create. He couldn't afford to show weakness. He ruled this school through intimidation, control, and power. But now? He's in a closed-off room somewhere, hyperventilating and looking weak, because of *you*. You ruined the most popular guy in school, merely by existing in his proximity. You're poison, possum. No, you're toxic waste, and it's high time you realized it."

Her invisible knife slips through the spaces between my ribs. My heart doesn't feel the blade at first—but it's so sharp, so expertly cut, that once it does, the blood pours.

Falyn dumps her champagne down my dress.

I gasp, but not at the liquid soaking through the gauze and the fumes going up my nose. I'm gulping for breath because what she says is true.

"Falyn!" Ivy cries.

Falyn shoves her empty flute at Violet, who fumbles to keep it from falling to the ground. "You're next, *Princess*. Better keep an eye on your position and make sure this rodent doesn't nuke it like she did Piper and Chase."

Falyn flounces away, gesturing at her friends to follow.

Willow, not to be excluded, also dumps her drink down my chest, and this time I gasp in surprise.

Giggling, she departs on a wave, but Violet pauses and unties her cloak.

"Here," she says, "to help you dry off."

My response comes out as an accusation. "Why are you being nice to me?"

"Because there was a time when I was you. And I wish I'd had someone to be kind to me in between all the cruelty."

"Then why do you stay?" I ask, while Ivy helps me wipe my chest with Violet's heavy cloak.

Violet's voice goes quiet, almost impossible to hear over the surrounding music and voices. "You heard Falyn. There's nowhere to go but up."

Falyn calls for Violet, a snappish, impatient sound. Violet drifts away, but I watch her departure with a sodden weight against my chest, unrelated to spilled champagne.

"Falyn's jealous she's wasn't chosen as the princess after Piper," Ivy says, swooping in and blocking my view of Violet. "And she's pissed she wasn't chosen as the crew captain after Piper, then Addisyn."

I collect more folds of fabric, wiping at my arms. "That's pretty misdirected rage, if Falyn's taking it all out on me. No —this is something else. She can't stand me and has hated me since the minute I walked into Briarcliff. It's Violet I'm most concerned about. She doesn't belong with them, does she?"

Ivy pauses with her dabbing long enough to peer over her shoulder. "She's too sweet for all this."

"Then why was she chosen?"

"She's beautiful and innocent. A lot of men would pay five figures for a night with a girl like that."

My hands freeze. My blood turns ice cold. "No," I whisper.

"It's not going to happen. She graduates this year and will no longer be an option."

"That's a relief," I breathe out, my heart rate leveling. But I've always questioned the chances of luck. "If that's why she was initiated, why hasn't Sabine used her?"

"Because I took her place."

And just like that, my heart crashes to the ground. I wrap my fingers around Ivy's wrists, stalling her from her busy-work and forcing her gaze back up. "I'm not mad at you. Okay? I'm fucking terrified for you. We have to stop this."

Her answering smile is wane. Empty. "I meet the bill for pretty innocence, too."

I fold her into a hard, *hard* hug. If I could absorb her, I would. If I could steal her away from this room, this world, I'd do it.

My chin digs into her hair, the wildflower wisps of it tickling my nose. Ivy wraps her arms around my waist, accepting the embrace, her chest heaving against mine. But no tears come.

I'm sure she learned her tears were wasted a long time ago.

A tug of warning prickles against my bare shoulders, and I lift my gaze. It doesn't take long to locate the source of my unease.

Sabine stands with Daniel at the front, toasting the room, everyone's masks off and faces on display. But as

Daniel's warm tone embraces all the members, Sabine keeps her eyes on mine.

She doesn't blink. She doesn't smile.

All she does is stare as I hold Ivy close.

Ivy and I manage to escape the Societal Ball without too much notice, after pretending to join in on the festivities and fake-drinking as much as the rest of them.

When Cloaks started splitting off and coupling against the walls or passing out in corners, one look from me and Ivy was more than eager to follow me up the stairs and through the hidden door into the Wolf's Den.

Sabine didn't stop us, but that's not a win. She got what she wanted from me tonight, but I've learned it will never be enough.

Ivy and I split up at Thorne House, Ivy assuring me that we'll talk tomorrow after class. With the horrors of tonight under our belts, neither of us feel like more confessions for forgiveness by candlelight.

My dorm room is silent when I close the door behind me, Emma's light off and bedroom door shut. I don't wake her for the same reasons I let Ivy go.

We all need to rest.

After stripping off my ruined dress, I kick it into the corner, hating the sight of it. I'm also happy to shower off the stench of tonight, and I wonder if I'll ever acquire the same taste for champagne ever again.

The pink flannel pajamas Lynda sent me never looked

so good, and I slip inside them, hugging the comfort close to my chest. It's with a *pang* of grief that I kiss the picture of my mom on my desk before switching off the lamp and tumbling into bed.

But do I sleep?

My tangled sheets and the pillow tossed across the room would tell you no. All I can think of is Chase. Every moment that passes has me wondering if he's tasted the salt of his tears for the first time in years.

I can't do this. I can't leave him.

I fumble my light back on and shove on my boots and winter coat. A hat and mittens soon follow. I throw my door open, and—

Run straight into Emma.

My resulting scream loosens all the remaining tension from my chest. Emma stumbles away in shock but regains her composure enough to clamp a hand across my mouth.

"Are you asking to bring Mr. Rent-A-Night-Cop to our door?"

I shake my head under her firm grip. She releases me, and I gulp in a breath.

"You scared me," I say tonelessly.

"Good. Stay scared. Because tonight is just the start of it."

I rub my eyes with my mittened hands. "I failed so bad, Emma."

"It wasn't just you." Emma places her hands on her plaid flannel hips. "It was goddamned Ivy and her inability to stay strong under pressure, and my cocky-ass brother who thinks he can take any punishment and survive, and fucking Eden for shrinking to the size of a mouse, instead of warning me, when Sabine burst through the library doors." Emma pauses. "And me. For being a pathetic waste of lard who couldn't bring her dreams of pummeling Sabine into a pulp to fruition as soon as she locked eyes with me. We're all fucking losers."

"I don't believe that." Emma's despondent speech sets my shoulders. "We underestimated her, but we haven't lost, yet."

"That's the problem. She keeps outsmarting me."

"I'm not giving up."

Emma sighs as she takes in my outdoor gear. "You're going to see him, aren't you?"

"I'm not leaving him to—"

"Relax. This is me supporting you. I don't want my brother hyperventilating alone any more than you do. And you're smaller than me, otherwise I'd go to him, too."

My brows crunch down. "What does my size have to do with it?"

"You can't go in the same way you left. Sabine'll kill you. Chase is in the old tombs, right?"

I nod, not bothering to ask her how she knew, since this is Emma, a former Stone and Virtuous princess. She knows things.

"It neighbors their old chapel," she continues. "A piece of the wall swings open just enough to fit you, if you shed your jacket. You can get in and out through there."

"A swinging wall?"

"Chase and his crew sneak in there often to smoke up.

James likes to take girls there to terrify them into screwing him."

I work like mad to memorize her instructions to a place I've never been before, shuffling them in with other morbid pieces I've had the bad fortune of collecting today. "Emma, Ivy showed me the bedroom."

Emma's features go flat. "Go. You only have so much time before James sobers up enough to figure out that's a route you might take. He's fast becoming Sabine's preferred righthand man, but nobody will leave the ball for a while yet."

"Thank you," I say, though our conversation is far from over.

"Use the key you swam under the docks for; it still works on a Virtue passageway at the academy. You remember the chemistry room?"

"Yep." My lips pop on the *p*, as I not so happily linger on the memories as to why I'm so familiar with it.

"There's a false door at the back. Find the row of textbooks published in the late 1800s Briarcliff likes to display as a sign of respect to the founders. The third spine has a tiny lock in the center. Slip your key in, turn, go down the stairs, and you should end up at the Nobles' tomb. Push on the third skull from the ground, and that'll lead you to where Chase is held."

"How am I supposed to gain access to the academy? After the chem lab was vandalized, Marron locked up tight."

Emma gives a sly smile. "Your Virtue key works on the side door, too."

She shoos me away, and I leave the dorm as fast and soundless as I possibly can.

It's with the help of my phone's flashlight that I make it to the academy through all the snow, and I use my Virtue key to open the side door at the east wing.

Puffing and shivering from cold, I scurry into the warmth of the silent halls, fly to the chem lab, reach the back where the line of books is, and—

Halt at the many, *many* spines facing out on a shelf above chemistry supplies.

I rip my hat off and toss it on the floor with a curse of frustration, but then think, *fuck it*. What do I have to lose by using my phone's flashlight to find a tiny, tiny keyhole in one of them?

Shockingly, I find it in the first two minutes, right when I'm about to text Emma if she remembers which book.

Probably because Sabine planned for this moment.

I don't care. *I don't care I don't care I don't care.*

Chase is suffering, and he's alone. I am not going to discard him. I *won't*.

When I push the false door open, I grab my hat and run through, wasting no time and following the secret stairs nestled between the school walls until I hit the bottom.

It takes a few missteps and a lot of flashlight to navigate the pitch-black corridors. I don't give up, and on the fourth try, I make it into what most resembles a neglected chapel— if a chapel decided on a skull-lined hearth as its centerpiece.

"So fucked up," I mutter as I peel off my jacket, but count the skulls and settle on the fourth one on the right.

It works. A slim, vertical piece of the wall swings open, and I slip through until it flips shut behind me.

I come to a stop in the honeycomb room I was in hours before, even though it seems like painful decades.

I shed my mittens and sprint first to the pile of broken wood. I choose one, then rest it against the door on an angle. If someone is standing guard, hears me, and tries to come in, the panel will crash to the ground, creating a cloud of dust. I'll be alerted and escape the way I came, ideally before I'm discovered.

After setting the boobytrap, I race over to the lever I saw Daniel use. I twist and pull and use my entire bodyweight to bring the rusted spike down...

And watch as the chains begin to clink. As they start to pull up the middle cage.

As Chase is slowly revealed.

23

———

At first, all I see is an empty cage.

The spaces between the bars are clear. There's no sign of Chase.

Did he escape?

That'd be insane. And amazing.

The pulleys keep whirring, but I've stopped searching the cage and debate running out of here, instead. What if this was all a trap? What if Chase was in on this the whole time and never expected to be punished?

That would explain his guileless demeanor as he allowed his father to lock him in. His casual insults to his future stepmother, his *fuck you* attitude to the room, and his sweet, calming assurances that *it'll be all right, Callie.*

A groan snaps my attention back to center. I didn't register the cage coming to a stop or the fading clink of chains.

Something shifts near the bottom, a dark, hunched-over form.

"I'm here." I rush over, falling to my knees and clinging to the bars. "You're not alone. I'm right next to you."

Another muffled sound comes from his collapsed form, a mix between a moan and a sigh. He shifts, his hands, originally wrapped around the back of his neck as he folded down, falling listless by his head.

"Chase, it's me," I whisper. "Can you hear me?"

His head lulls to the side. Half his profile comes into view, blotched, yet bloodless. His eyelashes flutter, as if coming back to consciousness. "C...Callie?"

"Yes." I pull myself flush against the bars, wishing I were boneless and could squeeze through. "I'm right here."

"You ... you shouldn't have come."

"I couldn't leave you."

"T-trouble..."

I glance up at each corner of the room. There are no blinking lights, no eerie black lens staring down. There may be a log of my mindless rush through the maze of corridors, but I doubt it. If the dust and decay is anything to go by, the original, hidden hallways and rooms of the academy haven't been updated in a long time.

I think of Sabine's secret bedroom. It's not just the Virtues who want to keep certain blueprints private.

I reach through the bars as much as I can, stroking his back, tracing the curve of his ear. "Breathe," I say. "Listen to my breaths. Follow them. In ... and out."

Chase's jaw spasms with the effort. "I c-can't open my eyes."

"You can. It's all open space here. Or keep your eyes closed and envision a field, or the peak of a mountain or—or a lake! You're on the water, just you and your scull. Breathe."

Chase's brows crash down. His chest seizes with forced, small inhales.

I rip in two at the sight of him, this unflappable force of will who'll gladly take punches to the jaw and withstand insidious insults by his father. This boy who will risk everything to avenge his sister and face his worst fear to protect ... someone who doesn't deserve it. Me.

I keep my voice calm, my inhales and exhales measured and leveled. Slowly, with great effort, he starts mimicking my breathing.

"Good," I say. "You're doing great."

"You need to ... leave. Before..."

"I'm not here to break you out." I swallow, staring at the thick, metal padlock keeping him in.

Chase follows my attention and gives a weak smile. "You'd sear that off with laser beam eyes if you could."

"Without a thought." I give him a resolute stare, but it crumbles the longer I take him in.

Chase trembles, pieces of hair stuck to his forehead with dried sweat. The snippets of voice I'm hearing from him sound raw and damaged.

"I put you in here." I can't keep the pain from my voice.

"No." Chase's throat moves with a hard swallow as he struggles to sit up. It reminds me, and I crawl over to my discarded jacket and pull out a water bottle.

His eyes spark with life, and he accepts the bottle and puts it to his lips, gulping greedily.

"Gently," I say, but scan his space between the bars. "Although, I'd piss all over this shit hole if I could, too."

Chase's lips curve over the bottle, then he lowers it, wiping his mouth with his tuxedo's sleeve. "This isn't your fault."

I cock my head. "That's sweet, coming from a boy trapped in a cage from the Medieval Times because of my botched plan."

"You think I would've avoided this if it weren't for you?"

I nod.

"Not true, sweet possum. Tempest told you about my claustrophobia because I asked him to."

I stare at him.

"There would come a time when Sabine or my father would force someone into a choice like this, pitting my sister and me against each other, and you against all of us."

"But..." I take in his sallow pallor, the red rimming his eyes, and the hoarseness surrounding his voice. "You *are* afraid of small spaces."

"Yes."

"Then why...?"

"Sabine asked if you knew our fears. Tell me, if you didn't know mine, would you have chosen me? Or would you have gone with Emma, who fears being trapped in a fire, or Eden, who is terrified of exposing herself to the entire school? What do you think Sabine would've made them do?"

"They're not members," I reason. "They wouldn't have—"

"Don't finish that sentence. They'd suffer. Sabine wouldn't tolerate any less."

"That woman," I seethe. "The second you're released, I'll throw my fucking Virtues' key in her *eyeball*."

"Callie." Shadows creep along the terrible hollows in his face, making him appear skeletal. "I will come out of this unscathed."

I catch my lower lip between my teeth. "You're suffering."

"Nothing I haven't been doing since the ripe old age of nine. Now go, sweet possum. Before my father comes and checks on his deplorable son."

My head whips to the door, and the *Home Alone* trap I've made. So far, it's undisturbed. "We have some time yet." Emotion blooms in my chest, then swells in my throat. "I don't want to go."

"I know."

"I can't put you back down there."

"You have to."

"I've weakened you in front of everyone."

Chase squints. "Don't think I won't make a splash when I get out of this fucking thing. I'm okay, sweet possum. *We* are okay." He motions to the bottle. "Thank you for the water. And..." His eyes soften. "Thank you for checking on me. I can't remember the last time someone's done that."

"I'll stay with you. Right here. Whatever happens."

Chase shifts, his hand coming between the iron bars

and drifting across my cheek. "You would, wouldn't you? Stay here until someone comes, damn the consequences."

I hold onto his wrist and squeeze. Answer enough.

"That's not the way," he murmurs, brushing the pad of his thumb along my lower lip. "Go pull that switch, then step on the iron lever by the wall you came through and get back to your room. Tell no one you've come here."

"You know how I got in."

"I'm aware of a lot of things, even when I'm put into the black."

"I—"

"Now, Callie." He hands me the empty bottle.

Though every muscle protests the command, I rise to my feet and move to the lever. I glance once more over my shoulder. Chase has risen to a stand, his arms folded. Though he looks in complete control, smudges of dirt mark his tuxedo and his white shirt is missing buttons, like he tore at it in the dark. The whites of his knuckles poke through his skin as he clutches his biceps.

"Do it."

I catalogue every tear, every mark of pain left on his body from having to endure being buried alive. "I won't let this happen to you again."

Chase nods, but his eyes have glazed over with a faraway look, committing to his entrapment by initiating a mental disappearance.

I yank on the lever, a rusted squeal bursting from my hands. The chains begin their rattle, and I'm seized with panic. I can't stay still and watch this. There's no way I can be a bystander for the second time.

I sprint to the cage, grab Chase by his lapels, and pull his lips to mine.

I kiss him, and kiss him deeply, our mouths rubbing together with desperate passion, and I sink along with him, bending my knees, then bowing forward, never breaking that kiss as he's lowered to the ground.

Not until the distance forces us apart.

24

I slink from the tomb, through the chem lab and deserted academy halls, and step outside into the dark, frozen tundra of the Briarcliff landscape, my ribs feeling like icepicks poking against my skin.

Snowflakes catch in my lashes, descending from the ink-black depths of the sky on a silent drift of wind.

My walk to Thorne House is heavier than when I left, my feet filled with leaden angst as I leave Chase in depths without snowflakes, without wind, without ... anything. He says it's the right thing to do, but I'm not sure it'll ever feel that way.

When I unlock my door, I'm surprised to find Emma staring into the creamy swirls of her mug. She looks up when I set my bag down beside her on the counter.

"You didn't have your phone," she says as greeting.

Shedding my outerwear, I say, "I had it. That looks good. Mind if I make myself a cup?"

"Why didn't you pick up? I thought something happened to you when you weren't answering."

"And I thought you were asleep."

"How could I sleep after sending you into the Nobles' tombs?"

I pause, lifting a mug from our little tree by the coffee machine. "There's no shortage of blame to go around, Emma. I shouldn't have asked you to be a part of tonight."

"You didn't ask. I demanded. I thought I could follow in Piper's footsteps." She wipes a hand down the unscarred portion of her face. "But I couldn't. I saw Sabine, and I couldn't."

I finish making my coffee, then sit beside her, my spoon clinking as I stir in cream. "If you were testing your willpower, that was a difficult way to do it. You went all-in. Maybe next time, see how you react if you spot her from a distance on campus."

"You made a joke." Emma huffs out a weary laugh. "Impressive, considering our circumstances."

"I'm not sure they'll get any better, so I try for gaps of time when I smile."

Emma slides a saddened gaze my way. "How was my brother?"

I start to lift the rim to my lips, then think better of it. "Surviving. Posturing. Pretending it's all good."

Emma breathes through tightened lips, but her shoulders slump. "He's continually protecting me, but when it comes to needing my help, I'm useless to him."

"I feel the same way. But he seems to think this is all for the greater good." I spin the mug, its hot ceramic searing the pads of my fingers until I lift them for relief, a maneuver I wish I could pull off in real life. "I can't imagine being forced to endure my greatest fear."

But I can, and I did. Drowning in the brackish water of Briarcliff Lake before Ivy saved me. It was the type of explosive, thundering feeling in my chest I never want to experience again.

And Chase has to endure hours and hours of it.

"I'm glad you saw him. I'm glad he was able to speak to you."

I nod. "It was almost too easy. Yes, I used the secret tunnels you suggested, but there was nothing. No one to get in my way."

Emma makes a sound in her throat before sipping her coffee. "I bet Sabine knew you'd go after him."

"And she let me." I lean on my elbows, the mug centered in my hands. "I wish I could get into that woman's head. She's hidden articles—"

I stop myself. The sickly sage color of the bedroom floats into my vision.

"What?" Emma asks, but her expression holds warning. *I'm not ready to talk about it.*

I say, quieter, "I found newspaper clippings and articles about my mother's death in a binder Sabine was hiding."

"She was researching your past."

"Well before I enrolled here. The dates are from more than a year ago."

"It makes a sick kind of sense. Your mom was having an affair with her ex-husband, right?"

"Yes, but remember when I confronted her tonight?

Sabine explained the binder was for Virtuous prospects. Why would she ever consider me as a Virtue, after what my mother and her husband did? I was his illegitimate child for a hot minute there."

Emma shrugs. "With that theory, why has she let you in now?"

"Because she assured me I'm *not* Mr. Harrington's bastard daughter. And hell, she could be enlisting me as a Virtue now as a sick sort of revenge on my dead mom's ghost, by making her daughter a kind of Virtue not even the Nobles know about—"

Again, I stop, inwardly cursing.

Emma visibly stiffens beside me, her fingers flattening against her mug.

She asks, her breaths shallow, "Where did you say you found those articles?"

My hair falls on either side of my face, and I find more solace in the dregs of my coffee than I do by looking up. "I didn't."

"Tell me, Callie."

I sigh. Tuck my hair back. "I mentioned it before I left to see Chase. It was in a kind of ... bedroom."

Emma's brows lower. "Is it the kind of bedroom that can only be accessed through the back of a fireplace?"

I lift my gaze in answer.

"So, it's official. Ivy showed you the irony of becoming a Virtuous princess. Did she tell you all of it?"

"Most. The rest I could glean for myself."

Emma moves to stare vacantly across the room.

"You don't have to talk about it." I lift my hand to offer

comfort, to rub her back or squeeze her shoulder, but instead of doing any of that, my arm comes back down. She's not the kind of person to seek comfort, only strength.

Her attention shifts, her eyes sharpening as they land on me. "Maybe it's time I did."

I'm wary of spooking her, so I say nothing.

"In ninth grade, Sabine awarded me the title of princess. I thought it was an honor. Took it as entitlement. For as long as I can remember, my family has drilled into my ears the importance of becoming royalty in the Nobles and Virtues. And it was about time, too. Chase had become prince two years prior."

I push my brows together. "In seventh grade?"

Emma shrugs. "The Nobles don't have the—responsibilities—that we do. To be prince means to be groomed for leadership and granted privileges unavailable even to other society members. Like the best dorm room, a rigged top of the class ranking, make-up exams when you don't feel like taking them at the time, first seat in Briarcliff's nationally renowned rowing team. All orchestrated by the Chancellor. *All* so it looks terrific on an Ivy League application."

I drum my fingers against the laminate counter. "He doesn't act like any of his positions were bought and paid for."

Emma offers a jaded smile. "Because they weren't. Chase gave the best boys' room to Tempest. He's at the top of the class because he earned it and is both captain and stroke of crew because he has the racing stats to prove it."

I smile. That sounds exactly like the Chase I've come to

care for. "And what about the Virtues? How is the princess awarded?"

Emma's chest concaves. Despite the thorns she rims around her body and the steel she wraps around her heart, she seems so fragile right now. So brittle and broken as she hunches over her cold coffee. "It used to be that way, too. When my grandmother guided the Virtues, we had all those privileges, but ... it's a man's world. We were never awarded the status of a Noble Prince. The princess was ranked second in the class, given stroke and captain of crew, but the girls' rowing team isn't as widely recognized as the boys'. And exams..." A mirthless laugh escapes her lips. "Most of the time, the princess did better than the prince. But who got the top marks?"

I nod. "My mom, she worked in a male-dominated industry and was made to feel like a bitch when she wanted to be seen as an equal, and a single mother when she needed to take time off when I was sick, like it was some kind of handicap to gaining respect. I'm pretty sure I was aware of gender norms when I was five."

Emma snorts in agreement. "Yeah, but what did your mom do to combat it?"

"She stayed the course, got together with the other two women at the precinct, demanded equal pay, and worked hard to change perceptions, even to the smallest degree."

"Yep. The hard way. And I'm sorry you're mom's dead, but she didn't make much headway, did she?"

I'm forced to agree.

"Sabine Harrington, or Sabine Moriarty, back then, when she took my grandmother's place, didn't want to work that hard for recognition. She wanted it now. She made deals behind the Nobles' backs—starting with Nobles who'd automatically graduate into top positions in the country. She married one. You'd think they'd stay loyal to their own society, and most did, but there were some willing to bend the rules, including Paul Harrington."

I force a deep breath, waiting for what will come next.

Emma whispers, "Sabine used the most ancient power a woman has over a man. Sex."

I wrap one hand around the back of my neck, massaging out the goosebumps. "She negotiated the bodies of the girls in the society to gain favors from these men?"

"Only some girls. The most innocent, the sweetest. The ones less likely to talk." Emma shakes her head, a hollow swing, side-to-side. "I wasn't like my brother. Not boisterous, or sociable, or aggressive. I preferred *Harry Potter* in bed to societal events, Comic-Cons over sports, Reddit forums to talking to friends in real life. That's why, when Sabine picked me, *me*, I was shocked and over-the-moon. Yes, I was a Stone, but for the most part, I went unnoticed as a Loughrey. I chose my mother's last name instead of becoming a Stone. I was a legacy in the Virtues, because I had to be, not because I earned it. And my dad, he was so proud I'd taken the Stone status. My mom, too. I'd never experienced so much warm attention, not to mention, the open respect it caused. And it's because of that I was willing to do anything to keep Sabine happy. Anything."

"Emma, I'm so sorry." Though it's never enough. The platitude, even genuine, will never bring back what was lost.

"It was Piper who figured out what was going on, first.

Why I always disappeared the first Tuesday of the month and came back quieter, lesser. And she wouldn't stop asking questions." Emma rubs her eyes, but a smile creeps along the edges of her mouth. "God, she was so fucking annoying. But I thought, being Sabine's daughter, she was on her mom's side. I thought she *supported* what Sabine was doing. Turns out I was wrong."

I bite my lip in thought. "Was Sabine keeping her daughters blind because she wanted to protect them?"

"Maybe. But remember the qualifications were innocent, quiet, sweet. Piper was none of those. She couldn't fake innocence if she tried. Same with Addisyn."

Remembering the Piper I met, I murmur, "Good point."

"I'll never understand it, not in a million years, but one night, I decided to tell Piper the truth. Scream it at her until it tore her open. I didn't care if she told the entire school. Didn't give a fuck if she called me a slut. I wanted it out." Emma clutches her chest, as if she can feel a bullet wound. "I wanted the *poison* out."

I ask, with bated breath, "What did she say?"

"Piper did the last thing I expected. She offered to help me."

The dorm is silent, but Emma's words trickle into my head with the steady drips of a faucet, pooling into a watery puddle of answers, growing hotter the longer I study Emma's face.

Her wounds.

Her scars.

"Back then, we only knew of one way to get out of

Sabine's control, and that was to make me no longer desirable for her needs."

I cover my mouth. "Oh Jesus, Emma..."

But Emma forges on. "We agreed to meet at the library—the old one. The Virtues original temple was underground, built almost as a mirror to the Nobles. We figured the best way to really piss off Sabine was to do this on her turf. Piper brought along a baseball bat."

"*She's* the one who attacked you?"

Emma raises her head. "With my permission. I didn't want to be me anymore. Didn't *want* to be desirable, or special, or Sabine's princess. The men, they were old, stinking, *vile*, and I couldn't take it. I needed it to stop. How else was I supposed to do it? Go to the school? Marron wouldn't believe me. My own *father* didn't. The one time I tried, he asked why I was back into reading fantasy again and that Sabine would never do such a thing to the future accessories to our country. That's what he called the Virtues. *Accessories* to the Nobles. Like we're the arm candy to the true leaders. And my brother ... Chase was too busy being Mr. Popular and proving to our father he deserved to be a prince on his own merits."

I scrape my hair back from my face. "Holy fuck. This is—I can't even."

Emma nods sagely. "I asked Piper to hit me as hard as she could. Multiple times. In the head, in the ribs ... if she killed me, I didn't care."

I reach for Emma, but she recoils, and I'm forced to sit there, arms hanging limp, as Emma's trauma unfolds in my head.

"She was scared at first, but it's like ... a switch went off in her once she really got going. I don't know what was going on in the Harrington home, and I still don't, but that night told me Piper had hidden rage in her, too." Emma takes a breath. I use that time to grab her mug and push it under the coffee machine. If she won't accept my comfort, then I'll give her another form of warmth.

"I blacked out and didn't come to until I was in the hospital, with Sabine leaning over me."

Tears pool in Emma's eyes, and I rush to set the fresh coffee down and rub between her shoulders. If she shrugs me off, so be it, but she doesn't.

"Guess what that bitch said? None of my injuries would cause too much scarring. And any that formed, she'd personally pay for a plastic surgeon to fix. I'd be back to beautiful in three months and could resume my princess duties after that time."

The coffee I'd gulped down rolls in my stomach. "I can't believe..."

"That's when I knew there was no escape. And that's when I decided to start the fire and burn the whole fucking place down."

I risk prodding, "You said you were trapped inside, against your will."

Emma looks down at her untouched coffee, but her hands wrap around the ceramic. "Sabine caught me before I lit the match, and the look on her face when she did... it was like she was some kind of demon. I saw her true self that night, just like I was showing her mine. She pulled out a lighter in her purse, sent the bookshelf next to her up in flames, then turned around and locked me in."

Black stars come across my vision. I need to lie down but can't. Won't. Not until Emma finishes.

"Piper followed me that night. She'd hidden behind a tree when her mother stormed out, saw the smoke, and ran to get Chase. I was cornered by fire and smoke. I couldn't see or move. They unlocked the door, dragged me upstairs, broke a window and escaped, and the next thing I know ... I'm scarred. Burned. The fire is labeled arson and connected to the same perp who attacked me a few weeks previously. It remained unsolved and then ... forgotten."

I stare unseeingly at the fridge, the conjured scenes of Emma's confession playing out in my head as if I were there. "This is terrible. Worse than I could ever have imagined."

"Which part?" Emma tries for a smile, the scarred ridge of her face moving with rediscovered mirth. "That Sabine is, at the very least, an attempted murderer and pimp, or that Piper was nice and saved my life?"

I answer honestly. "Both."

"Piper changed after that. She took the role of the princess, which Sabine accepted, since my situation was so costly to the Virtue reputation she'd garnered. While Piper was princess, there were no 'meetings' with men. I guess Sabine had a line—her own flesh and blood couldn't be trafficked. I could've spoken my truth. Piper would've backed me up, adding heavy credibility as the queen's daughter. But we both decided to stay quiet and bide our time, because we only had my word as evidence. Piper was working to find more. She went all the way back to the origins and Rose Briar, started collecting secret messages Rose had written to Theodore and even unearthed a Briar's birth certificate she wanted to talk to me about, but then she..." Emma changes tactics. "She'd be the expected bitch by day and the Virtuous princess by night. But in between, Piper was my savior. And she was working to save all of us before she died. Then she was pushed off Lover's Leap, and ... it's like a reset button was hit. Sabine could begin again."

This time, I really am going to be sick. "And she started with Ivy."

Emma spins to watch me as I fly into our bathroom and dry heave into the toilet. When nothing comes up and my stomach proves its dire emptiness, I rise, wiping my mouth with a hand-towel.

"Now you're aware of Sabine's motives and how she can so easily manipulate. Even the Noble King isn't aware of the influence Sabine wreaks inside this school and out. My only question is this." Emma comes up to the bathroom, folding her arms, but looking upon me with desolate wisdom. "What is she planning to do with you?"

25

I greet the next morning with a massive headache and roll over to check the time with a wince.

The over-extension of my body, my mind, my *emotions* last night shouldn't come as a surprise, but I'd argue that I shouldn't feel like a 90-year-old woman creaking out of bed at the crack of dawn.

Then it hits me.

Chase.

He doesn't have a morning to greet. His time consists of preventing his black environment from seeping into his soul.

Picturing how the rest of this day is going to go, I don't think I'll be able to take my mind off his suffering in order to properly listen to Professor Dawson in biology.

"Morning," Emma says as I pull my door open. She lifts a mug.

I garble a sound close to *yes, please*, and yank the hot coffee from her hand.

"You gonna be okay today?" she asks.

"I'd rather ask you the same thing. Are you okay after what we talked about last night?"

Emma purses her lips. "I doubt you or I will be able to focus on our studies while my brother is buried in a basement."

I nod, and my shoulders *finally* relax. Out of everyone, Emma gets me the most. "Let's not go through this day alone."

"You mean..." Emma arches a brow. "We'll have each other's backs?"

"Maybe." I flap my hand. "Let's not get ahead of ourselves."

"Thank you."

The room goes quiet. I stare at her.

"For last night. For everything." Emma continues, "I thought I knew what to expect when I returned to Briarcliff, and I gotta say, you weren't it."

I give her a half-smile.

"But it's been easier with you—if you can call what we're going through easy. I don't have a lot of friends, and I'm not saying you're, like, my bestie or anything, but it felt good to tell you my story last night and not have you judge me. There hasn't been anyone like that in my life, not since Piper, and—"

"Emma." I lay a hand on her shoulder. "I like you, too."

Emma fights off a smile. "Yeah, yeah."

She pushes my hand away and absconds into her room.

I snort, buoyed by this small moment of normalcy, but Briarcliff doesn't award an average day without a price.

A knock sounds at our door.

"Hey," I greet Ivy, but she brushes past me, her cheeks flushed, and her hair tangled. "What's ... up?"

"I was hoping you wouldn't be at school yet." Ivy tears off her winter coat and tosses it on the couch. "Is Emma here?"

Emma pops her head out of her bedroom. She takes one look at Ivy and says, "What's wrong?"

Ivy turns to me instead. "Have you ever looked at past Briarcliff yearbooks?"

"That's random." I arch an eyebrow, but answer. "I was thinking of looking up Howard Mason at some point but haven't gotten the chance." I lean forward, resting my forearms on the counter. "Why?"

"Well, after you found those news articles Sabine saved about your mom, it got me thinking."

Emma comes out of her room and stands beside me. If I didn't know any better, I'd say she was taking a protective stance, her suspicions of Ivy coming to a head after last night. Emma says, "I figured the mystery stopped at Callie's mom having an affair with Sabine's husband."

"Me too, or so I thought," Ivy says. She thumps her backpack on the counter and unzips it. "But Sabine is rarely that surface-level. You assume she wants one thing, until she turns it around on you at the very last second and slits your throat, amirite?"

Emma makes a sound of agreement. "Couldn't have put it better myself."

"I went to the library as soon as it opened." Ivy pulls out a yearbook, the silver foil flashing 2002. "To look up Sabine's class."

Ivy cracks open the yearbook, both Emma and me hovering behind her shoulders. She flips it until she finds the graduating class. Her finger lands on one photo in particular. "Look."

I squint. Then, I hiss in a breath. "That's Lynda."

"Yep. And there's more." Ivy flips to another page, points to another teen.

Emma says, "And Mr. Harrington."

"Makes sense," I murmur, "Since Sabine would've been pregnant with Piper around this time."

Picturing Sabine as a teen mom is an entirely different image than the one I have of my own. Mom had me at nineteen, but she didn't have a rich boy to fall on or a billion-dollar furniture company to inherit by forcing his hand.

Except ... wasn't Sabine part of an oil family? *Moriarty Oil*, that's right. So, why would she—

The answer comes to me in a harsh wave. *She made deals behind the Nobles' backs,* Emma had said. *Starting with Nobles who'd automatically graduate to top positions in the country. She married one.*

Sabine started her control of the Nobles early, using Piper as her first weapon.

I blink out of my fugue when Ivy finds another face, to which I say, "Daniel Stone."

Then, with the slow, careful push like the triangular pointer on a Ouija board, Ivy lands on one last photo.

I stumble back as if scalded. "That's—that's not possible."

"Holy shit," Emma says, her eyes as wide as the mugs we've forgotten to drink out of. "Callie, your mom went to Briarcliff?"

"No way." I shrink away, like the yearbook is about to rear up and bite me with traitorous fangs. "That's someone else named Meredith Ryan. It has to be."

"But her face," Ivy supplies, lifting the book so I can see. "She looks just like you."

The denial shrivels inside my throat the longer Mom smiles back at me. "She never told me ... she never ... how could she not have said anything about attending an elite private school?"

"Callie," Emma says. "Your mother kept a decades-long affair from you. She was murdered in a way that seems personal, and her killer has never been caught. And now she attended an exclusive school she never mentioned. Looks like your mom didn't tell you a lot of things."

"But why?" My voice cracks. "We lived in a one bedroom and shared instant ramen for *years*. We told each other everything. She was my best friend—my *only* friend for so, so long. I trusted her. I—I *loved* her. How could she have...?"

I trail off, the rest too difficult to comprehend.

"Callie." Ivy grabs my attention by gripping me by the shoulders. "That's not all."

"What?" I ask, pressing my hands to my cheeks. The ground tilts, Chase is below dirt level, and my mother, the only person I trusted in the *world*, is a certified liar. "What could be worse than that?"

Though it clearly pains her, Ivy turns back to the yearbook. "There are so many players in this class, I had to look at the underclassmen, too. Just to be sure I'm not missing anyone. And here. In the tenth grade. Do you recognize this guy?"

Ivy lifts the yearbook again, and I force the papery lump in my throat to dissolve.

I look.

When I do, the lump comes back twice its size.

Emma leans over me and asks, "Who's that?"

I lick my lips, but they're so cracked and dry, I only cause a sting of pain. "That's my stepdad. Peter Spencer."

flex my hand above my notebook, the pen bouncing across the page. The new history professor drones on, and up until now, I'd been furiously taking notes. Who knew such desperation would provide copious amounts of energy to focus, my ears tunneling to the professor's voice and my handwriting following suit?

It was easier to avoid Chase's empty chair that way.

The vicious noise between my ears quieted down, and the images of my mother's Briarcliff Academy yearbook photo became a backyard blur in my head.

That is, until the bell rang.

I jolt, glance around, blink. Then pack my things like everyone else.

A heavy hand hits my shoulder the instant I stand. Tempest leans forward, his breath hot. "Are you done fucking around in our lives? Chase asks me to do him a solid, and I do, only to find out hacking security systems are pointless when the head honcho is already aware of the hamburglars. You not only put my boy at risk, but me, too. I don't like being duped by pretty faces."

I stare straight ahead, but his breath wafts strands of my hair near my cheeks. My voice comes out steady through the intimidating shivers. "I'll be done when you people stop fucking around with *my* life."

Tempest backs off, and I regain my own oxygen. "That supposed to mean something, possum?" he asks.

Shoving the textbook in my bag, I say, "Not to you," and storm away from him.

Tempest doesn't follow, but I'm forced to pass James, then Riordan, both with flat, predatory stares.

"Chase should've laid you to waste the minute he got the chance," Riordan mutters.

"She must have a lollipop pussy," James replies, "for him to take a day off for her."

I slam my hand on the doorframe. "If you idiots had the decency to really learn about your stupid club, if you're so protective and proud of being members, then you should recognize the stink. It's not Chase's fault, but it's not mine, either." I hiss, "Figure out your *shit*," before exiting the room.

I storm down the hallway, furious and already wishing for hindsight. I should've told them what Sabine is doing to the Virtues. Should've told them what Ivy will go through —*again*—on the first Tuesday of the coming year.

Except, when I snuck into the Nobles' ritual room, there were those women in purple robes. I recall the look on

James's face as he presented those women to the new initiates.

James won't care and is probably well aware of Sabine's embellishments to the Virtues, and while Tempest and Riordan were hooded and ambivalent when the women shed their cloaks, I doubt they'd give a shit, either.

It's up to us girls to put a stop to this. And it's up to me to figure out why my mother cloaked her past in the same secrets that are shrouding me now.

I spin the lock and open my locker, transferring my texts for the next class, but I pause when my phone lights up on my shelf.

Lynda.

Snatching it, I press the green button before I think too hard on it. "Lynda, I need you to—"

"Hey, girl!" Lynda trills on the other line. "I'm in labor!"

"I—huh?"

"Blair's coming a week early! Your dad's driving me to the hospital now."

"Shit," I breathe out, and Lynda laughs.

"Don't worry, sweetheart, this pain is easy-peasy considering the bulldozer I've been carting around in my belly for 38 weeks. I'll take a few hours of screeching cramps over one more week of this waddle I've got going on—*oh*. Oh, here comes another one!"

"I—should I come?" All thoughts of the past dissolve as I picture my future—my *sister*. "I can get on a train and be there by tonight—"

"Cal, we're fine!" my dad calls out. "Finish your exams. I don't want you missing out on this semester!"

My exams? "Oh *shit*, exams are next week."

I envision my father's deep, drawn-out sigh. Lynda says, "Exactly, hun—*ooooh*. Faaaaaaaack. Okay. I'm good. Come when exams are finished. Once Blair's out, she's out, but she's not going anywhere. And I'll be able to introduce you two in much better conditions than *aaaaaaaaaaaaaagh!*"

I grimace and hold the phone tighter against my ear, as if that could help. "Okay. As long as you're sure."

"I didn't get you into Briarcliff to coast by, Callie," Lynda says, panting. "You get those A's, then come meet a B. God*dammit*, she's a bitch!"

"I can't wait," I say, "though I figure I also got into Briarcliff because I'm my mom's legacy."

Lynda breathes heavily into the phone. "Um, what, hun?"

I respond with a grim smile. Her words are too carefully placed between her gasps.

She knows.

"Can you put Dad on the phone?"

"Sure. I need to recline and scream now. Bye, love."

"You got this, Lynda."

"All good, Cal?" my father asks when he comes on the line.

"I should ask you the same thing. You ready to be a baby-daddy?"

He gives a shy laugh. Pete came into my life when I was nine, and I doubt he's been around a kid, since. "I hear the whole afraid-to-hurt-the-baby is natural and will go away after the first fifty diaper changes in a day."

I can't help but smile at the true terror in his tone.

"You'll do great. And you'll be there for Lynda the entire time. That's something my mom didn't have."

"Ah, Cal." Dad's voice goes thick. "If I could've been there for her, too, I would've."

"But you didn't know each other back then, so I get it."

"That's right, honey."

"Well, good luck, Dad. Facetime me once everything goes well."

"Will do. Love you."

"You, too," I say through a forced smile, ensuring the feigned brightness transmits through my voice.

Then I hang up and toss the phone into the locker with a *thunk* and slam my locker shut.

I clued Lynda into the unraveling of their lie, and I caught Dad in the same, sticky web.

Lynda may be screaming her face off at the moment, but once things calm down, let them figure out how much they fucked up in that one, simple conversation.

27

The sheer intensity of the stars in the black sky tells me that it must be close to midnight, but sleep was never an option.

I chew my lip, watching the night grow darker and darker, lights on the student paths flickering out one by one, and the night security's flashlights bouncing against the white snowdrifts less and less.

He has to be out by now.

Chase, not my sister, but yes, I do see the parallels in both scenarios. If I really wanted to think about it, I could postulate about a newborn being dragged from the black into a new life, and Chase being pulled from the pit because of old traditions, but I'm not interested in getting philosophical.

I just want him.

Unable to hurry-up-and-wait any longer, I shoot from

my chair and don my winter gear, prepared to wait outside Rose House all night.

I grab the thickest scarf I own and wrap it around my face while clomping into the main room, until I come to an abrupt halt, and not by my own volition.

I look down at Emma's hand, firmly encased around my puffy jacket as she slams it against my chest.

"What the hell?" I ask.

"Where are you going?" Emma retorts.

"To—" *see Chase*, but from the look in her eyes, I've been caught doing something stupid. "I don't want him recovering alone," I finish lamely.

"He won't. He has his friends, probably even my dad. You won't be welcome there."

She's right, but it doesn't lessen the pain of hearing it.

At my expression, Emma moderates her tone. "You care about him. And I'm sure he wants to see you, too. But you guys can't do this anymore. Not until we understand why Sabine and Daniel want you two apart."

The ends of my scarf flop over my hands. "Because he's Piper's, and I can't compete with a secret society's soulmate, in life or in death."

"It's true no one can escape the society, but that reasoning is off," Emma muses. "My dad following Sabine's every whim is off. He's a horrible man, but he has excellent business sense. He'd never approve of what she's doing with the Virtues. He'd see it as devaluing currency. Diluting assets. And because of that, I don't think he has any idea what she's up to."

My hands drop to my sides. "Does that mean your dad has no idea what Sabine did to you?" *You never told him?* Is my next question, but I wisely keep it to myself.

"No. He and Chase have no clue. I've made certain."

"But, why?"

"Because, despite what Sabine's done to the Virtues, they'd try to keep the society. Restore it, make it beautiful again—whatever. I don't want that." Emma's eyes go hard. "I've worked my ass off to regain their trust and get back at Briarcliff to destroy, not repair. Those two noblemen would only get in my way."

I see her point but my heart sinks for Chase. He'd want to know. Perhaps if he did, his whole perspective would change and he'd see the truth of these societies. The deadly, irrevocable poison seeping into us.

I ask, "Does that mean you don't think he truly understands why Chase and I can't be together?"

"Not a damn clue," Emma intones. "Strip yourself out of this marshmallow you've encased yourself in. You have no time to pine over my brother. We have work to do."

"Like go back to the yearbook."

Emma's hand smacks down on the silver crest of the Briarcliff yearbook on our coffee table. "Yep. And since Sabine and your mom probably knew each other..."

I pull my lips in, stare hard at the seemingly innocent maroon and silver hardcover and toss my jacket. "Let's search the internet for anything we can find."

Emma smiles, slow and cat-like. "I'll make the coffee."

✦

Two hours and a thorough delve into the dusty pages of a three-decades-old yearbook later, we have as much to go on as we did when we started. Mom isn't in any additional pictures—no clubs, sports, or written honors. It's like she was a ghost haunting these halls, taking her classes, then quietly blending into the stone—unremembered, intangible.

That sounds nothing like my mother. I flipped through the yearbook and did over a thousand internet searches to prove the theory wrong, but it's like she popped into existence when she became a crime scene photographer. Everything before is an empty data mystery.

It's hard to believe I missed such an important gap in her life while she was alive.

I've been staring at the 74 faces surrounding her, wondering if my dad is also in here somewhere.

Fuck. That's a barrel I do *not* want tumbling down the waterfall of emotions I have right now.

"You're sure your mom never mentioned Briarcliff?"

Emma sits with one hand squished against her cheek as she rests her elbow on the counter, half falling off her stool.

"Positive," I reply. "As far back as my memories go, at least. I can call Ahmar in the morning. He knew her best—as far as I can tell."

I slump in my seat. *As far as* is becoming the new preface whenever I talk about my mother. *As far as I knew, as far as I can tell, as far as I understand...*

It feels thick in my mouth. It weakens our relationship. But I must utter those words and prove to the world that I didn't know my mother as well as she knew me.

My fingers drift over her smiling face in her class photo. Her long, kinky, reddish brown hair. The pert nose I never inherited, and the large, close-set eyes that reflect my own.

I stroke her cheek.

And I pretend not to hurt at the idea that I'm the same age she's frozen in, her uncertain future encased in a grin.

"I'm sorry she died."

Emma's quiet words bring my eyes up.

"I don't think I ever said that. I'm sorry you're entrenched in Briarcliff as much as I am and that it's caused you the exact amount of pain needed to keep you here."

Her sincerity circles in my head, less like vultures and more like seagulls searching for an offering. "My sister's being born today."

Emma blinks. "What?"

"Yeah. My dad's at the hospital with Lynda right now. Last they texted, she's still in labor, but all signs point to Blair coming today."

Emma hums in thought. "So, she's not blood-related to you."

Emma's bluntness doesn't grind against me like it used to. "We may not share DNA, but this one beats the imaginary one, named Dragoon, I concocted as a kid."

Emma's lips even out in a smile—a symmetry of muscles Emma rarely deploys. Usually, she holds the scarred side of her face frozen, unmoving.

"My mom was seriously concerned when I started blaming Dragoon for all the dead cockroaches around the house."

A beat of silence passes, then Emma laughs. "You were

one creepy kid. But that comes with sibling territory as well as imaginary. Chase *constantly* pinned shit on me that I didn't do."

I almost grin, but the mention of Chase sobers us both.

"Running isn't the way to solve this," I murmur, stroking my mom's picture. "And I think that's what my mom tried to do."

Emma sighs. "You might be right. And since she's not here to explain, we'll have to figure out the rest of her story ourselves."

I manage a small smile. "Thank you."

"For what?"

"For not judging. For having my mom's back when you never met her. For trusting me when I say she was a good person."

Emma's lips press shut, trapping whatever she almost said next. Instead, she says, "Maybe we should sleep."

I gaze out the bay windows, wondering if Chase is in his bed, thrashing, sweating, his mouth stretched wide with silent screams. "I don't think I can."

"You've barely slept since the formal." Emma slides off her stool, then all but wrestles me out of mine. "If we're meant to take down the biggest, most dangerous bully Briarcliff has to offer, I can't have your bleary, googly-eyes beside me when we do."

"Fair point," I say.

I do as she asks and head to my room, going through the motions, changing into my pajamas, and turning off my bedside lamp, revealing the grayish, dusky sky leaking through my windows.

I lay in my bed, convinced I won't be able to find solace in sleep.

Three hours later, my eyes are still wide open, staring into the creeping dawn.

28

---

a locker slams shut beside me, and I jump. The girl responsible sneers at me with her tongue on her upper lip, then saunters away.

Rubbing the sleepless grit from my eyes, I mutter to her back, "You must be friends with Falyn," then resume collecting my notes and books for my next class.

I've coasted through the day in a hazy, here-but-floating state. Emma, my wise night owl, is right, and if I don't find time to sleep soon, I might timber over in the middle of a confrontation with Sabine.

My mind doesn't seem to care about my body's needs. It wants justice, it demands to *think*. About my mother, the Virtues, the Nobles, and Chase.

I haven't seen Chase all day. He didn't show up to the classes we share, and I can't ask his friends about him without raising suspicion. All there is to go on is Tempest's expression, and it's like he's been raised by a gargoyle, with his flat, one-note expressions and stone-heavy eyes.

Sighing, I heft my bag from the floor and head to English Lit.

"Hey there, sweet possum."

Tingles prickle along the back of my neck as I spin around. Every piece of me itches to jump into Chase's arms, but we're in the middle of a crowded hallway. I settle for a breathy, "Hey," but know my eyes shine with relief.

He tucks his hands in his pockets, his blazer flaring out behind his wrists. "I'm okay."

I take in all his parts, starting with his face—fatigued, pale, flawless—and his slightly stooped but otherwise strong and confident posture. After a quick check to see who's around us, I risk one step closer.

Chase's eyes run over me as I move. "As for you, I'm now wondering if you're worse for wear."

"I'm fine." The tremble in my voice indicates just how much I'm *not*.

A strand of hair falls into his eyes when he tilts his head. "I've been gone twenty-four hours, sweet possum, not deployed to Afghanistan. What have I missed? Don't lie," he adds, as I open my mouth to do just that.

"Now's not the time," I say instead.

"It's never the time." Chase clamps onto my elbow and drags me into a blind corner, hidden from view of the hallway. "Tell me, anyway."

I release a breath, staring past his shoulder as I force my heart to stop its pounding, traitorous beats.

Chase tips my chin, forcing my eyes to his. "Tell me, Callie."

Leaning into his fingers, I close my eyes. His warmth, his presence, he's *here*. And he's in one piece.

My brows come down over my deliberate blindness. Maybe it's the sadness inside me that makes my heart want to speak, because I blurt, "All I want is to wrap my arms around you."

Chase growls, low in his throat. "We can't."

"It's stupid, and I wish I—"

Strong arms envelop my body, and my eyes flutter open when my cheek hits his clothed chest. Chase's freshwater fragrance hits my nose, and I burrow into him, just like I said I wouldn't. His chin comes down on my head. He strokes my hair. Chase holds me so tight I can't breathe, and my own grip on his waist will leave bruises.

"I'm so glad you made it through." My voice breaks on the last word.

He kisses the top of my head. "I've been around worse." Chase traces a final trail down my cheek, then releases me.

Cold air replaces the heat of his body, and I shiver with sudden emptiness. Instead of buckling, I siphon Chase's burst of emotion until I mimic it.

Lifting my head, I tell him about the news articles Sabine's hoarding.

Throughout the exchange, Chase's lips turn down, harder, deeper. By the end, he's forced his mouth down so hard, he's revealed a small dimple I never knew he had.

"It could be related to your sniffing around the Virtues when they didn't want you to," Chase says.

"I initially thought that, too, but she has clippings and print-outs from well before I enrolled at Briarcliff." Then I tell him about his father, my stepdad, and Lynda all attending Briarcliff at the same time. "Chase—my mother was a student here, too."

I expect a widening of eyes, at least, but all I get from my big reveal is a slight tic of an eyebrow.

"Don't you think that's a little suspect?" I prod. "What if they're all part of the secret societies? What if my *mother* was a Virtue?"

"That's taking it a little far, don't you think?"

"Sabine's remodel of the Virtues is taking it too far. Putting you in a glorified coffin. Dumping me in the Briarcliff Lake in winter. Assuming our parents all knew each other? That's a drop in the fucking bucket." I take a closer look at him. "Why aren't you as surprised as your sister was?"

"Surprise looks different on me. And I'm wondering..." Chase trails off, deep in thought. "My father's study. He has files there relating to the societies related to our quarterly reporting. Financials, official documents, and records of membership dating back to the beginning."

My heart leaps. "Could I see them?"

Chase licks his lips. "My father's doing business in New York for the next few days. I believe Sabine's going with him." His eyes flash with freshly forged bronze. "I'll take a look tonight."

"I'm going with you."

"Hell no, sweet possum."

"Hell to the *yes*. This is my mother." My shoulders heave

with my determined breaths. "And she's not here anymore. Anything that's found out about her, I want to be there. Read it *first*. I deserve that."

Chase shakes his head, releasing a heavy sigh. "It's not a good idea. We're being watched. And this conversation has to end."

"Then be mean to me," I blurt out.

Chase narrows his eyes.

"All day. All week. Do your worst. Enlist James and Rio, even Tempest. Be assholes, and get Falyn off my scent. I'll even cry."

Chase rumbles his disagreement, but I continue.

"I'll convince Ivy, Eden, your sister, that I'm devastated. Then I'll sneak out with you tonight."

"It's not a good idea."

"None of this is good or right."

Chase takes a longer assessment of me. "Are you sure? I won't be easy on you. Or humane. I'll have to make your day brutal, and sweet possum, after the past twenty-four hours, I'm fucking hellbent on letting loose right about now."

I set my shoulders. "I can handle it."

Chase grunts. "And if we get caught?"

I smile when I have him. "Sabine and Daniel aren't here. Who would dole out our immediate punishment? Falyn? Marron?"

"They'd wait."

"Then I'll gladly take the repercussions, because I would've read everything your father had on the secret societies."

Chase rubs a hand down his face, and a twinge of guilt

follows the movement. He's gone through so much and has only recently been taken out of a hole of his nightmares. How much more can I ask of him?

But this is about my mother. Not him. Not us.

"Fine," he says, then glances to the side at a noise echoing from down the hall. "We need to get to class."

I give a resolute nod, but my voice isn't nearly as strong. "Thank you."

"Don't thank me yet." The forged bronze dies out the longer he looks at me. "You may not like what you find."

"So be it if it's the truth. Because so far, everything I have has been built on other people's lies."

※

Chase starts off mild.

I endure a few muttered vermin insults during class, but having heard it all before, I don't grow concerned over the increased participation he's gathering—first from his boys, then Falyn and her girls, then the rest of the class.

Professor Lacey turns to write something on the board. The slogan "slut muncher" is uttered nearby, but I steel my shoulders and feign detachment, writing down every single letter the professor scribbles on the board.

Then something wet hits my temple. I raise my chin but keep my expression blank, despite all the gasps. And I wipe it away, assuming it's a spitball.

The girl next to me screeches, scooting herself and her entire desk away. Hoots and laughter follow.

My stomach pitches, and a hot, scorching blush creeps into my cheeks before I even figure out what the cause is.

"Gross, possum!" a male student cries.

"Wipe your fucking face!"

My gaze skirts to Ivy. She flips around in her chair and stares at me, her face white.

Oh God, I don't want to look.

...but I do.

A used tampon lays near my feet. I scrape my chair away, vomit surging in my throat, but all of this is too late. It's already hit my skin. *I have someone's period blood on my face!*

A strained whimper escapes my lips at the same time someone else says, "Period possum!" and starts applauding.

The rest of the class makes gagging and retching noises, but I can't bear to scan the room to see which voice belongs to who.

Professor Lacey spins around. "Class, what the heck's going on—oh. Oh, Christ. Miss Ryan, what...?"

She scrutinizes the mess in the aisle, and when I follow her gaze, I realize someone has dared to kick the tampon under my seat, leaving a bloody streak on the white marble.

"Dig into your vagina in the bathroom like a normal chick," James cries, then stands, plugging his nose while he stands. "Should we call her bloody possum twat or rat vagina now? I can't decide."

"*Mr. Windsor!*" Professor Lacey cries, her voice so high, it screeches. "Chancellor Marron's office, *now*."

James grins. He slams his palms on his desk, then high-fives Riordan on the way out. "Worth it."

As his final encore, he winks at Chase then gives the thumbs up.

I swallow thickly.

Chase leans back in his seat, his gaze cold and inscrutable, but directed at me. With a face that blank, eyes that dead, Chase's stare can only mean one thing: *I warned you.*

You did, I silently respond. Tears betray my vision, but I wipe them away and turn in my seat, facing forward. "Professor, can I go to the—?"

"Yes. Absolutely. Go, go." Professor Lacey eyes the mess on the floor with appalled trepidation. "In fact, class is dismissed. A custodian must get in here immediately."

I scurry out of my seat as the class whistles and claps at the dismissal, but most choose to keep commenting on the mess.

Ivy tries to grab my hand as I pass, but I sprint out of class, find the nearest bathroom, and scrub my cheek until it's raw.

$\mathcal{A}$ knock sounds at my bedroom door.

Ivy's hesitant voice calls through the wood, "Callie? You in there?"

I burrow deeper under my covers, the sheets scratching against my tender cheeks and wicking away the lingering tears.

I'm supposed to be devastated, but to be honest, it's not difficult to play sad this evening.

"Can I come in?" she asks.

I sniff and rise out of my hovel, brushing away pieces of hair stuck to my face. "Sure."

"Oh, Callie." Ivy rushes over, the mattress dipping when she sits, and she wraps her arm around me. "I wanted to comfort you sooner, but you ran away so fast."

I nod, sniffling into her shoulder. "It was easier to escape."

She rests her head against mine. "Want me to bring some chocolate and vodka so we can really commit?"

I chuckle, pulling away and wiping my eyes. "I just needed a few minutes to cry. I'll be okay."

"That was brutal. And *ugh*." Ivy makes a face. "Whose tampon was that? Did she just—" Ivy mimes pulling a string from between her legs "—and *plop*? Like what? How is *she* not ridiculed for that?"

Ivy is so appalled with herself for even mimicking the maneuver that she gags. I laugh, and that laughter travels to my belly. "Can you picture Falyn resorting to that level?"

Ivy topples over in a fit of laughter. "My goodness, imagine the horror of anyone who *saw* it happening."

I fall next to her, joining her in laidback repose. "Right when I thought the Witches of Briarcliff had given me all they had."

"No way, this was part warlock." Ivy props herself up on her elbow. "This isn't something Falyn or her cohorts would think up on their own. This, my friend, is dead rat territory."

I recall the mass of rat corpses slopping out of my locker mere days after coming to Briarcliff Academy. "What girl would willingly do that in public? And smack me in the face with it?"

"A girl who was blackmailed." Ivy grows serious. "Callie, Chase has picked his side. Only someone like him could make a girl be so grotesque. He either promised her a world of sex, or..." Ivy purses her lips, "used her worst nightmare against her, same as what happened to him."

I roll and stare at the ceiling, folding my hands over my

stomach. I'm worried if I look at Ivy, the smallest tic of inner knowledge will show on my face.

It doesn't feel great to dupe my friend, but Chase's and my deal is working. Ivy believes he's turned.

"He's angry," Ivy continues. "After what happened to him, I was worried he'd take his anger out on you, and it looks like I'm right. I think you should be sick for the rest of the week. Catch up on some sleep. Stay away from him and wait for his rage hurricane to end."

"I would," I murmur, "but I'm failing my classes and finals are in a few days. I can't miss them."

Ivy grabs my hand and squeezes. "Then I will do everything I can to help you stay out of his way."

My mother, I think as a wave of guilt crashes inside me. *Think about getting answers. Not about hurting Ivy.*

I turn to her and envelop her in a side-hug. "Thank you. I love you ... you know that?"

"*Ack.*" Ivy laughs tightly. "You sure you don't want to row? You're squeezing me like you *want* me to be an oar."

"Maybe next year," I say as I release her.

Ivy frowns. "But we graduate this spring."

"Exactly."

Ivy smacks me on the arm as I roll and pull the covers over my head. "I'm glad to see you sassy, at least. Get some sleep. I'll come by tomorrow morning and walk with you to class. As the Virtuous princess, I can order Falyn to stand down. But Chase and the Nobles..."

"You have your own shit to worry about, too. I can handle stupid school pranks."

"That's just it," Ivy says, her pensive face growing

smaller as my lids get heavier. "We've moved way beyond hazing."

"Mm?" I mumble sleepily.

"I'm worried about you, Callie. The Virtues and Nobles are out of control."

"Callie? Possum. *Possum.* Hey. Baby."

My shoulder's jostled a few more times, the last few shoves so hard, I'm positive I'm no longer running toward a cliff with ravens nipping at my back.

"Wha...?" I crack open an eye, but I shouldn't have bothered, since my room is as dark as my dreams.

"There you are." A vague outline of Chase's large body takes shape. "You were so KO'd, I was about to leave you to the Sandman."

I sit up, scrubbing my eyes, then scraping my hair back. "I'm ready. Just give me..."

"Callie." His hand falls on my shoulder, a leveler on most occasions, but it feels like an unwanted anchor tonight. "You should stay here. It's obvious you need the sleep."

I throw the covers off and my feet hit the floor. "I want answers more than a few more hours of rest. I'll get dressed, and we can go."

"If you say so."

Chase backs off, but his residual grumble makes it clear he's not happy about it.

I pad around my bedroom, finding my sweats and socks

and pretending I don't see the cool, unbothered Chase reclined in class today instead of his current shadow waiting along the edges of my room.

His lack of features in the night makes that impossible, and my movements are stilted and clumsy, reflecting the emotions toiling away in my chest.

"You good?" he asks after my third curse when I bang my toe against my bedside table.

"Fine." I fumble for my hair-tie and call myself ready. "Let's go."

"You can change your mind."

"Nope."

I lead the way from my bedroom into the low-lit gloom of our kitchen appliances. Emma's light is off, and while she spent time eating with me at our counter tonight, I was so shell-shocked and desolate, she wisely left me alone with my feelings for the rest of the evening.

"Emma doesn't know?" I whisper over my shoulder, verifying that she's sleeping on the other side of her door.

Chase's voice, rough even when controlled, responds, "Not a clue. And I'd like to keep it that way."

These twins keep too much from each other, I think sadly. But right now, my mother is the priority.

Chase cuts past me at the apartment door while I'm putting on my coat and pushes the stair's door open to slide through. We silently descend the three flights, and when we burst into the frigid, winter air, I let myself squeal into the collar of my coat as I follow him to his car.

We take a hidden path through the forest to a back road, probably for vendors and staff to travel unnoticed around the edges of the academy. Chase's car lurks quietly on the plowed drive, shining iridescent black against the opaque darkness of the trees and sky.

He opens the passenger door, and I'm thrown into the memory of the last time I rode in his car, with the smell of caramel, fresh-baked bread, and *him* permeating the interior, stimulating both my stomach and pheromones.

Just the thought has saliva building in my mouth and clenches my core. I'm desperate to tighten myself around him again. Rules be damned—I want him to take me in his car, surrounded by forest, and out of sight from our enemies.

Chase gets in on the other side, his eyes dark but shining when they land on mine. Every line of his shadowed expression communicates his same need.

"Chase, I—"

He growls, then clamps his hand on the back of my neck and pulls me in for a hard kiss. Chase's tongue plunges, explores, and I part for him easily. A needy mewl sounds from my throat, and I guide his free hand between my legs, aching for him to fill me and for my walls to clench around something other than emptiness, but he rips away with a curse.

"I knew this was a bad idea." Chase swipes the back of his hand over his mouth, staring straight ahead.

"I told you, I have to be the one to discover anything about my mother. She's mine, Chase. She was everything to me."

"That's not what I'm referring to." His gaze slides over me but flicks away the minute heat builds between us. "If

I'm to follow orders to keep my hands off you, we can't keep finding ourselves alone." His tone falls into velvet when he continues, "Because I will take every advantage. I'll have you naked before the end of the night. I won't be able to bring you home until I've tasted you again. Fuck, I miss your taste."

I lick my lips, but they're not the flavor he's looking for.

A tingling hollowness builds low in my belly. I squirm in my seat.

"Drive," I manage to garble out. "Before I climb on top of you and end this charade."

The engine rumbles to life, and my head falls back on a sigh when the vibrations hit my seat.

It's not enough, it will never be Chase, but it takes off the keening edge building at my middle.

We don't talk as he navigates the private road and onto the main passage of Briarcliff Academy, and I'm grateful, because that time of quiet allows me to regain rationale and logic. And memories of today.

"You're quiet," Chase muses as he turns out of the academy gates. "But I can hear you thinking."

I stare out my window. "It's nothing."

He turns left, the wheel gliding between his skilled fingers. "You come better than you lie."

My cheeks grow hot.

"Fine. I don't need your words to be confident in your hatred for me at the same time you want to jump my bones."

"Don't simplify it like that."

"Why not? It's exactly how you're feeling."

"I had a used *tampon* thrown at my face."

Chase arches a brow. "I told you I wouldn't be kind."

I rear away from my seat, so incensed, it's difficult to form a sentence. "What the hell is the matter with you? I expected name-calling. I practically guaranteed Falyn's bitchy involvement in some way. Hell, I wouldn't have been surprised if James joined in and my locker was fucked with again. But you convinced a girl to yank on a string between her legs in the middle of class and *toss* it, then you sat back and enjoyed the show. That's fucking gross, Chase. It's despicable. And you orchestrated it."

Chase's hands relax on the wheel, and I note the small smile playing against his profile. I'm about to punch it off his face.

"Did we not agree to convince the Nobles and Virtues that I've taken their side? Bowed to their rules after a night in a cage? I couldn't play by the normal bullying rules. It was the only way, and the reason you're in my car right now. Sabine's cronies won't be tailing us after that display—and even if they are, I went through a lot of bullshit and dollar bills to make it look like I've locked myself in my room with a random sophomore tonight."

The thought of Chase with someone else—even pretend —makes me sick. But I can't argue the point, so I fold my arms and counter, "Don't be surprised if I pee in your sports bottle before your next rowing practice."

"Now, Callie," Chase says as he pulls into the driveway of his lake house. "That's just gross."

30

The lake house is quiet and undisturbed, the small porch light offering mild illumination of the front steps, and I follow Chase through the front door.

We don't stop in the kitchen and talk over coffee like last time. I try not to reminisce on how close he was when we sat next to each other and how the heat of his skin acted like a magnet to the little hairs on my arms, drawing me closer, my lips softer, my body on fire.

Chase tosses his jacket on the couch and descends the stairs two at a time. I scamper to keep up with his long legs and sure footing. He turns on the study's light before I arrive at the bottom, and I swing into the office right as he's rounded the desk and started typing on the keyboard.

I come up beside him, admiring the toned bulges of his muscles through his shirt as he bends, but getting to the task at hand. "I thought you said your dad used hardcopies."

"He does, but he keeps a catalogued system on his computer. Rather than search through all his file cabinets, I'm going to locate the ones we need in his spreadsheet."

"And he's given you his password?"

"He gave Sabine his password. Piper watched her type it in one night, then she told me."

Piper's name causes a squeamishness in my gut, more because of my inability to see just how good she was at working the room while being a completely different person behind the scenes.

"I underestimated her," I say, folding my arms.

"If you're wishing you had the time to get to know the real Piper Harrington," Chase says, while a spreadsheet pops onto the screen, "I tend to agree with you."

My lips pull into a sad smile. "I'm hoping I can properly avenge her instead by picking up where she was forced to stop."

Chase turns to me. "I love you for it."

I shift on my feet, unsure of his proclamation and where it should land. Chase has never said anything *near* that level before.

And, because I'm a coward, I pretend I didn't hear it and ramble, "What's your opinion on Addisyn being the killer? Now that I'm an initiate, I'm seeing all these holes..."

"Nah. Piper may have been a double agent, but she wasn't killed by her mother. Addisyn did it. To be sure, I visited Addy in holding. Ah. Here we go."

Chase taps the screen and straightens.

"Wait, you visited Addisyn?"

He nods, his posture loose, like he just told me he had a

burger for lunch. "I had the same misgivings you did and needed to hear it from Addisyn's lips. Why she killed Piper. *Why* she worked so hard to eliminate her sister."

I raise my brows. "And?"

"It was jealousy, through and through. Over Piper being a Virtue before her, then becoming the princess. Then, Piper sleeping with Addisyn's boyfriend and getting pregnant. Those two ... Addy and Piper ... they didn't have the best upbringing."

I think back to Sabine's graduation photo, and the realization of what Piper was to her. Addisyn might've been the same thing. A weapon. A leg-up. A *power* play. It must have affected those girls. So much so that it ended it murder. Both their lives, over.

I say, "It's just so hard to believe, especially after hearing about what Sabine is doing to the Virtue name and to her princesses..."

I stare at Chase, watching for his reaction. It's hard to believe that he'd be aware of the trafficking and not become an apocalyptic incendiary device. Emma's keeping the worst from him to protect her cause. Can I take away her right to confess when she's ready?

In this office, surrounded by the Stones' trinkets and deadly creatures, I dare to add, "Chase, do you know the full story of Emma's—?"

He spins to the wall of books behind us. "The files we need are in the panic room."

I allow the change in topic, since I haven't even collected more information on Mom yet. "Oh, so it's not just for robberies, huh?"

Chase sends me an unamused look before typing in the code. "That was before you stuck your nose in this shit and got yourself initiated into a dangerous secret society."

I stand back as the wall pushes out, then slides apart to reveal an industrial gray door.

Chase motions to follow him through the door. "In here."

Despite my resolve, guilt remains heavy in my gut. I can't *know* these things about Emma and not lay down clues for him. "Addisyn was made a Virtue after killing Piper. Don't you find that suspect? Wouldn't you think Sabine was complicit in the murder by protecting Addisyn?"

"Both are her daughters, and both had deep-seated issues with their family. I believe Sabine was shielding the one legacy she had left, regardless of whether she saw Addisyn as her second favorite. Her favorite was gone. And as a mom..." Chase shrugs but continues striding to the back of the panic room where a set of file cabinets are built into the wall. "I'll never say what she did is forgivable. I miss my friend a whole fucking lot. But when it comes to family, to my sister, I would do anything to protect her."

"That's different. You did that out of love. I don't think Sabine's capable of that. Every action she makes comes with a plan."

Chase pauses near the gray cabinets. "You're right. But I thought we were here about your mother, not Addisyn or Sabine."

"Pretty sure it's all relative," I mutter as I sidle up to him, but he's so focused on locating the correct cabinet, he doesn't hear me.

"Got it." He pulls one open on a squeal of metal wheels. "These are the members from the 1980s and before. After that, we were put into a computerized system, but after Y2K, my father preferred to keep the originals, too."

"Thank God for that," I say, and lift my hands to dive in. I'd heard about that strange year in 2000 when everyone was terrified computers would either crash forever or take over the world.

Chase blocks me with half his body as he sifts through the files with sure fingers. "Your mom was in the same class as my dad. If she was a Virtue, it'll be in here."

My heart leaps, but it leaves a nauseous wake. "And my stepdad. Peter Spencer. And stepmom, Lynda Meyer."

Chase nods, pieces of hair falling into his eyes as he focuses on the files. "I'll find them."

I swivel to the opposite side of the open drawer. He tracks me with his eyes. "Let me do this. I'm familiar with my dad's system."

"Sure. But I want a front row seat."

Chase stares at me, setting his jaw as if preparing for an argument, but must second-guess himself, because he returns to his search.

After a few seconds of rifling paper and the low hum of air vents, Chase speaks. "I found her."

"Oh my God," bursts out of me, and I reach for the file before he's pulled it all the way out. "Let me see."

"Hang on." He lifts it out of my reach.

"*Chase*," I warn. My muscles are primed to leap. "I will tear that thing out of your hands with my teeth. Give it."

Chase levels me with a look. "Despite you being here,

the Nobles require plenty of confidentiality. I need to make sure there's nothing in here you're not meant to see."

"Like what? My mother would've been a Virtue, not a Noble, and that negates any confidentiality you may have, because I'm a—"

"You're not a Virtue yet. And at the rate you're going..." Chase gives me a droll look.

"I don't give a shit, so long as I understand why my mother *died*."

Chase freezes with the file dangling high above my head. "What did you just say?"

I clamp my mouth shut, but my chest heaves. "I didn't mean to say that. You have to understand. With Piper's death, and all these secrets surrounding my mom and Briarcliff, can you blame me for thinking her death might be related? Her killer's never been found."

"The societies don't murder."

I scoff, shaking my head. "Even now, after all they've done to you, you're still loyal to the Nobles."

"I've told you before, sweet possum. I will lead them. In a different way than my father, sure, but I'll never leave them." His voice goes quiet. "I don't bow to them. They submit to *me*."

"I ... just give me the file, Chase. Let me see what the Nobles have on my mother."

Chase lowers the file, but with the open cabinet still between us, he's able to fan it open and read it before I can get to him.

"She was a Virtue," he says, right as I'm about to snatch the papers away. "Says it right here."

He points to a list of the graduating class of 2002. After their full names, the students are ranked by status.

And there, right in the middle, is my mother in typed font. **Meredith Ryan.** "She was a marquess?"

"Meaning she was initiated into the Virtues, but not as a legacy. Instead, she was a promising achiever."

I run my finger along my mother's name. She was never one to talk of academics or brain power. I remembered her with an insane work ethic and an encouraging smile whenever she caught me struggling over homework. She always assisted me with the harder problems and the heftier math equations, but I never, for one moment, assumed she was a genius achiever great enough to be noticed by a coveted secret society.

I suppose all kids just think of their parents as starting their lives once their kids are born. Anything previous to that is an unnecessary blur, because they now exist to care about and protect you, their own goals and dreams dull in comparison.

But this goes beyond thinking your mother is just your mother. She lived a completely different life than what she set up in my brain.

I close my eyes, lingering in the dark for a moment. After a breath, I open them. "And my stepdad? He was two years below her."

Chase flips the 2002 file shut, but I grab it from him and press it close to my chest. "I just want to hold onto it for a minute. Before you put it away."

Chase's lips twitch in what might be understanding. He nods. "2004 should be..."

"Wait." I put a hand to his wrist to stop him before he keeps shuffling the files. "What's that?"

He surveys the cabinet. "What? I don't see anything."

"That. Right there." I push his hand away and pull out what caught my eye. "Is this a birth certificate? And … holy shit, it's old. Emma said Piper wanted to talk to her about a Briar birth certificate…"

The single piece of paper is laminated. I'm not worried I'll crumble it with the oils of my fingers, but it's yellowed with age, and covered in ash.

"It probably has to do with the origins of the societies." Chase moves to pluck it from my fingers. "Which we already know."

"No, it's…" I squint at the same time I spin to keep it away from Chase's sticky fingers. "Rose Briar is listed as the *mother*. Oh my God—I remember. The librarian in town said there was some kind of illegitimate child born between Rose and Theodore Briar."

"Callie, this has nothing to do with your mom."

"Yeah, but it's near her file and … I thought this child was adopted out and made to not exist. Thorne Briar exiled it, right? I shouldn't say 'it.'" I correct myself. "Says here it's a girl. A Daphne Wilmington. Maybe that's Rose's maiden name, since a father isn't listed … wait. Why does your dad have this? Isn't this Virtue property, since it's related to Rose Briar?"

"Callie, we need to go."

"Does Sabine have any idea this exists? I mean, yeah, she has the password to the location of these files, but was this listed as an item on your dad's spreadsheet?"

Chase sighs. "Not that I saw."

"Let me just get a picture of this."

"Do you really think that's necessary?"

I nail him with a look. "If you know what I know about the Virtues, *everything* is necessary."

That stops him. "Fine. But be quick about it."

I pull out my phone and take a photo. I also take a snapshot of my mom's listing. Chase doesn't find anything with regard to my stepdad, but he does find Lynda's name, and I take a snapshot of that, too.

"Let's go," he says, stuffing the file back in. "I had the motion detectors turned off in the room, but Tempest can only keep them black for so long."

"Way to tell me that now."

"You'd've been skittish and set them off with all your twitching had I told you earlier."

Frowning, I turn with him to the door, but the faded edges of the birth certificate linger in my mind.

Where did the baby girl go after leaving Briarcliff?

And ... why is it considered so important that Daniel Stone has it safely stored *away* from Sabine?

31

Chase drops me off in the woods near campus. He offers to walk me through the forested pathway to the back of Thorne House, but I decline, my head too filled with my mother's cloaked past and my body too attuned to him to withstand more of his presence with no pay-off.

Yet, his headlights carve my way back to the dorms and don't wink out until I'm safely in Thorne House's backyard.

Once I'm sure no security guards are idling outside, I sneak in through the side-door I propped open with a rock, then creep up the stairs into my dorm room.

It's close to 4 AM, a time when Emma begins to stir. I tip-toe into my bedroom and shut my door with a soft click.

Then turn on my laptop.

Sleep is not a priority. I pull out my phone and flip to the photo proving my mother's involvement in the Virtues.

It doesn't stop there. Lynda is a Virtue. And my stepdad

may not be a Noble, but he went to school here, too. Two years below them.

Why didn't my mom tell me she met my stepdad in Briarcliff's high school and they both graduated from BU? And why did Lynda and Dad send me here without cluing me in that Dad was an alumnus, too? Is my dad's second marriage to another Briarcliff alum a coincidence, or a secret society set-up?

I'm staring at a blank search screen, but so many questions flit through my head. I don't know where to begin, other than to call the responsible parties, but it's too early for that.

I straighten from my computer. *Or is it?*

Swiping through my contacts, I find the number I'm looking for and call.

"Calla? Everything okay?"

Unanswered questions may be swirling through my mind with suspicions cast over my every move, and suspects are more involved in my life than friends, but Ahmar? He will always be my heartening escape.

"Everything's fine—well, sort of. I can't sleep."

"What's wrong?"

Ahmar's voice sounds tight. Clipped. "Are you busy right now? At a crime scene? I can call back."

"No, no, you're good, kid. I just got home after a rough one, is all. But I have the morning off, so I'll sleep in a bit. Which means I have the time to hear you out on why you're calling me before dawn."

I cut to the thick of it. "It's about Mom."

Ahmar goes quiet. "Shoulda figured. How can I help?"

"I've just found out she was a student here at Briarcliff."
I decide to leave out the Virtue part, since Ahmar has no
idea about the societies. I'm starting to wonder how much
longer I should keep it from him. "And so were Dad and
Lynda."

"Really."

I shuffle into a cross-legged position on my bed. "That
wasn't the exclamation of surprise I was expecting."

"No, kid, it's not." Ahmar sighs.

My thigh muscles clench. "You *knew*?"

"About your mom? Yeah, honey. Don't freak out on me. I
plan on explaining that. As for your dad and Lynda, I knew
about them, too, but it's high school, honey, that they went
to decades ago. Nothing at Meredith's crime scene pointed
to Briarcliff."

I rub my forehead, the friction causing a small, needed
amount of pain. "Why didn't you tell me? Why didn't Mom
open up to me? What the hell is going on behind the scenes
of my *life*?"

"Calla, honey, calm down. I'll tell you what I know. And
I'm sorry, I'm so sorry, you're hearing this from me and not
from your momma."

"I feel like she's a stranger." My throat constricts. "Like I
never knew her. Like she's this girl who became this woman
who had a child, then decided to erase her past life. Is the
person I grew up with the woman she always was? Or was it
all an act for my benefit? Who *is* she, Ahmar?"

"She was happy with you. Don't you ever think she lost
herself when she had you. There were times when I was
over, and you were playing at our feet, that I'd catch your

mom—in the middle of one of our serious conversations—staring at you, and she'd smile with this special curve to her lips. It lit up her whole face, that grin. The *pride* she took in you, baby girl, was unlike any kind of love I'd seen before.

"Looking back, it's the reason why I let her get away with her secrets, because she worked so hard to be good at the mother thing and the single parent rap she got served with. Part of me also knew there'd come a day when you'd find out, especially once I heard you were being sent to Briarcliff Academy."

"Did you ask Dad about why he chose Briarcliff?"

"It never occurred to me to ask them about it. Briarcliff is a top tier school, and parents across the city try their damnedest to get their kids enrolled. As alumni, they had an easy in. I figured it was his effort to give you something more, especially after the friction between you two and how much you were suffering in the city. It seemed like a good idea."

"But you're a detective. You don't believe in coincidences." My hand squeezes the phone against my ear. "What about my mom? What did she tell you about this school?"

"She mentioned it one night, I think. You were, I dunno, two? She'd just put you to bed, and we'd had a rough day on a scene. It was a teenaged girl ... she was brutally murdered, and the entire time your mom took photos, there was this glazed look in her eye. Like she'd checked out. So, when we got home and she relieved the babysitter, I poured us a stiff drink and asked her, point blank, what the fuck was going on with her that day. We'd had bad scenes before, with younger victims.

"She told me it had to do with her past, and while she wanted to get it off her chest, she swore me to secrecy. I swear, kid, it's like she knew her future, 'cause she stared at your bedroom door the entire time."

I fold my hand over my eyes, bowing forward. "She wouldn't have wanted me to attend Briarcliff Academy. But you encouraged me to go."

"No." Ahmar's hard exhale causes static against my ear. "But Pete had a different experience at Briarcliff. He loved it. That kind of diploma is prestigious, an honor, all that bullshit. And frankly, I thought your mom was taking it a bit too far, closeting her high school and university education like this. These are buildings, for chrissake. Not haunted houses."

If only you knew...

"On that same night, your mom told me she had some bad blood with kids she went to school with. She was involved in some kind of extracurricular, she called it, that didn't go well for her. Somehow, she got on the wrong side of some popular chick. Meredith was ostracized, bullied, her freshman year made into a living hell. Your basic elitist bullshit."

"It's not basic at all."

"Ah, kid, I didn't mean to simplify it like that, especially while you're going through something similar—but that's what I mean. It's like a rite of passage at that snob school, am I right? Girls who don't come from much are the first to be kicked down. And shoved, and belittled, until they start fighting back.

"That's what your momma did. She told me she had grown fed up and enlisted the help of some guy. It only pissed this popular chick off more. Your mom's grades dropped, she barely graduated, and the way she told it, this girl made her suffer long after she left Briarcliff, until she was forced to become incognito and live—in her words—an unaccomplished, boring life where she no longer made any waves. When that happened, this chick got bored and moved on. In my mind, at least. Mer made it clear to me that this chick didn't know you existed and wanted to keep it that way."

"Why didn't she want anyone in this town to know about me?"

"Unfortunately, the answer to that lived in your mom. She made me promise, if anyone from her past ever reached out to me, never to mention your name. But you see, no one did, Calla. And everyone she was involved with graduated. You went to Briarcliff on a clean slate. Your mom and you, you guys had a great life, but that night, she acted like this school had fingers that could grab you in your sleep. It was ... unsettling."

"Paranoia," I finish. "Just like when I went after Dad for her murder and was dead wrong. So, you decided it was easier to go with Dad and Lynda's perspective of Briarcliff, huh?"

"Baby girl, I ain't saying what you think I am. You are all the best parts of your momma, don't you ever forget that. And I loved her. She was my sister, my best friend. And you're like a daughter to me. I promised to protect you, but I couldn't keep you away from a school that showed no evidence of being a danger to you. Meredith's experience there was decades ago. *Decades*, Calla."

I cast my eyes to the ceiling, the popcorn pattern becoming a watery blur. "Tell me you looked into Briarcliff before sending me, anyway."

"What do you take me for? Of course I did. That request she made, that I never tell any of her past classmates about you? Strange as fuck, considering she married Pete, who while not her classmate, was a graduate of Briarcliff. I was on this school like spunk—I mean, like glue—the minute your momma was murdered. I made the calls, even visited the campus. I conducted interviews with her former classmates, though she wasn't friends with many. At that time, Lynda Meyer came up in the investigation but was ultimately dismissed as a suspect. She hadn't reunited with Pete at that banquet yet, and she and Meredith didn't run in the same circles at school. And, when she and Pete *did* start dating, I looked into her again, since she was gonna be around you, but she has no criminal background. Lynda was a straight A student and didn't participate in any drama at Briarcliff. She barely knew your momma. The rest of the people I interviewed from your mom's class couldn't say much about Meredith. She wasn't outspoken or extroverted. Nice and polite but didn't seek attention. I will say, though, she was Winter Court Queen in her junior year."

"Why didn't you tell me any of this?"

"Because I wanted you to be a kid, kid. You went to Briarcliff to start a new life and heal. If I told you your momma walked the same halls, went through some shit, and graduated by the skin of her teeth, what would you have done?"

"That should've been my choice to make. I should've been able to make the decision to go here based on my mom's experience."

"I did what was best for you, Calla. You were in a rough place. I wasn't about to add to your pain. I ain't standing down from that."

My phone grows hot in my hands. I don't want to argue with him. "What about Sabine Harrington? She would've been called Sabine Moriarty back then."

"Funny you should mention her. She was the chick who went after your mom in school."

"And the mother of my dead roommate." I go quiet, allowing the dominos to settle in place in Ahmar's mind. Although, knowing him, they probably already had.

"Remember, kid, Rhode Island isn't my jurisdiction. Your roommate's death wasn't something I could investigate officially. I did compare it to my notes on your mom, back in the beginning stages when I'd interviewed Sabine—who, while a bitch at BU and a real doozy now, had no contact with your mother since and has an airtight alibi on the night Meredith was killed."

I rub my eyes with my free hand. "Did my real father go here, too?"

Dead silence. Then: "I wish I could tell you the answer to that."

"She was nineteen when she had me. Eighteen when she got pregnant. Ahmar, my dad..."

Ahmar's response is gentle, yet firm. "None of my interviews raised red flags. Your momma was a loner, honey. There were no guys she was noticeably close with that I could find. She never told me who your father was."

"What about the Winter Court King?"

"Some senior. I'll look him up, but that shit is based on votes, and she wasn't in a relationship with the dude."

"I should've been told this. All of it, while you were investigating."

"Kiddo, because you're like a daughter to me, I treated you like one and protected you from unnecessary stress." Ahmar no longer sounds like he's satisfied with his answer, and the aching hole in my heart is glad for it. Then he ruins it all by saying, "I hear your relationship with Pete is better now since enrolling at Briarcliff. Am I wrong?"

I don't enjoy proving Ahmar right, so I follow up with, "It could've improved faster if I were kept in school in the city."

"Calla."

My shoulders fall. "Fine. Dad and I are back on track. But there's more to this story ... more than what anyone involved is telling you."

"Kid, me and my team squeezed that school dry. I hate to tell you, it's a dead end."

I take a deep breath. "What I've found out won't be on any records. It's not spoken about publicly. And anyone involved will deny it well after their death."

"I think you need to get some sleep. You're making me a little worried, kid."

My stomach flips, my throat so thick with fear, but I

forge on. "That extracurricular my mom was talking about? It's more of a cult. And I think she tried to back out of it, which is why Sabine took her as such a threat."

"Let's not get ahead of ourselves. We're talking school shenanigans. After time passed, your momma lived a good life—"

"Until someone took it away. Someone took her from *me*. I'm going to send you some documents, Ahmar. And before I'm labeled as a psychiatric threat again, I want you to not just read them, but research them. This is so much more than a school club. It's a rigged college acceptance scheme, interference with the economy and political agendas, and a sex ring. *That's* what my mom was running from, and what Sabine is in charge of now."

My breath *whooshes* out. My heart slams, pounds, ricochets off my chest and races all the way down to my fingers and toes. But I said it. I put it out there.

And I pray I haven't just handed Ahmar a bomb that could put him in serious trouble.

At first, I think the line's gone dead. I hear nothing from Ahmar's side.

Then: "Those are some heavy accusations, kid."

"Please believe me. Or, if you don't, look into it and prove me wrong. *Please,* Ahmar. I'm in over my head. I need help."

I squeeze my eyes shut, remembering the last time I begged for his help, and he cuffed my dad and arrested the wrong man. Ruining my dad's reputation, and destroying his trust in me.

"This is different," I add. "I have proof. Evidence."

He doesn't answer. Too much silence has passed since I last spoke. "Ahmar?"

Ahmar breathes audibly. Soon, careful words follow. "Kid, I didn't need to promise your momma I'd be there for you forever. I'd do it anyway. Yes, I will look into it. Send me what you have, but I can't promise you there will be a change."

This time, when I close my eyes, it's with a sigh of relief. "I appreciate it."

"Do something for me. Get some sleep before school."

"I will," I lie. But my next words hold nothing but the truth. "I love you."

"Love you, too, kiddo. Too much, sometimes. Talk soon."

When we hang up, the first thing I do is send him the Virtue Member List containing Mom and Lynda's names, proving Lynda could know more than she said. Then Dad's class photo. And, as a mysterious cherry on top that I'd love to know the flavor of, the birth certificate of Rose Briar's illegitimate baby girl. Maybe Ahmar could trace the lineage. His knowledge of Rose Briar's family could perhaps lead him to physical proof of the existence of the Nobles and Virtues.

Balling my hands into fists, I curse losing my copies of Piper's diary. I mourn the brief existence of Howard Mason's writings hidden in my calc textbook before it was stolen and given back to the societies.

I'm relying on my gut to lead me in the right direction, at the same time it churns with uncertainty.

And for the second time, I've used that instinct to involve Ahmar.

bounce on the balls of my feet, waiting for Ivy to notice me. When she finally turns into the hallway, she yelps and trips to a stop seconds before bumping into me.

"Lord, Callie! Save the creeping around in the shadows for our nighttime adventures, would you?"

I offer up lamely, "I wanted to catch you before our next class."

Ivy shifts the pile of books in her arms. "For what?"

"I'm wondering when I get the rulebook."

Ivy clutches her texts to her chest, then elbows me into the empty classroom. "Are you out of your mind? Don't ask for things like that in public!"

Expecting that answer, I interlace my fingers, and ask, with innocent charm, "I take that as a *not any time soon*?"

"Your third trial's complete. Sabine will schedule a date

for the ceremony where you'll pledge your loyalty, accept your robe, and become an official Virtue."

"I assume Sabine's scheduling is at her leisure."

Ivy responds with a pained look. "Sorry."

"There's no time to wait for her. I might have a lead on something. Can I borrow yours?"

Ivy squints at me. "This was a setup, wasn't it?"

I give an offhand shrug. "Do you have it handy?"

"It's in my room, in the locked drawer of my bedside table. Here." Ivy digs in her blazer pocket and pulls out a silver key. "Go and satisfy your curiosity, but don't tell anyone I gave you access."

"Never. We're on the same side, Ivy."

Ivy's fingers tighten around the key before releasing it into my hand. "I hope you're right."

When the key drops into my palm, I hold her hand and squeeze. She looks up at me in surprise.

"I will not let Sabine schedule another Tuesday, do you understand?"

Ivy blinks. Swallows.

"However I can stop this, I will. You are no longer Sabine's slave."

Ivy holds my stare and whispers, "How can you be so sure?"

"My mother was a Virtue. She and Sabine had beef long before you and I were born. And like us, my mother tried to leave them. They punished her, made her suffer the rest of her year here, but ... she went into hiding and was able to live a life without them. Up until my enrollment, she kept me from becoming a legacy."

Ivy shakes her head. "That's not possible. Once you become a Virtue and accept their privileges, you're indebted to their cause for life."

"Which is why I need that rulebook. I don't think my mom became invisible like she thought she did. The societies must have kept track of her somehow. She married my stepdad, who went here. And now he's married to her classmate. And after her death, I became a freshman at the very school she ran away from. It took me a while to figure out, but ... it isn't just about Sabine bringing me under the society's control to stop me from exposing the Virtues. This is about my mother. Whatever's in those pages might tell me what *she* found to get them to let her go."

My confession to Ivy leaves me out of breath but determined to trek through the bitter cold to Richardson Place. The afternoon air is so frigid, it's like walking through a block of ice, and I pull my faux fur-lined hood closer around my face as I clomp down a paved walkway that's begging for another snowplow to come around again.

It's supposed to blizzard tonight. I forgot that nugget of relevancy when I shot up in bed this morning. My dreams were so relaxed (for once) that my mind was able to toil away behind the scenes, picking up jagged pieces of collected information and fitting them just right before the answer slapped me awake.

And when I stared blindly at the wall across from my

bed, my eyes stretched wide, I thought, *There it is. The missing clue.*

There is a deeper connection to this school and my mother than I was initially willing to consider. A festering one. Why else would Meredith Ryan, the strongest, most independent, and fiercely loyal woman I knew, capitulate to a mean girl like Sabine?

Mom worked herself ragged when I was young. Her hands were nothing but reddened, knobby stubs from all the detergent she was forced to work with while she cleaned office buildings at night. It wasn't until she began cleaning the precinct, that she noticed someone left a folded newspaper by their computer with a half-completed crossword. During one break, she finished that crossword and left it on the desk. The following night, that day's newspaper was left open again, this time a quarter completed. She filled in the words once more. It became a nightly ritual that eventually had her meeting Ahmar, working late, and he used her innate strategic abilities to help convince her to be more.

Looking back, I see that my mom was a broken version of herself. Somebody swung down a power stick, and it shattered across my mother's back. And a woman like my mother—boisterous, pragmatic, sincere, smart, and an expert at spotting the smallest details—would never have been put in that position unless she was given no choice.

She may not be alive anymore, but I'd like to gift her that freedom back.

When she died, and after the initial investigation was over, Dad packed up her things and put them in storage to go through later, when I felt ready. More clues might lie in the items she left behind, and I make a mental note to call Dad and ask him to send a few boxes over—once I've prepared myself enough to talk to him.

He and Lynda are on my list, but I must see this theory through, first. Ahmar may have thought it a coincidence, but I never inherited my mother's pragmatism, nor did his wash off on me.

The last time I confronted my dad, it ended horribly and with me on a mental hold. This time, I'll be holding evidence of Briarcliff Academy's duplicity in my hands before I accuse him of helping the Nobles and possibly *marrying* my mother to ensure her continued docility.

The thought makes me unsteady, and I walk faster through the falling snow, eager to breathe air that isn't filled with microscopic icicles taking up space in my lungs.

I key open Ivy's door, but since my departure from the academy, the wind kicked up, and a boatload of snow follows me in.

"Damn it, Callie!" Eden pops up from her desk chair, runs past me, and slams the door shut. "I *just* got the room to a decent heat level!"

"I didn't think anyone would be here."

"It's independent study this afternoon. Remember? Exams start tomorrow."

"Oh." I blow a lank, half-frozen strand of hair from my face while I pull my hood back. "Right."

"What are you doing here?"

I hold up Ivy's key with numbed fingers. "Her copy of the Virtues' rulebook is by her bed. I'm here to read it."

Eden blinks. "Points for blunt honesty. Fine, go ahead."

While Eden goes back to studying at her desk, I slip off my coat and make sure to hang it on the coatrack under Eden's hairy eyeball. My socked feet make no sound as I head over to Ivy's side, sit on her bed, and unlock her bedside table.

The rulebook is where she said it would be, and I pull it out, sliding a palm down the buttery leather and gold foil lettering of her full name: *Ivara Alling.*

How must it have felt to receive this kind of belonging? I trace the edges of her name. How must it have felt to have that belonging ripped away from you and replaced with fear?

I carefully open the book, my head bowed over the pages.

My hovering doesn't stop the watchful prickles from heating my neck, however.

"Eden, are you interested in reading this, too?" I ask without moving.

After a creak and a shuffle, the bed dips under me when Eden takes a seat. "What are you looking for?"

"Anything relating to my mother," I say, turning the page.

"Your mom?"

"Oh yeah, she's a Virtue." I read the next page, containing the rules and decorum of a Virtuous member.

"Jeez, I miss one day with you guys and already I'm way behind on the revelations. She went to Briarcliff?"

"That's the theory." I flip to another page, my brows growing tauter the more I find block paragraphs of etiquette and appropriate dress codes. "When was this written?"

Eden slams her hand on the open pages, smacking it into my lap. "The 1820s. And your confused face is correct. The moral code is way out-of-date from current Virtue practices. Mrs. Harrington thinks these books are wasted materials modern women don't need. Ivy didn't tell you that?"

"She didn't have to," I say on a sigh. "I told her I wanted the rules, and I guess I have them. But I thought it would give me more clues. This is so *frustrating*." I push the heels of my hands against my temples. "I feel like all I do is sift through papers written in a secret code I can't read."

"You haven't tried asking me." Eden stares at me attentively. "I've broken into Ivy's drawer and read that thing a thousand times. Whatever you're looking for, I might be able to save you a ton of wasted reading time."

"You go through Ivy's things?"

"You went through Piper's. Now ask me your question."

Touché. "I've just found out my mother went to school here with Sabine and Daniel."

"The two current leaders of the secret societies," Eden muses. "Interesting."

"It's why I'm scouring the Virtues' rulebook, because I think my mom was also a member of the Virtues." I lift my head and stare at the ceiling, allowing my thoughts to take over. "When I first came here, I found the societies' crest, hidden in the trophy case by Marron's office."

Eden nods. "I've seen it."

"It had a familiarity to it ... one I couldn't put my finger on. It might be because I recognize it from somewhere in my past. I plan to go through Mom's boxes when I'm home for Christmas. See if I can find ... something."

"Well." Eden lifts the rulebook from my hands. "A lot of this is moot because of Sabine's overhaul of the Virtues' record-keeping. Back when your mom was attending, it wasn't. So, hmm..." Eden fans through the book, running her finger down the pages as she skims. "Here it is."

I lean over her shoulder.

"The Virtues have differing opinions from the Nobles, even back then. When these societies were first created, Rose Briar adopted the same rules and initiation rites as the Nobles."

"Like what?"

"Tradition over change. The men handled all the money, like alumni donations, robe purchases, site maintenance. If the Virtues had a leaky pipe in their toilets, they had to go to the Nobles for approval to obtain funding to fix it. That sort of thing."

I wrinkle my nose.

"Exactly," Eden says. "The women members wanted to carve their own paths and obtain independent power over the men. So, while they used *this* in obvious sight of the Nobles, secretly, they created rules to reflect their views, *not* the Nobles'. The queen who replaced Rose figured out a way to siphon money from the main bank account into a secret one, only for the Virtues." Eden brightens. "Which, I think, is the first documented case of embezzlement in Briarcliff history."

I laugh under my breath. "Good for her."

"Back then it was good. *They* were good, decent, and damn smart. That's what you get for harboring the best and brightest women under your wings but become blind to what goes on in between the thick feathers. These women toiled, conspired, and fought for their independent rights. They married CEOs but handled the bank accounts. Started dating future presidents while advising them under her breath in their ear. Founded their own companies, spearheaded some of the most successful non-profits in the world ... all under the Nobles' unassuming eye."

"That's wonderful." And I mean it. "I always thought Rose had good intentions creating the Virtues."

Eden side-eyes me but doesn't expand on the topic. I wonder if she knows, whether by going through Ivy's stuff, or because she keeps an ear to the ground, what Sabine asks of her top girls in order to keep those accessory positions these days.

"Getting to my point," Eden says, then taps a section of the rulebook. I peer closer. "Most of these rules are inapplicable except for this one."

I squint, then reread the bold title. "The rules of succession?"

Eden reads the paragraph out loud. "'A direct descendent of the blood of a Briar will forever maintain leadership and accord over the prestigious Virtuous members.' And look here." Eden skims over the requirements of being considered a Briar blood-relation to subsection (c). "'If a member of the Briar lost lineage is subsequently revealed, herein after referred to as a 'Hidden Briar,' that Hidden Briar has the automatic right to overthrow a Queen in power over the Virtues, provided the Hidden Briar possesses a relation stronger than the current Queen."

I straighten. "This is to be expected. From what I've

gleaned of the Briars, they were egotistical, power-hungry males, willing to leave anyone considered below them behind."

Eden looks up from the book, her cheeks blooming in a flush of excitement the longer she studies me. "Uh-huh. Keep going."

I give an uncertain smile, unused to friendly encouragement from her. "Okay. Well, does the blood-relation requirement include illegitimate children?"

Eden's smile stretches wide. "Yes! It's like you said—the Nobles were assholes with a hero complex, and they gave rights to their illegitimate heirs. Granted, the rightful heir had a stronger hold on the throne, but an illegitimate son, born to Thorne Briar for example, had more of a claim to leading the Nobles than, say, a distant cousin."

I lose my breath for a moment when I latch on to Eden's explanation. "And the Virtues copied the text directly from the Nobles' rulebook."

Eden's answering smile shows a row of bright, white teeth. "And never changed it."

My heart pounds in my ears. "Rose Briar had an illegitimate daughter with Theodore Briar, Thorne's brother. I found the birth certificate hidden in Daniel Stone's personal files."

"Looks like you've found yourself a Hidden Briar. Buried into nonexistence. You discovered it in Daniel Stone's study, but where was it before? Why have the Nobles been keeping it a secret?"

I whisper, finishing, "Instead of destroying it?"

Eden snaps the book shut. "It's the Nobles' leverage over

the queen. I guarantee it. Because I will bet you more naked pictures of me that Mrs. Harrington is not a descendent of the Briars. In fact, ever since Rose died, there hasn't *been* a direct descendent in power for almost two-hundred years. The Briar brothers all had sons."

"Holy shit." I stand, move, my footsteps matching the pace of this revelation pounding into my brain. "So that means we have—"

"A traceable way of finding the true Virtue queen." Eden spears up from the bed, throwing her arms wide. "And kicking Sabine to the curb. Holy fuck, Callie. Holy, fucking, FUCK."

"Wait." I raise my hand, though my heart is slamming into my throat. "This is big. We have to think this through. If we have a weapon to overthrow Sabine, we need to protect it. I *have* to tell Chase how important that birth certificate is before he accidentaly reveals it to Tempest or someone else."

Eden cocks her head. "Wait, you think the birth certificate is the weapon?"

"Well, yeah."

"Oh, dear." Eden comes up and puts her hands on my shoulders, searching my face. "You haven't thought this through as much as I hoped."

I search her eyes just as thoroughly. "I've had two minutes since reading the succession rules."

A harsh laugh leaves Eden's throat, but she doesn't let go. "I've grown to like you, so I'll say this quick. Think about every minute of your stay here at Briarcliff and who glued themselves to you. Your stepdad went here. So did your stepmom. Your best friend is the Virtue princess. Your not-so-secret crush is the Noble prince. It's all been orchestrated. Ivy *knows,* Callie. Chase does, too. Daniel Stone has probably long ago traced the lineage of Baby Girl Briar."

I lick my lips, but realize my tongue is numb. The weight I thought was coming from Eden's hands has moved into my belly, dragging me down, sinking me through the ground.

The longer Eden stares, the more the weight claims a name. Dread. Sick, inhuman, soul-eating dread.

I try to get the answer out, my lips are stiff, uncooperative. "Y-you think..."

"That your mom was Rose Briar's descendent? At this point and with the people we're dealing with, I'd be surprised if she wasn't. Or ... *dude.*"

"What?" I practically shriek.

"This dad you don't know about. What if *he's* the tie to the Briar line? Either way..."

"That would mean..."

"That you are, too." Eden's smile turns grim. "Your coming to Briarcliff was not a coincidence, Callie. Someone wanted to keep tabs on you and keep their enemies close."

"No." But it comes out soundless, and I spin out of Eden's grip. My features contort as I twist back to my friend. "*No*, Eden. That can't be right. Because that also means—that means—"

"Your mom's murder may not have been so random," Eden says. "Especially if, through Daniel Stone, Sabine discovered who Meredith Ryan could be the mother of."

Hot, sticky tears well in my eyes. I don't wipe them away

when they fall. I stand my ground. Stare soullessly at Eden. Then I give voice to the demon blackening my bones.

"If I'm a descendent of Rose Briar, and Sabine found out … she killed her. Sabine killed my mom to force me to go to Briarcliff."

33

———

Betrayal isn't supposed to make me blind.

Yet, I can't see anything as I shoot out of Eden and Ivy's dorm and into the frigid evening air, the stars so dim, they vaguely light my way home.

Snow crunches beneath my boots as I finish zipping my jacket and stumble up the jagged walkway to Thorne House. My fingers shake as I pull out my phone and try to send a text, but the screen is too bright, and I can't read the message chain even when I squint.

Eden doesn't cry out for me to come back. If I turn and take one last look at Richardson Place, I doubt I'll see her in the doorway I left open when I flew out of there. She dropped her nuggets of wisdom, then sat back to see what I would do.

It's not her mother whose past has been broken open. Eden had never heard of Meredith Ryan before she was brutally murdered in her own bedroom.

By the Virtues.

"No," I whisper, shaking my head. "It's not true. It's not real."

My paranoia's taking over. My unfounded convictions are building in my throat, desperate to be torn out with one long, never-ending scream.

I blink, and I'm in the psych ward, restrained and flailing in my hospital bed.

I open my eyes, and my stepdad faces me, until he's marched out of our home, his hands cuffed behind his back.

I trip, my hands plowing into a mound of snow, and I'm blinded by the white noise of my actions, the wrongness of them swirling around my head and telling me to *stay down.*

"I-I can't," I tremble out while resting on my haunches. My bare hands have immediately gone red and ache with cold. "I can't be silenced this time."

I can't be wrong.

My phone bounced into a snowdrift nearby when I stumbled, and on a hitched sob, I reach back into the cold and grab it. I say into its speaker, "C-call Dad."

Lifting the phone to my ear, I wait for him to answer.

And when a bubbly, audibly exhausted new father answers, the stone in my gut sinks deeper. "Cal, hey!"

"H-hi."

His tone immediately changes. "Honey? You okay? You sound a little distant."

"I'm..." I breathe out, my exhale turning white against the darkness before dissipating. "I'm outside, walking back to the dorms. That's all."

"Ah. Okay, good. Say, why don't we FaceTime? I have someone who'd love to meet you."

I squeeze my eyes against the ache at the same time I say, "Dad, did you go to Briarcliff?"

A few seconds pass. Something squeaks in the background, and though I've never heard a newborn before, my baser instincts tell me its Blair. "What's that, hon?"

I stumble out of the snowdrift. "You're a graduate of Briarcliff Academy. Class of '04."

"That's—"

"And so is Lynda. 2002, the same year as *Mom*." My voice becomes pitchy, my steps uneven. "The three of you went to this school, and neither you nor Lynda told me you did before sending me here. Why?"

"I didn't want to skew your view of the academy by admitting your mother went there. You were hit so hard by her death, honey. We all were. But when Lynda said she could get you in—through no urging of mine—I couldn't pass it up. It could open so many doors for you. It provided so many possibilities you weren't getting—"

"Like it did for Mom? We were *hermits*, Dad." I bare my teeth despite the flickers of snowflakes coming at my face. "Before we met you, Mom was barely getting by. She had me dumpster diving for our dinner so she could work two jobs. I'd wait up for her every night until she came home because I wasn't sure how safe she was. We had nobody, *no one,* to call a friend. Not until Ahmar. And then ... you."

I hear Dad's sharp inhale at the insinuation. "What are you getting at?"

"Were you told to meet my mom? To seduce her and marry her?"

"Oh, Jesus. Honey, don't do this. Not again."

There's true terror in his voice, but I can't contain myself. Not after I held in my hands the very reason my mother could've been killed. My voice crackles in the air, splits and divides into scattered explosions, and I don't relent. "Did the Virtues tell you to find her, to make us feel safe, then for you to step aside while they *killed* her?"

"Callie—"

"And then assured you Lynda would be waiting for you on the other side, with her wealth and privilege and safe haven, so you could forget about the murder you helped commit—"

"Calm down. Calm down this *instant*, Calla Lily!" Dad roars.

"*She's dead because of them!*" I shriek. *Because of me.* "The Virtues! The Nobles! They killed her because of some *rulebook!*"

"CALLA LILY RYAN!"

I yank the phone from my ear, grimacing, crying, howling with the building wind.

"That's it," his small voice says from the phone's earpiece. "I'm coming over there and we're packing you up early. You're coming home, young lady. Briarcliff was a mistake."

"It was," I sob, then crumble to the ground, my knees sinking into the snow. "It's shown me too much. I didn't want to know my mom went here. I want the mom I knew. I want my mom..."

My sentences fade away, taken by the winter air, and my head bows, tears trickling down the tip of my nose and splashing into the snow.

"Give me the phone, Pete."

An argument sounds out on the other end, Lynda jumping in with indecipherable sentences, until the phone shuffles between them and she becomes clearer.

"Pete may be afraid, but I'm not anymore, honey."

My head lifts. "W-what?"

"You are not crazy, okay? I don't think you're having a break down. I don't believe you need any medical intervention." Her voice is soft, soothing.

Until Dad argues something I can't catch.

"*Enough* of this, Pete. I'm tired. You're exhausted. We have a new baby. I'm not playing this game anymore. Are you still with us, Callie?"

I wipe my sleeve across my nose, my breathing coming out in faster puffs. "I'm here."

"You mentioned the Virtues. You know they exist."

I swallow through the swollen, aching emotion in my throat. "Yes."

"Then I'll tell you what you don't know." Lynda's tone, so matter-of-fact, sets me on a bated edge. "A few weeks ago, Pete lost his job when he did nothing wrong. There was no warning, no list of circumstances offered as to why he was being let go. All he understood was the subtle crest of the raven imprinted on one of his boss's office photos."

I think back to when Chase was punished for my breaking into the temple. I thought it ended there. What a fool I was. "The Nobles fired him?"

"I'm convinced it was under the Virtues' direction. Honey, I'm a Virtue, too. And I never spoke to her much, but I ... I knew your mom."

Though I'm not surprised, my face still falls. "You never said a word."

"For your protection. I figured out, pretty early, Sabine's hatred for Meredith—your mom. At that time, I couldn't do much about it. We were just freshmen. Powerless. And Sabine, while a freshman, had the ear of the queen of the Virtues. Her grandmother. For reasons I don't quite gather, Sabine was able to convince her grandmother to make Meredith's initiation difficult, almost impossible, to pass. Meredith and I weren't close, and I was never a witness to her initiation rituals, but I ... I saw her fading away. Bit by bit, as the days passed, and the hazing didn't stop. It's hard to explain, but I saw Sabine grow healthier, glowing, enjoying every moment of your mom's torture."

My lips tremble, and it takes everything I have left to hold them closed. I imagine my mother, forcing herself to continue the ritual because of the promise of being a Virtue. The possibilities. The prospects.

The forced sexual favors.

"Did she ... was part of her initiation being involved in a sex ring?"

For a moment, all Lynda does is breathe. "Honey, I wish I could explain what really happened between her and Sabine, but your mom didn't tell a soul. When she passed the trials and became a Virtue, she never spoke about her initiation. But she—it's so hard to be an outsider for this, and I'm so *sorry* I didn't do more at the time. Meredith left abruptly during our freshmen year and finished her schooling through distance learning. I was never sure why. Not until I received a phone call, a few months ago, to transfer you into Briarcliff Academy."

I scrub my eyes. I still can't *see* straight. "Why didn't you go to the police? If the Virtues threatened your family, why didn't you tell Ahmar? Or me? Or *someone*, that this was going on?"

"You and I both know that I couldn't."

Blair cries out. Dad's quiet shushing follows.

I say what Lynda doesn't. "You didn't want to say anything because you were making a family. They threatened you when you were pregnant."

"*You* are part of this family, Callie. We did this to keep you safe. Please believe me. If I didn't do as they said, if I ignored their orders..."

"They would've gotten me here another way." I stare off into the white-washed forest, a strange dullness taking over my body. They'd already moved my mother, the one force blocking my entry into Briarcliff, out of the picture.

"Not all of them, honey," Lynda says quietly. "You have allies."

None of her assurances hit where they're supposed to. "Was Sabine responsible for this? For getting me here, watching me, and making sure I didn't solve my mom's murder?"

"I assume your presence there is related to your mother, but I can't tell you if Sabine is responsible for your mother's death."

Though I'm so stiff with cold, I push to a stand. "So,

what *do* you know? What were you and Dad planning behind my back?"

"Oh, honey." Lynda sighs, the saddened vibration tickling my ears. "We were at a loss on what to do. Pete was terrified. When it came to the Briarcliff societies, we couldn't escape. And a part of him—a part of *me*—hoped you were just as much protected as you were monitored at that school. Not all Virtues are cruel. Not all Nobles allow the rules to bend until they're non-existent. I know, because I'm one of those members."

I hold my breath, then blow it out, the sifting cloud of my exhale dissipating in the frosty air. "What about Dad?"

"Pete's not one of them, honey. I had to explain the existence of Briarcliff secret societies when we received that phone call over the summer."

I close my eyes and massage my forehead, but it feels like being soothed by frozen ice-pops on my skin.

"Meredith died nineteen years after high school, honey. I had no contact with her after she left Briarcliff. And your father and I, we recognized each other at the banquet as alumnus from Briarcliff. It's how we struck up a conversation. Pete and I getting together had nothing to do with my or your mother's involvement with the Virtues."

My boots crunch into the packed snow as I resume a shaking, unsteady walk. I believe Lynda when she says she had no ulterior motives when meeting my stepdad. She's sweet, open, kind. And so far, she's the sole Virtue, who, when pressed, has told me everything she could.

I can't disregard that.

I also can't ignore the niggling in the back of my mind.

"That banquet you and Dad attended at the Met. Was Sabine there, too?"

I sense more than hear Lynda's hesitation. Blair whimpers in the background. "Yes. Yes, she was."

My eyes fall shut. "How sure are you that your reunion with Dad was a coincidence?"

"I ... oh." Lynda trails off, her voice trembling.

"It's okay." I look up at the lights of Thorne House, growing closer with each step. "Go back to Blair and Dad."

"Honey—"

"It's almost the holidays. I'll see you then. I love you."

"Are you safe? Why don't you come home?"

"Not yet." My breathing grows steadier, my strides longer, as I hit the entryway to Thorne House.

I don't leave room for more argument, or for my dad to come on the line and order I come home. They put me here.

And now it's up to me to figure out how to best utilize the remainder of my time at Briarcliff Academy.

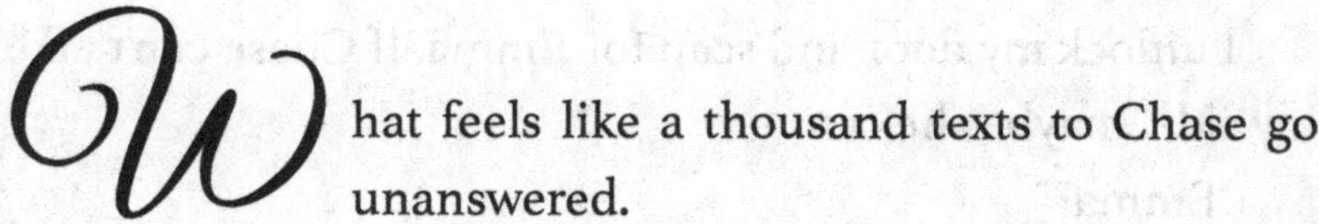

34

What feels like a thousand texts to Chase go unanswered.

He won't pick up his phone, either. I chew on my thumbnail, staring at my screen, waiting for the elevator to open onto my floor.

I wish he were here. I ache for his reassuring weight against my side, or the way he tucks my head under his chin, squeezing me close.

I'm empty without him. There's no one to receive my worries or help figure out just how the Virtues got to my mother.

As if called upon, logic sifts through my frantic thoughts, asking, *Whose side would he take?*

Chase has never once proclaimed his separation from the Nobles. He wants to stay a member and become their leader. He's sure of his ability to turn them around.

Would my belief that the Virtues killed her ruin his plans to preserve the Nobles?

Yes.

That singular conclusion leaves me standing in an elevator, bleak and alone.

Providing exam answers and manipulating college acceptances is one thing. But murder? If proven right, I could never keep that from Ahmar. I'd happily expose the secret societies in order to avenge my mother.

I stare down at my phone.

Chase must've figured that out, which is why he isn't answering.

I unlock my door and scan for Emma. If Chase can't take my side, maybe she can.

"Emma?"

No answer.

I hang up my damp winter coat, melted snowflakes landing silently on the floorboards.

Scraping back my hair, I finish my brief search of the central area and her room, both empty. Phone still in my hand, I walk to my side of the apartment and text:

Emma, where are you? I need to

When I glance up to enter my bedroom, I stop mid-sentence.

There, on my bedspread, sits a perfect white rose with a note attached.

I don't want to know is my first thought, but I quench it as quickly as I drop my phone beside the flower. After the revelation of my mother, I must keep up the pretense and play to Sabine in hopes I'll find something more concrete to hand over to Ahmar or Detective Haskins.

Your death won't go unnoticed anymore, Mom. I swear it.

Grimly, I pick up the letter and unfold it at the single crease.

You are hereby summoned to the temple post haste.

My cheeks puff out with an exhale, and I throw the note back on the bed. Sabine wants me on her turf? Fine.

I spin to my closet.

This time, I refuse to face her unprepared.

After pressing my finger on the hidden panel, the back wall of the library opens to the Virtue's Temple.

It's incredibly well-lit compared to the darkness of the closed library, and I squint at the unexpected brightness, costing me precious seconds.

I step through, my gaze adjusting and landing on three figures in the center, one taller than the rest.

I tread faster, the figures snapping into focus—

"That's far enough, my dear."

Sabine's liquid voice soaks into the air, and my feet

follow the order before my mind has a chance to catch up to the scene. When it does...

I shake my head as if to dislodge a hazy dream clinging to me as I wake. Yet, ice water shock floods my system, proving my wishes wrong.

Sabine smiles coyly as she lays her hands on the heads of Chase and Ivy. Both on their knees. Both with their arms tied behind them.

I meet Chase's eyes first, so intense, so level, and filled with the promise of impending fury. His rebellious will soaks into my bones the longer I hold the connection, and I pull on that strength and hold it close. It hurts to drag my gaze away from him, but I have to see if Ivy's okay.

She is, but her stance isn't nearly as defiant. Her entire body shakes, and her eyes turn wet at the sight of me.

Both Ivy and Chase's mouths are unbound, yet neither say a word.

I meet Sabine's stare last. "What is this?"

"My sweet Virtues tell me you've learned a secret."

I don't let the surprise show on my face, but my thoughts tick back in time frantically, wondering where, how, Sabine could have heard.

Eden? Would *Eden* have said something?

"Where's my sister?" Chase growls.

Sabine takes her time looking down at him, but her warning is imprinted in every subtle, cruel line on her face. "One more word, little prince, and I'll show her to you."

That isn't a reassurance. Chase's expression grows dark, black caverns forming under his eyes, but he tears his attention from Sabine and turns to me. "Let her do whatever she wants to me, Callie. Just save my sister."

I nod, my face numbed with terror, but I force my voice strong when I say to Sabine, "What's to stop me from calling the Nobles? You can't treat their prince this way. Not without consequence. And your own princess? What are you doing, Sabine?"

"Ah yes," Sabine says, her voice tranquil and light. "We societies do have our rules, don't we? We follow them rigorously. To the letter. At least, my counterparts do. As for me? I prefer to do whatever it takes to stay in power. Look around, Calla Lily."

I do, noticing the empty balcony above. The closed temple door behind me.

"This is not for my society to witness, nor is it for the Nobles to take part in. The Virtues have claimed independence with my rule, and what can the Nobles do about it? *We* have the highest positions in the country. *We* have the longest reaching influence. And if the Nobles want to continue, they'll curtsy to my commands."

"*You* have committed murder!" My voice ricochets off the walls, echoing my vitriol.

"My, my, you've been busy."

"You killed my mother." I'm not as steady now, but I call upon Chase's fury and absorb it into mine.

Ivy gasps, but one look from Sabine, and she droops, hiding her face in her hair. She's so afraid, so desperate to save her family, she'll fall to her knees and allow her queen to tie her up despite everything Sabine's done to her. *Oh, Ivy...*

"You put your girls up as prostitutes," I continue, fueled and hungry for hate. "Emma had to disfigure herself to get away from you."

Chase goes white, a marble statue carved in rage. *He really didn't know* hits me between the eyes, but I barrel forward.

"Your own daughter turned against you and helped Emma. Then you locked Emma in a fire in case she talked, but you failed, because she survived. Your *other* daughter will rot in prison for the rest of her life. What kind of leader does that make you? No wonder my mother wanted nothing to do with you. No *wonder* she was willing to give up her natural-born right to the Virtues and escape the filth your family created—"

"*How dare you*," Sabine hisses, her venom permeating the air. "You think reading some old papers gives you the right to question my leadership? My abilities to turn these girls into strong, hardened women who bow to no man? It is because of me they thrive outside of this school. It's because of the Virtues' continued reach that we possess power, prestige, *riches*, for lifetimes after."

"My mom wouldn't know about that. Ivy sure doesn't." I angle my head. "And neither do your daughters."

Sabine's cheeks splotch with rage, a sound like a death rattle emitting from her throat. "You mistake the reason for your presence here, dear girl. You will never smite me. You *will* bow to my will, just like every other girl who's attempted to thwart me, and dares question my reign."

I level my shoulders, notch my chin, but I look to Ivy,

and then Chase. "You didn't kill all the Ryans. The societal crown belongs to me."

Chase doesn't blink. His granite eyes are hard and his jaw tauter than a predator's on its prey. And as I speak, his expression holds.

Eden was right.

He knows.

My frantic blinks can't be helped, my heart hammering for my body to respond to the shock. I move to Ivy, my sweet, loyal friend ... and her forehead creases. Her eyes slant with sadness. But her mouth doesn't go slack.

This entire time, they knew about my heritage.

"Child." Sabine laughs, but it is brittle and empty in such a vast room. "You truly believe I killed Meredith?"

I stand my ground, fuming silently.

"I take that as a yes. Well, dear, I have more important tasks than hunting down a former housekeeper turned smut photographer."

Outrage spirals into my throat. "You don't have the right to lead the Virtues, and you haven't for a long time. You hid the truth, Sabine. And you indoctrinated those who'd continue hiding it for you." I take a long look at Ivy, at Chase. "Not anymore."

"And what will you do about it, little lamb? I have years of experience over you. Decades of duplicity. You. Are. Mine."

"I'll never be yours to control."

"Nor will you ever reach your full potential then, I'm afraid. Already you've shown your crutch." Sabine's expression grows sly. "You came here thinking both you and your mother were meant to be killed. I'll provide you a counter-argument. Your mother proved her unwillingness to surrender to the new Virtue rule when she ran and left Briarcliff far behind, thus becoming expendable. But you, my dear, you are young. Impressionable. Moldable. And if Rose's child's birth certificate ever surfaced, it was best to manipulate you onto the right side. Isn't that right, Chase?"

My heartbeat thrashes so hard, it pulses in my fingertips and booms in my soul. I can't move, because I'm quaking.

Chase seethes, but as he replies to Sabine, he only has eyes for me. "We had that birth certificate under Noble protection for a reason. It was meant to keep the Virtues under our thumb."

"So, dear, did you seduce Calla Lily for the Nobles, or the Virtues?" Sabine smiles. "That's a lovely thought, that the boy you love has manipulated you either way."

I feel sick, yet I'm starving. Aching for the truth, I ask Chase, "Did you know? What she was doing to her top girls? To Ivy, to *Emma*?"

"No." Chase's answer is almost a howl, grinding against his teeth.

"Did your father?"

Chase opens his mouth to respond but can't.

"Daniel understands the importance of power as much as I do," Sabine supplies. "He and I agreed, so long as I was successful, there was no need to reveal Rose Briar's secret line."

"Until your daughter found out." I dare to step forward. "First Piper discovered what you'd done to Emma and the men you expected her to have sex with. Then she found out about Rose's baby. Didn't she?"

"Callie," Ivy pleads. "Stop. You're saying too much. Please."

"Why?" I ask my friend. "The secret's out. I'm not the only one who plans to stop her." I raise my eyes to Sabine. "Do what you want to me, but it's too late. People outside this room are coming for you."

Instead of backing into my trap, Sabine's stare glitters with malice. "Dear girl. When will you finally concede that I will always be one step ahead?"

Suddenly, I tune into the sounds of my breaths, loud and extraordinary in a room that houses at least four people.

Then, realization hits.

Because Chase has stopped breathing. And Ivy looks on with a sickly, silent, dreadful cast.

I anxiously search their faces for answers. *What am I missing?*

Too soon, Sabine provides the missing link. "Shutting you up is much too easy. I can't kill you, but I do want to hurt you, and I don't have to pierce your body to know I've torn out your heart."

My mouth forms on a *W.* But I don't give my question voice. My shock doesn't have sound. Sabine draws a knife from her bodice, and it glints in the sconce's light. Lances down. My scream unleashes with the steel.

"*No!*"

I fly forward, rushing for them both, desperate to save

them *both*, but instinct tells me who Sabine is after before my feet hit the air.

I hit Chase, and he braces for me. I topple him, sending us to the floor and digging my chin into his neck, prepared for the blade to sink into my back...

But nothing comes.

35

A wet gasp sounds out to my left.

I raise my head, hair falling into my face. Through the tangled strands, I meet widened, glistening, terrified blue eyes.

"*Ivy*," I whisper, but her name is so raw with emotion, it comes out as a desolate moan.

"M ... my..." Ivy's hands skate to her neck, where a thin, intricately carved silver handle sticks out of her flawless, white flesh.

Sabine backs away with a cruel twist to her lips, her eyes alight with a vulturine thrill as she watches Ivy flail. I launch to Ivy's side, heedless of any impending danger, and bring my fingers up to Ivy's neck as hers dance around the wound.

"P-pressure," I stutter out. Somehow, my voice can be heard through the desperate swelling in my throat. "We need to put pressure on it. Ivy, stay with me. Look at me. Don't ... no, Ivy, don't close your eyes..."

But Ivy's lids flutter closed, and she collapses to her side as she gasps for breath. A keening wail escapes my mouth as I follow her to the ground, tearing off my coat and holding the fabric close to her throat.

"She's choking on her blood. Call 911!" I scream at Chase. I glance over my shoulder and see him standing, but his expression is so sad, his demeanor so dismally accepting, that I screech, *"Call an ambulance!"*

He comes to his knees beside me. "Callie. It's too late."

"It's not! Look at her! She's—she's—Ivy, no. Why isn't she breathing? Wake up. *Wake her up.*" My face crumples. I lean over her, stroking her temple, brushing her hair off her forehead, tracing her cheeks. I croak out, "Please, Ivy, open your eyes."

"Understand this, dear child." Sabine's voice comes from the depths of the temple, despite every section of the circular room being illuminated. Her voice alone brings the darkness, shrouding my hold over Ivy, skittering along the tenuous grip I have on my mind.

She continues, "I have the control over the Virtues, Briarcliff, the Noble prince, *you.* Anyone you attempt to turn against me, I will ruin. I don't have any ties. No reasons to withstand the Nobles or any uprising within my own society. My daughters are gone. You are the daughter to no one. It is essential you understand that, if you wish for any kind of future."

Chase grips my shoulders, but I wrench out of his hold.

"Don't you dare drag me away. I'm not leaving. *I'm not leaving!*"

"We have to go." Chase's command is so unsettling, offering a gravity I have no desire to sink into.

"You're *hers*," I hiss. "I refuse to go anywhere with y—"

Chase swallows the space between us, bringing us almost nose-to-nose. "I will *never* follow Sabine's rules." His guttural whisper coats my lips. "But if we don't get out of here, we'll have to follow Briarcliff PD's. Sabine's probably called the police."

I tear my attention from his face, scanning our surroundings, my hand tightening on Ivy's lifeless, slackened fingers. "She's not gone."

Chase grasps my arm. "Get up, Callie. *Now.*"

"I don't care!" I sob, folding over Ivy, my forehead pressing into her still chest. "She's not dead. *She's not dead!*"

"Swallow the emotion. I know it hurts. Keep the grief inside for just a few minutes. Can you do that for me? We need to get out of here. Get. *Up.*"

My fingers knot in the fabric of Ivy's school uniform. "I can't—I can't leave her. She'd never leave me. I left my mom. It's so cold in here. I have to—"

Strong hands hook under my arms. Chase lifts, but I fight off his grip.

"If I have to drag you out by your fucking hair," he bellows, "*I fucking will!*"

"Ivy!" I sob, scream, howl, my hands clutching at air as Chase encircles my waist and pulls me from the temple.

By the time we burst through the library doors, sirens wail in the distance and red takes over the night sky.

Callie's final REIGN begins in Book 4.
TAKE ME THERE.
(keep reading for a sneak peek)

SNEAK PEEK OF REIGN

Chase and I sprint down the pathway, keeping to the pedestrian trails so our footsteps can't be tracked. Somehow, Chase managed to snag my coat as he struggled to get me out of the building and throws it over my shoulders as we escape.

A sodden piece of the coat hits my cheek.

Ivy's spilled blood is still warm.

My tears are frozen, turning into salted ice that stiffen my cheeks as we fight through the winter chill, but Chase doesn't leave my side. He's so close, I feel his hot breath on my neck every time he exhales, his steady hand landing between my shoulders and coaxing me forward every time a fresh image of a dying Ivy hits the backs of my eyes and I buckle between sprints.

"Almost there," he says, his breaths heavy. "Keep going."

My breath hitches on a sob.

"Don't fall apart yet. I promise, baby, as soon as we get to your room, you can fall apart in my arms. I'm right here. I'm not leaving."

I grip his arm as we run, the hard sinew of muscle bulging against my fingers as he uses every ounce of energy his body has to get us out of there.

There's a tickle of realization as I hold onto his arm. He has no jacket. The thin material of his white button-up Briarcliff shirt is all that separates him from the December winter moon.

He must be freezing.

I think this fact, but it doesn't register past the surface of my brain. The only worry I can come up with has to do with Ivy. The only anxiety I'm concerned about has to do with my friend.

My former friend.

My dead friend.

"Oh, God," I moan, and Chase takes my weight for his own.

He half-carries me the last few feet to Thorne House and hauls me against his side as we sneak through the back. Chase props me up just inside the door, then exits briefly to use a fallen tree branch to obscure our footsteps in the snow.

He brings the cold with him when he shuts the door and carries me up three flights. I grip his neck like a lifeline, breathing in his familiar scent laced with snowflakes, and work to calm my broken heart.

"Almost there," he says into my ear.

I bury my face into his neck, but hear when the lock turns at my apartment door and register the blanket of warmth as soon as he steps out of the hallway.

"What happened?"

Emma's soft voice floats in my periphery, but I've yet to lift my hanging head.

In fact, I've yet to register Chase depositing me on a kitchen stool as he goes to talk to his sister.

"Thank fuck you're here," Chase says, and my eyes lift from the floorboards enough to see him embrace his sister in a hard, emotional hug. "Are you all right?"

"It was the strangest thing," Emma says once they pull apart. "I got a text from Ivy to meet her at the lobster shack in town, but when I went, it was Falyn and Willow waiting for me."

"Goddammit." Chase scrapes a hand down his face. "We thought she had you. That Sabine had taken you."

"Hell no. Just a couple of bitches thinking they could dangle my re-entry into the Virtues like it'd be something I'd desire. Why? What's going on?"

It's here I see the cracks in Chase's glacial demeanor, the stricken lines around his eyes and mouth as he speaks close to Emma's ear.

Emma gasps and rips from his hold. She's immediately at my side, pushing my hair back and eclipsing my vision.

"Callie? Callie, can you hear me?"

I say nothing. Do nothing. Do I blink?

Emma pulls her lips in. "She's in shock."

Chase's presence, as soon as it comes close again, fills my soul and my arms ache to tangle around his neck again. Yet no part of me moves.

His voice carries above my head. "What were you think-ing, Callie?" His tone dips and dives with emotion. "I should've taken the blade. Not Ivy. Not *you*. Why did you get in Sabine's path? *Why* did you protect me?"

My only answer is motionless lips, soaked in tears.

"It should've been me," he whispers. "It should've fucking been me on that floor. I should've protected you both."

Emma cuts in, "Chase. Please. Look at her."

Chase stills. Gives me the once-over. Something at my middle catches his eye. I curl my fingers, but they're stiffer than normal, like a new layer of skin has caked over them.

Not skin. Blood. Dried blood. Ivy's.

I'm lifted in a *whoosh* of strength and carried into the bathroom where Chase resolutely shuts the door in his sister's face.

I want to tell him Emma's seen me in this state before. Naked, shivering, scared. But I can't.

Chase sets me on my feet, running his hands up my arms as he straightens, so gentle, so barely there. He searches my eyes for a moment.

His stare hardens, coming to a decision. Delicately, he unbuttons my blouse and strips it off my form. My skirt is next, my bra, my underwear.

When I'm naked in front of him, his expression doesn't waver or flush with need. He doesn't grit his jaw or indent my skin with his hard grip before he can't contain himself anymore and he covers me with his body.

He does none of that, and I wish he would. I wish for normalcy, for a regular day, for a rewind.

Chase turns on the shower, then strips off his shirt and pants.

Bared, beautiful, he steps up to me, trailing a finger down my cheek. "We'll get through this," he murmurs. "I got you."

I'm lifted into the shower the same way he swept me off my feet in the main room, the warm spray covering my shoulders and splashing his chest as he steps in.

In silence, Chase lathers my body, his sweeping strokes as effective as sweet, whispered *shushes* against my ear. He soothes as well as he commands, and I wonder if Chase knows that.

He cleans my hair, rubs the blood from my fingernails, and massages the tender spots of my body with athletic expertise. He doesn't stop until he hears a relieved, long sigh leave my lips.

When he's toweling me off, he asks, "Can I carry you to bed?"

It takes effort, will, my every fiber, but I meet his eyes and give him the barest of nods.

His chin lowers. "Okay."

He settles me against his chest, his heartbeat falling into my ear.

It's fast, hard, and relentless in its pulse, but it's soothing compared to my erratic rhythm.

I'm laid on top of my covers, my pajama shirt and shorts slipped on with the same ease he peeled my clothes off.

"I'm staying with her," Chase says above me.

"I wasn't about to question it," Emma responds. Somewhere during our trip from the bathroom to my room, she reappeared. "Sleep, if you can. We'll talk more in the morning. Is there any chance the police will knock on our door tonight?"

Chase sighs. "Likely. Callie was Ivy's best friend."

"I still can't believe it. Sabine's out of control." Emma pauses. Then she asks, in a much softer tone, "Did you leave her body there?"

"Yes, but I doubt Sabine wants Ivy discovered in temple. She could've used some Virtues to move Ivy in the library when we left. These girls ... Jesus Christ, Ems. These girls do anything for her."

"This is what our father has missed for *years*. Even with his own daughter. Sabine cultivates us like a predator. She has complete manipulation and control. And..." Emma pauses. "Maybe Father's encouraged it. He certainly encouraged me, in no uncertain terms, to return to the Virtues' fold when I re-enrolled at Briarcliff."

"I had no idea. No fucking clue you were being used like this. And what you did to yourself? What Piper helped do to you? She beat you with your permission. *Emma*." Chase's tone breaks off at the end, the first, and only, clue of grief he's allowed to permeate the air. "Why didn't you tell me? I could've done something. Exposed the Virtues to the rest of the Nobles. I can guarantee not every one of us would be so accepting of our sisters used as fucking *sex* slaves."

"Some of those very Nobles you speak of stepped up to the side of my bed."

Chase's breaths heave in response, a bull readying his horns for a disemboweling.

Emma continues, "Would it have stopped Sabine from

using you to seduce Callie for her own means? From Piper falling off a cliff? From the Virtues threatening, blackmailing, then killing Ivy? I don't know, Chase. This is what I think about every day. But you've been following Father's rules for so long. I couldn't be sure you'd be on my side."

"How could you think that? I *pulled* you from that goddamned fire!"

"And there, right there, is your damned hero complex bursting out of the gates without any reins. You always have to save the girl, don't you? You ran into those flames without giving a damn about yourself, when really, you should've given thought to the fact that I didn't want to be pulled out."

Chase sucks in air. "Emma. You don't mean that."

But she's relentless. "You even have the gall to blame yourself for Piper's death. *You* didn't push her off the cliff. *You* didn't get her pregnant. It was Piper's choice to dig into the Virtues. *Her* decision to become the Virtuous princess instead of me. But because you just can't stop yourself, now you go after Callie for daring to try to sacrifice herself for you. Maybe she wanted to. *Maybe* it's not all about your sacrifices, Chase. We needed to have our own. I needed to save other girls from becoming Sabine's puppets. Piper needed to save me. Callie needed to save her friend and *you*. For once in your fucking life, allow us to be the selfless ones."

"I'm not going to apologize for wanting to protect the girls I care about."

"You guys are fighting about who has the right to die first," I whisper, "when Ivy's already dead."

Both go silent.

Emma's the first to speak. She covers her face with her hands. "I'm sorry. My brain is everywhere. I'm so sorry about Ivy. And I'm terrified for my brother, for you, and I'm taking it out on anything that moves."

"It's okay," I murmur, but the tears well anyway.

Emma lays a hand on my shoulder. "You'll tell me tomorrow. Try to rest." She then lays a hand on Chase's cheek, staring long and hard into his eyes. "You, too."

"Yeah, sis." Chase squeezes her wrist.

Emma hobbles out of the room and the bed dips as Chase settles beside me. His body molds to mine, and he says, close to my ear, "Can I stay?"

I turn into him, my damp lashes cool against my tender skin as I close my eyes. "Don't leave."

"I won't." He brings an arm around me, tugging me close. "I'm so—I should've—"

I nudge my nose with his. "Your sister's right. You take on too much. Let us have our faults. I could've saved Ivy, too."

"I wish you had."

I squeeze my eyes shut, asking, for just this moment, that my crying stops. "Sabine was aiming for you. I know it in my bones. And I couldn't stop myself from protecting you if I tried."

"Callie." My name sounds so pained on his tongue. He kisses the hair at my temple. "I hear the guilt in your voice. There's no way you could've saved us both. One of us was dying tonight. There was no way out."

"There's always a way."

I'm surprised at the grit in my tone, the instant anger.

Yet, the more I stew on the words, the more certain I become.

"Tomorrow will be rough." Chase fits me against him. "Rest. Sabine's not touching a hair on your fucking head."

I lick my lips, truly wondering if Chase can claim such invincibility when tonight has shown us there's no such thing.

My best friend is dead. That caring, smiling, bursting-with-joy person is dead. Because she wanted to save her family. Because of Sabine.

Those thoughts grow vulture's feathers until they form into jagged, black wings, and they silently circle my mind, flying lower and lower, ready to eat into the carrion I've become.

But with Chase's arms around me, I manage to avoid their gnarled beaks and fall into a fitful sleep.

Callie's REIGN starts now.
TAKE ME THERE.

A NOTE FROM KETLEY

Thank you so much for reading FIEND!

If you have the time, I'd love for you to leave a review on your preferred platform, or tag me on social media to let me know your thoughts. Those golden little stars are what drive me to keep writing.

You can also join my new readers' group, <u>Ketley's Crew</u>, on Facebook! I'd love to meet you!

xoxo, Ket.

ALSO BY KETLEY ALLISON

all in kindle unlimited

If you want more villains and secret societies, read:

Rival

Virtue

Fiend

Reign

Thorne

Crush

Liar

Tempest

If you like your bad boys and bullies as standalones (no series, one book, a happy ending), read:

Rebel

Crave

If you like mafia men, read

Underground Prince

Jaded Princess

If you like a grump turned into protective, read:

Rock

Lover

If you like your playboys with big hearts and bigger secrets, read:

Trust

Dare

Play

If you like a psychological thriller with a side of romance, read:

To Have

To Hold

ABOUT THE AUTHOR

Ketley Allison has always been a romantic at heart and loves writing over-the-top, plot-twisty romance and characters. Ketley was born in Canada, moved to Australia, then to California, and finally to New York City to attend law school, but most of that time was spent in coffee shops thinking about her next book.

Her other passions include her two daughters, wine, coffee, Big Macs, her cat, and her husband, possibly in that order.

tiktok.com/@ketleyallison

instagram.com/ketleyallison

facebook.com/ketleyallison

bookbub.com/authors/ketleyallison

amazon.com/author/ketleyallison

goodreads.com/ketleyallison

pinterest.com/ketleyallison

www.ingramcontent.com/pod-product-compliance
Lightning Source LLC
Chambersburg PA
CBHW011206190726

48288CB00013B/3338